Party of Two

Center Point
Large Print

Also by Jasmine Guillory and available from
Center Point Large Print:

The Wedding Date
The Proposal
The Wedding Party
Royal Holiday

**This Large Print Book carries the
Seal of Approval of N.A.V.H.**

Party of Two

JASMINE GUILLORY

CENTER POINT LARGE PRINT
THORNDIKE, MAINE

To Simi Patnaik and Nicole Clouse
You two are worth all the champagne
and fries in the world.

Chapter One

✴

Olivia Monroe sat down at the hotel bar and grinned at the bartender, who grinned back. Thank God for a friendly face after such a long day.

She'd almost gone straight to her room to put on one of those cozy hotel robes and order room service to eat on her bed, but what she wanted more than anything tonight was a huge pile of french fries and an ice-cold martini, and she knew from experience that room service was the least optimal way to get both of those things. Fries always arrived soggy and martinis never arrived chilled enough. Better to get the best version of both and a conversation with Krystal the bartender that had nothing to do with intellectual property or law.

"Hendrick's martini, two olives?" Krystal asked her, already filling the cocktail shaker with ice. Olivia had been staying in this hotel for a week now, ever since she'd packed all of her worldly belongings and flown out to L.A. to start this new chapter in her life.

"Yes please." Olivia slipped off her blazer.

"And a Caesar salad and a large order of fries."

"You got it. How was work today? You look like you've earned this martini."

Olivia laughed and twisted her mass of dark curly hair up into a knot on top of her head.

"Well, I left the hotel at eight this morning, and I'm just getting back now at . . ." She checked her watch. "Nine at night, so yes, I've earned that martini. But I've had worse twelve-hour days."

Much worse, actually. After years of considering it, she'd moved from New York to L.A., and she and her friend Ellie had formed their own law firm: Monroe & Spencer. Olivia had spent the last month anxious she'd made the wrong decision, about both the move and starting a new firm. She was still terrified about that—so much so that she'd woken up at four a.m. the night before and worried for an hour. But, God, she'd loved every minute of her workday today. She'd been on an adrenaline high from the moment she walked into the office that morning—hell, from the moment her plane had landed last week. She was thrilled to be back in California, it was great to have Ellie as her partner, and it felt incredible to be her own boss, finally, after all these years.

When her martini arrived, she raised it to Krystal in thanks, and silently toasted herself. She took a sip and smiled. Perfect.

She inhaled her salad and half of her fries as soon as they arrived, and realized she couldn't remember the last time she'd eaten. Oh right, Ellie had handed her some sort of green smoothie at eleven a.m. when they left for a meeting together, and Olivia had laughed at her. Ellie had been in L.A. ever since law school graduation, so she did things like drink green smoothies and go to seven a.m. yoga classes before she got into the office. The smoothie was terrible; no wonder Olivia had eaten those fries so fast. As it was, the gin plus all of that adrenaline from their meetings and calls today had left her feeling very euphoric. Maybe she should eat something else.

She waved Krystal over and asked for the dessert menu. Chocolate cake, that's what she needed right now. A big slice of chocolate layer cake. Ooh, or apple pie, warm, with a big scoop of ice cream on the side. That would also hit the spot.

Krystal hesitated before she handed her the dessert menu.

"There's a new pastry chef here, and . . . well, at least the cookies are good."

Olivia scanned the list and shook her head.

"What *is* all of this?" she asked Krystal. "I understand that pastry chefs need to feel like they're expressing their emotions in their pastry or whatever, but why are all of these desserts so incomprehensible and confusing? Basil ice cream? I don't want herbs in my dessert!" Krystal laughed at that, which only inspired Olivia to keep going. "Deconstructed banana cream pie? What even is that, a banana just rolling back and forth on a plate, with some whipped cream on the side? A cookie plate? I don't want a cookie plate! What happened to a nice layer cake? Chocolate, or carrot, or for the love of God, yellow cake with chocolate frosting? Everyone loves yellow cake with chocolate frosting! Or a delicious pie—an actual one, not any deconstructed nonsense. Apple pie, or chocolate mousse pie, or my favorite, strawberry rhubarb—the whole world would come here for dessert if you had those things!"

"I could not agree with you more."

Olivia glanced over at the guy a few seats down who had chimed in on her rant. White dude, far too attractive, baseball cap, jeans, blue T-shirt, expression on his face like he thought he was hot shit. She rolled her eyes and turned back to Krystal, who was still laughing.

"See? Even this guy agrees with me. Everyone loves a good cake—a real one, not any of this fancy, elaborate, delicate stuff that doesn't even deserve the name 'cake.' What does L.A. have against a good cake?"

"You really are passionate about dessert, aren't you?" Krystal set the dude's beer down in front of him. "The cookies are good, though, I swear."

Olivia pursed her lips.

"Are they really, though?" she asked Krystal. *Really?* Are they real cookies, or those thin, crispy, fragile cookies that are more crumb than actual cookie? Or, God, are they biscotti? I bet they're biscotti, aren't they?"

"I hate biscotti so much," the dude said, with a shake of his head. "The first time I ever tried one, I almost cracked a tooth. Then someone told me you were supposed to dip it in coffee first—whoever came up with a cookie you had to dip in liquid before eating it?"

Olivia pointed at him and nodded.

"Yes, exactly! Why would I want a soggy cookie? Please, say they aren't biscotti, Krystal."

Krystal shook her head at them.

"I promise, they aren't biscotti. I'll bring you some, you'll see."

Krystal disappeared, and the baseball cap dude smiled at Olivia.

"What are the chances these cookies are actually good?" he asked.

Olivia couldn't help herself from smiling back at him.

"Oh, slim to none," she said.

Normally, Olivia wouldn't give this guy the time of day. He was too good looking, with big dark eyes, strong jaw, and wide smile. His hair was probably in perfect, tousled waves underneath that baseball cap, too. She knew guys like this all too well—they'd been told their whole lives they were smart and charming, and they got away with everything. She'd gone to school with this guy, she'd worked with him, she'd worked for him. But tonight she was in a good mood and full of gin and french fries.

And she didn't work for guys like this, or anyone else, anymore. Her smile grew wider.

"Hi, I'm Olivia." She reached out her hand to him.

He glanced down at the stool in between them, occupied by her bag, thank goodness. Just because she'd told this guy her name didn't mean she wanted him to sit next to her.

"Hi, Olivia. I'm . . . Max." His handshake was firm, but not that death grip that so many men had, like they were trying to prove they were so big and strong. "So, where do you stand on the cake-versus-pie argument?"

Olivia waved a french fry at him.

"I reject the whole idea that I have to choose between them! I love both cake and pie. An excellent version of either is a perfect food; a bad version of either is a crime against humanity. I don't know why people always want you to choose a team when you can love both."

Oh no. She was shouting about dessert again. That martini had hit her hard. Well, at least she was shouting to this guy she'd never see after tonight.

"People are definitely pretty partisan these

days about everything, that's for sure," he said. "I tend to be more of a pie person, but I agree, an excellent cake can make me very happy." He gave her that slow smile again, and she tried not to let it affect her. "So what are you here in L.A. for? Assuming you're a guest here at the hotel?"

Olivia fished the last olive out of her martini glass.

"I am a guest here, but I'm also here in L.A. for good—I just moved here for work, but I can't move into my new place yet." She supposed she had to ask him, too. "Where are you visiting from?"

He laughed, slightly too loudly.

"Oh, I'm not visiting; I live here, too. Water main break on my street, and I have a lot to do first thing in the morning, so I came over here for the night."

She wondered what "a lot to do" in his world was. Did he work in the industry? Probably. Half of L.A. was connected to TV and movies in some way or another. As a matter of fact, this guy looked vaguely familiar. Maybe he was in a commercial she'd seen or something.

She wasn't going to ask him what he did; people like this were way too pleased to tell you they were An Actor.

Krystal set down a plate of cookies between the two of them.

"See, no biscotti." She glanced at Olivia's drink. "Another drink, either of you?"

They both shook their heads.

"I wish, but I have an early day tomorrow, and more work I should get done tonight," Olivia said. "But I'll have some coffee to go with the cookies."

"Coffee for me, too, please, but decaf," Max said.

When Krystal went to get their coffees, Max turned back to her.

"So what brought you to L.A. and is giving you a late night?" he asked her.

"Oh, I'm an accountant," she said. "Busy time of year for us."

As a rule, Olivia didn't like to lie. But she was having a pleasant evening drinking gin and ranting about food with a stranger, and she didn't want him to ruin the fun vibe they had going by cracking a stupid lawyer joke she'd heard a million times before. Accountant was a good, solid, boring job, and the best part of it was it was such a boring job no one ever asked her any follow-up questions.

"Oh, really?" he asked. "That's so interesting. What do you think of the new tax laws? Have they made your job more difficult?"

This guy, of course, would be the exception.

She reached for a cookie and bit into it so she

14

had more time to think of an answer. She would have never figured a pretty actor would ask for details about her nonexistent accountant job, especially not details about the tax code.

"It's been a little more challenging," she said, after thoroughly chewing her cookie. "And personally, I'm not a huge fan of the new laws. But the good part is business is up."

He nodded.

"I'm not a huge fan of the new laws, either, but I'm glad that—"

"Oh wow, you should try these." Olivia held up the cookie. "Krystal was right, they're actually good."

She didn't only say that because she wanted to end this digression about tax laws, but sure, that was part of it.

Just then, Krystal brought their coffees.

"See, what did I tell you?" she said.

Max bit into a cookie and nodded.

"Sure, these are good," he said. "But just think of how much better they'd be if this was an ice-cream sandwich."

Olivia gasped and dropped her cookie.

"Yes! This is exactly what I'm talking about—dessert menus should have ice-cream sandwiches with cookies like this, and cakes, and pies, instead of this pistachio tart nonsense."

Max laughed.

"I'll add that to my platform," he said.

Olivia took the last sip of her drink and pushed the glass toward Krystal.

"You joke, but I think someone needs to start a movement here."

That had been a close one. Max added cream to his coffee and mentally kicked himself for his stupid "platform" comment. This woman obviously didn't know who he was; why would he say something to help her figure it out?

Granted, most people didn't recognize him when he wasn't in uniform as Maxwell Stewart Powell III, junior United States Senator from California, at least not immediately, and that's the way he liked it. Sometimes it dawned on them after a while, though, especially if he'd been on TV recently, and he'd been on TV a lot these days.

But Olivia obviously had no idea who he was—that had been clear from her withering "even this guy agrees with me" comment when he'd joined her conversation. No one had talked down to him like that in years.

Why did he like it so much?

He had no idea, but he knew he didn't want this woman to figure out who he was and laugh at all of his stupid jokes like everyone else did these days. She barely even smiled at him, and the one time she had, he felt like he'd won a prize. It was weirdly nice to have to fight for a smile for the first time in a long time.

"So, Olivia, where did you move from? To move to L.A., I mean."

She pushed some of her curly hair back into her bun and gave him that half-suspicious look again.

"New York. But I'm a native Californian—I grew up in the Bay Area."

He lifted his coffee cup to toast to her.

"Well, welcome home."

She touched her cup to his.

"Thanks. It's good to be back. Even though L.A. is a lot different from the Bay Area, it still feels like coming home. But I've realized I only know L.A. from the perspective of a visitor, not a resident, so I have a lot to figure out. I haven't even bought a car yet."

He shook his head.

"You let yourself get too New York when you moved away. Soon you're going to start lamenting the state of the bagels and pizza in California, and insisting you really *can* get good tacos in New York if you know where to look."

Olivia burst out laughing.

He'd made her laugh. What a victory. Now all he wanted was to do it again.

"I swear, I'll never, ever do that last thing, cross my heart! People kept trying to pretend there was actual good Mexican food in New York—and in Boston, too, for that matter. It gave me a lot of trust issues, let me tell you."

Max grinned at her. The way she'd joked and

laughed with the bartender was one of the reasons he'd initially eavesdropped on their conversation. He was so glad that smile on her face now was because of something he'd said.

"What about the bagels, though? Are you going to complain about the bagels?"

She shook her head, a smile still on her face.

"I won't, I promise. I hate it when people do that—I didn't even complain about the bad Mexican food on the East Coast . . . well, not until someone dragged me to a place they promised was good. Not to be weirdly patriotic, but one of the things I love about America is the regional specialties; it would feel too bland and same-same if you could get everything in the right form everywhere. I love visiting other states and finding something I've never had a real version of—or sometimes, never even heard of—where I live. I don't want to change that."

She'd put something into words he'd always felt.

"I could not agree more," he said. He barely stopped himself from putting his hand on her shoulder, but instead just swiveled his stool around all the way to face her. "Even the Northern California–versus–Southern California burrito fights—I think it's great that even different parts of the state have such strong views on burritos, and I happily eat them all."

She picked up another cookie.

"So do I, but I have to admit that my loyalties lie with the Mission burrito. It's going to be hard to get used to the Los Angeles version, but I'll try." She raised an eyebrow at him. "So, Max, any favorite local places for me?"

He reached across the bar and grabbed Krystal's pen.

"Find me some paper and I'll make you a list. But first, you're moving out of this hotel soon, I imagine? Where will you be living? I have favorites all over L.A., but if you live on the Westside, you won't spend a lot of time east, and vice versa."

She pulled a legal pad out of her bag and tore off a sheet for him.

"That's a detail about living in L.A. that I already knew—I'll be on the Eastside. Silver Lake."

He started writing.

"Good choice. And there are even a few places over that way where I can recommend the desserts."

He scribbled down the names of all of the places he could remember, and vague location markers for the ones he couldn't—"that taco truck on Olympic" was one of his notes. He knew if he pulled his phone out, he could look up exact names and addresses, but he didn't want to deal with his phone right now. There would be so many crises—texts and emails and news alerts he needed a break from. He was enjoying this moment of pretending he was just Max. He needed at least thirty more minutes off from being Senator Powell.

And at least thirty more minutes to talk to, and look at, Olivia. He'd noticed her as soon as he walked in; she looked so joyful and alive, he couldn't help but notice. Her warm brown skin glowed as she laughed, her eyes lit up as she talked, and her hair refused to stay in the bun she'd tried to trap it in, her curls dancing in a halo around her face. Most of the time when she looked at him, she wasn't smiling, but that just made it all the more valuable when she did. She wore a silky pink shirt, and a thin gold necklace that disappeared under it, and he found the entire combination incredibly alluring. He wanted to follow that necklace down, but he forced his eyes back to his list so he wouldn't stare.

Olivia asked questions as he wrote, and they chatted about food and Los Angeles and hotel horror stories. This fun, easy conversation was the most relaxed he'd been in months. How was it that someone like him, who spent all day every day talking to people, felt so lonely for personal connection, and so happy to have found it, if only for a little while? The whole time they talked, he was afraid she'd ask him what he did—he didn't want to lie to her, but he also didn't want to tell her the truth and break this spell. But while they talked about a lot of other things, she never asked him that, thank goodness.

"Anything else for either of you?" Krystal picked up their long-ago-drained coffee cups and the empty cookie plate.

Olivia shook her head and glanced at her wrist. "Oh God, it's after eleven. I didn't realize it was so late. I'll take the check, thanks, Krystal."

Max sighed and nodded. This night had to end sometime.

"Me, too."

They each signed their checks and walked together to the elevator. He pressed twelve; she pressed eight. They were silent for the first few floors.

He could see more of her now that they were off those bar stools. She was shorter than he'd assumed, with generous hips, that incredible chest he'd noticed before, and very sexy black high heels. She had a tiny smile that hovered around her soft pink lips. He wondered if it was about him.

He didn't want her floor to come, he realized. He didn't want her to get off. Right now he'd welcome a power outage, an earthquake, any emergency that would cause them to get stuck together in this elevator so he could spend a few more minutes talking to this woman who made him laugh, and relax, and who had no idea who he was. Maybe after that they'd go out for a drink on purpose. Maybe after the drink he'd pull her close, and kiss her, and she'd wrap an arm around his waist and kiss him back. And then maybe . . .

But the elevator kept moving.

"It was great to meet you, Olivia," he said in a rush. "And welcome back to California."

She smiled at him one last time as the elevator doors opened on her floor.

"Thanks, Max. Have a good night."

The doors closed behind her, and he dropped his head in his hands. He'd lost all of his game in these past few years, hadn't he? He'd spent hours chatting up a hot, smart, funny woman at a bar, and hadn't even asked for her number? He'd written her a list of restaurants in Los Angeles, for God's sake, and hadn't even thought to put his number at the top of it? Or—what was wrong with him?—he could have asked for her email address to send her more restaurants, and then found a way to ask her out then.

He shook his head as he let himself into his room. This was the first woman who had sparked his interest in over two years, and he'd just let her get off the elevator? Sure, he was attracted to her for lots of reasons, but he also really missed having someone around who treated him normally—someone who made fun of him a little, laughed at him, was relaxed with him, in that way Olivia had been tonight.

He should have asked for her number.

• • •

Olivia shook her head as she walked into her hotel room. For a minute there in the elevator, she'd thought Max in the baseball hat was going to ask her out. And honestly, for a minute there in the elevator, she would have said yes. She hadn't realized until they'd gotten in the elevator how tall he was. Or how nicely his T-shirt gripped his biceps. Or how warm those dark brown eyes of his were. Thank goodness her floor had arrived when it had. What was it about elevators, anyway?

It really was for the best that Max hadn't asked her out. Sure, he could give good banter at a bar, but what in the world would she do on a date with a guy like him? She'd eventually have to ask him what he did, he'd say he was an actor, and then she'd have to ask him what he'd been in, and he'd say that one commercial and that other episode of *Law & Order* and she'd say, "Ohhh, that's where I know you from!" And then he'd go off on another long list of his acting credits and bore her to tears and that would be the end of it.

Plus, she didn't have time for men right now! Her firm was her first—really her only—priority; she had to get it all set up, keep her handful of existing clients happy, network with local lawyers and potential clients, and do everything she could to drum up new business. She actually *wanted* to concentrate on all that! Not some guy who charmed her at a bar after she'd had a little too much gin, but likely had nothing to his credit other than that perfect smile.

Okay, and those biceps. And those big, warm, nicely manicured hands.

Why hadn't he just invited her up to his room? That would have been the best of both worlds. Sure, she didn't have time to *date* men right now, but she had time for a few hours of stress relief. Ah well. Too late for that.

She kicked off her heels, turned on the TV to the local news, and went into the bathroom to wash her face and take out her contacts. When she came out, the reporter was saying something about the homeless problem in L.A., and she listened as she changed into her pajamas.

"Earlier today, senator Max Powell had a press conference on Skid Row that some are calling just a publicity stunt. But others are grateful to the senator for shining light on this problem."

"It's shameful the way we've treated our fellow citizens, many of whom are veterans," a strangely familiar voice said.

Olivia looked up at the TV and promptly dropped her pajama pants on the floor.

Was that . . . ?

Could that be?

She sank down onto the edge of the bed. Yes, it was. It could be. Max in the baseball hat from

24

the bar was not some C-list actor. He was United States senator Max Powell.

Holy shit.

She laughed out loud and picked up the phone to call her sister.

"You are *never* going to believe what happened to me tonight."

Chapter Two

✳

Max walked toward the hotel ballroom, his staffer Andy by his side. They were there for the anniversary fundraiser for a newish community center in an underserved part of L.A. He was happy to help salute this place, and plus, his speech would be a good opportunity to push his big criminal justice reform bill. He hoped that when the Senate came back after this recess, he'd be able to get some traction on it.

He took a deep breath and straightened his tie. He loved doing events like the one today— he always had. He loved the part of his job that was speeches and shaking hands and talking to people; he found people and their stories end-lessly interesting. But he had to be at least twenty-five percent *more* for these things: louder, friendlier, more intense, with a firmer handshake. People were coming to see Senator Powell, after all—he needed to give them what they were looking for. But sometimes when he walked into these rooms, he felt he had to push his ON button.

He and the community center's board president

walked into the ballroom to a round of applause. Max sat patiently through his introduction, dropped his speech on the podium, and smiled at the crowd before he started talking.

He glanced around the room a lot as he spoke. It helped him to connect with the people there, and to see if his speech was landing well or not. If he saw people on their phones for most of the speech, he knew he had to go back and make some changes before the next time. This one was going well; there were lots of smiles and laughs all around the room. Midway through, he looked at a table to the right of the stage, and that's when he saw her, staring straight at him, with that knowing look on her face he remembered so well.

Olivia. The woman from the hotel, three weeks ago. He'd spent the whole next day full of regret that he hadn't at least gotten her number. He'd even gone back to the hotel bar the next night to see if she was there, but Krystal had told him Olivia had come to say good-bye and had checked out of the hotel. He'd thought he would never see her again, and here she was.

They made eye contact, and he grinned at her. She grinned back at him with that same cocky smile on her face she'd had at the bar. He really liked that smile. And once again, he felt like he'd won the lottery when it was directed at him.

The crowd laughed, which reminded him he

was in the middle of a speech and he should really pay attention to what he was saying. Thank God he'd done this kind of thing enough that he could daydream about the woman in front of him when he was halfway through a speech and still keep talking and making sense. But now he needed to concentrate.

He took a sip of water, looked at the other side of the room from Olivia, and cracked a joke that got the whole ballroom laughing again. He was going to finish this speech, and then he wasn't going to let that woman leave the room until he'd gotten to talk to her again.

To what end, though? Was he really going to ask her out? Did he really have the time and energy to try to navigate dating someone not even two years into his first (and hopefully not only) six-year Senate term?

He wasn't sure. But he'd thought about her every day for the past three weeks. He'd gotten a second chance; he couldn't waste it.

He finished his speech to a round of applause and made his way off the stage and down into the ballroom to chat with the crowd . . . and to find someone to introduce him to Olivia. It would help if he positioned himself by her table . . . like so.

He didn't have long to wait.

"Senator, can I introduce you to Olivia Monroe?" The board president had his hand on

Olivia's shoulder. "She's an old friend of mine and a fantastic attorney who just moved to L.A., and I'm trying to convince her to join our board. I know she could be a wonderful asset to us."

She's a fantastic . . . attorney? But she'd said she was an accountant.

He kept the bland, professional smile on his face and shook her hand.

"Ms. Monroe, it's so nice to meet you. What law firm are you with?"

Her smile turned wry for just a split second. Ah yes, she remembered that she'd told him she was an accountant.

"My own," she said. He saw the pride in her eyes. "Monroe and Spencer. A friend and I started it last month."

Well, she *had* moved to L.A. for work; that part had been true.

"Congratulations," he said. "And welcome to Los Angeles."

Olivia smiled at him, then glanced over at the executive director.

"Thank you. It's very exciting but also very busy. Which is why, as I told Bruce here, I might be too swamped to join the board for a while, but I'll be thrilled to be involved in any way I can."

Bruce shook his head.

"I was hoping the senator here would be able to convince you to join the board, but I understand."

She looked back at Max. She had on a gray pantsuit with a blue blouse and black high heels—the kind of standard outfit he was used to seeing women in. So why did it look so special on her? Why was that row of buttons on her blouse—buttoned high enough so they almost, but didn't, show more of her curves underneath—so enticing?

"I was excited to hear about all of your programs with teenagers," she said. "And, Senator, I'm thrilled about your bill to demolish the school-to-prison pipeline."

Yes, yes, right, he was here to talk about his criminal justice reform bill, the entire reason he'd run for the Senate in the first place.

"I'm so glad to hear that," he said. "It's by far my biggest priority in Washington."

Bruce beamed at Max.

"We're thrilled about your bill as well, Senator." He glanced around the room and jumped. "Oh! Gloria is here, wonderful! Let me bring her over to meet you, just stay right here!"

He scurried away, and Max and Olivia were finally left alone.

"So you're an accountant, huh?" he said under his breath.

She shook her head, but with a smile on her face.

"I'm sorry I lied to you about that. But my God, the things people say when you tell them you're a lawyer! Sometimes I can't deal with one more stupid lawyer joke."

He'd been thinking about this woman for weeks; he couldn't believe he'd actually found her again. And that she was just as gorgeous and funny as he'd remembered.

"Well, I certainly understand that."

She laughed. He liked how he could tell that was a real laugh, not an "I'm talking to a senator, better make him feel good about himself" kind of laugh.

At least, he hoped so. He *thought* he was still able to distinguish between the two.

"A while ago I started coming up with different jobs to tell cabdrivers, bartenders, and . . ." She glanced up at him with that grin again. "Friendly strangers sitting next to you at bars. Accountant is a good one, because no one ever asks questions." She shook her head. "Well, except for you. But then, I didn't realize at the time that I was lying to my senator."

He laughed.

"Sorry for ruining it for you. I can't help it if my job makes me have questions about things most people don't care about." He lowered his voice. "Accountant or attorney, I'm glad we ran into each other again. I wondered . . ."

"Senator." Andy was by his side again. "Apologies for the interruption, but we're already running late to the event with Congresswoman Watson."

He held in a sigh. Andy was going to swoop him off to the next event, and he absolutely wouldn't get another second to talk to Olivia Monroe without at least three people surrounding them. Oh great, now there were four. Honestly, it was a miracle they'd gotten about sixty seconds alone; he had to be grateful for that.

"Yes, of course. Ms. Monroe, it was a pleasure to meet you today."

Her bland professional smile matched his.

"Likewise, Senator."

They shook hands. He wished he could hold on to her hand longer, but he forced himself to let go.

He turned to leave, just as Bruce raced over with someone else to introduce him to. Yes, he was very thankful he'd had that brief time alone with Olivia Monroe. Especially because now he knew not only her name but where she worked.

Olivia turned back to her table to grab her purse with a smile still on her face. When she'd seen that senator Max Powell was going to be the keynote speaker for this luncheon, she wondered if he would remember her; that was, if he even noticed her in the crowd. And then, in the middle of his speech, he'd looked straight at her, and she could tell from his very unpolitician-like grin that he'd recognized her.

If he were a normal person, and not a senator,

she would have thought he was flirting with her when he smiled at her like that, and also when he talked to her just now. But politicians were charmers in that way—everyone must think Max Powell flirted with them. That was probably how he'd managed to win the Senate seat in the first place.

She tried to put Max Powell out of her mind and made her slow way out of the ballroom. She hated that she couldn't accept Bruce's invitation to be on the board; it was exactly the kind of thing she'd love to do, and would be a great way to get to know her new city. But nonprofit board seats meant hefty donations, and she had to be careful with money right now. She wasn't in a position to give any more than a nominal amount until she and Ellie truly got this firm off the ground. However, luncheons like this were prime networking opportunities—before she left the ballroom, she'd given out over twenty business cards to other lawyers and made coffee dates with three people she hadn't seen in years. You never knew which connections could bring some sorely needed business to Monroe & Spencer.

She got back to the office to find Ellie in the middle of hanging up artwork on the walls. Olivia looked around at the frames on the floor, the tools on the bookshelf, and the glee on Ellie's face as she banged hooks into the wall with a hammer.

"Having fun?"

Ellie paused, hammer in the air.

"Absolutely." She brushed her immaculate hair back. "I love a chance to use a hammer in the middle of the workday. I'm going to have to keep this and a piece of wood and a pile of nails in my office, just to work off my rage for those times opposing counsel tries to talk down to me."

Olivia laughed.

" 'Tries' is the operative word there, Ellie. I don't think anyone has actually gotten away with that in years."

Ellie lifted a painting and hung it carefully.

"Oh, I know, but I still have to be diplomatic and all honey voiced as I hand their asses to them. Sometimes I just wish I could tell them to go fuck themselves—when those impulses come over me, I'll just look at this hammer and feel better."

Ellie looked like the gentle, blond, polite, per- fectly coiffed Southern girl that she was. Which is why it was all the more fun when people underestimated her.

She and Olivia made an excellent team.

Olivia sat down at her desk and spent the next few hours jumping back and forth between emails and phone calls with potential and existing clients, tinkering with their brand-new internal filing system, updating their website, and jumping on a quick call with their accountant.

Back when she was a big-firm lawyer, she'd have only done the client work and nothing else; all of her administrative work was done for her like magic by her secretary and the firm. But she and Ellie had decided not to have any support staff, at least at the beginning, so they were learning how to do all of this themselves . . . some of it better than others.

Just before five, Ellie knocked at her open office door with a twinkle in her eye.

"Delivery for you, and it looks fun."

Olivia looked away from her computer screen for the first time in over an hour and blinked.

"Ooh, is it the pens I ordered?" It made her feel very boring to be so excited, but she really had been looking forward to those pens.

Ellie shook her head.

"Nope." She held up a big white handled bag. "Looks like something from a bakery."

Olivia stood up from her desk and frowned.

"I didn't order anything from a bakery. It must be some mistake."

Ellie held up the delivery slip.

"It says Olivia Monroe, Monroe and Spencer, and our address, right here."

Olivia took the bag from her and set it on her desk.

"That's weird. Maybe my sister sent me something?"

Ellie's phone rang, and she rushed to pick it up.

"I'm coming back to see what that is!" she shouted on her way into her office.

Olivia took the bakery box out of the bag. There was an envelope taped to the top, and she pulled it open with a smile on her face. What a nice thing for Alexa to do.

To Olivia Monroe—just in case you're still in search of some excellent cake. Good seeing you today. Maybe we can do it on purpose next time?
Max
213-555-4857

No.

This could not be.

This was her sister playing a trick on her, right?

She flipped open the box. Inside was a big layer cake, covered in chocolate frosting, with "Welcome to California" written on it in blue.

She looked from the cake, to the note in her hand, back to the cake.

This must be her sister. Except her sister didn't know she'd seen Max today. No one did, as a matter of fact, except for the people who'd seen them talking for about forty-five seconds in the ballroom after the luncheon. And none of those people knew they'd met before. Or what they'd talked about.

Olivia walked back around her desk and sat

down, still staring at the note clutched in her hand.

Had United States senator Max Powell really sent her a cake?

And, in his note along with the cake . . .

He couldn't be asking her out, right?

Yes, when she'd walked out of that elevator, she sort of thought that the hot white dude in the baseball cap she'd been flirting with for the past hour or so had been about to ask her out, sure. But that's when she didn't know the hot white dude in the baseball cap was Max Powell, hotshot junior senator from California.

Was he really asking her out? From anyone else, this note would mean an unequivocal yes, but he was a senator!

Was he some sort of scumbag who went around doing this all the time? It had only been—she looked at her watch—four hours from when she'd seen him at the luncheon and when the cake had arrived at her office. Only someone who was really practiced in this kind of thing would work that fast.

Okay, maybe, but he'd obviously remembered their conversation at the bar three weeks ago—did scumbags do that? And if he was a scumbag, why hadn't he pounced on her at the bar, anyway? She'd had enough experience with men to usually identify the creepy ones right off the bat—she wouldn't have spent that long talking to him at the bar, gin or no gin, if he'd given her bad vibes.

And yes, fine, she had spent more than a few moments in the last few weeks fantasizing about what could have happened if he'd invited her up to his room. And she had to admit he'd been pretty hot in his very-well-tailored suit and tie. Apparently she found both senator Max Powell and Max in the baseball cap equally attractive. A fling with him could definitely be fun . . . Wait. Was she actually considering this?

Who was this guy even? All she knew about him was from the times she'd seen him on MSNBC, where he'd been appropriately respectful to Rachel Maddow and dodged questions about his presidential aspirations, but she needed to find out more. About both his politics and his personal life.

But before she did any of that, she needed to eat a piece of this cake.

Olivia found a knife and cut a fat slice of the cake. Three layers. Had she mentioned to Max that she loved a three-layer cake the best? She couldn't remember.

She took a bite, and closed her eyes in a silent celebration. This was exactly what she'd been craving that night—rich, tender, chocolaty cake, between layers of dark chocolate frosting. It was perfect.

Now, to see if the man measured up to the cake.

Unlikely.

She turned to her computer.

Senator Max Powell girlfriend was her first Google search. There she discovered that he'd had a serious girlfriend when he was DA here in L.A., but they'd broken up before he started his bid for the Senate, so almost three years ago. She couldn't find any evidence of his dating someone since then. Okay, so—if he was indeed asking her out—he obviously just wanted something casual. Which was fine with her.

Hmmm, what about *Senator Max Powell scandal?*

There were a bunch of hits for that, and she was seconds from knocking the cake on the floor, until she realized they were all about his comments about a sexual harassment scandal in the Senate last year.

I firmly and vigorously denounce the behavior of my colleague, and I insist that this chamber put into place a better procedure for reporting sexual harassment for employees.

Okay. Well, that was an excellent statement. She'd read a lot of statements like this over the past few years, ones by a guy getting asked questions about another guy they worked with, and she wasn't sure if she'd seen a better one. The cake was safe, thank God.

Now to see how she felt about his policies.

She knew instead of googling this she could just pick up the phone and call her sister, who had a seemingly encyclopedic knowledge of every California politician, and Alexa would tell her everything she needed to know. But she wasn't quite ready to tell Alexa about the cake from Senator Powell, and especially not the note along with the cake. She'd told her about the night at the bar, because it was funny, and she knew Alexa would appreciate it more than anyone else in her life. But that she was considering going out with him? Not yet. At a minimum, not until she'd at least made up her mind about that.

However . . . she needed to find out how this man felt about a few key issues.

"Oh my God, who sent you that cake?"

Olivia looked up from her *Senator Max Powell Black Lives Matter* search to see Ellie standing at her office door.

"Do you want some? It's really good. We need to remember the name of this bakery."

Ellie had already picked up the knife and sliced herself a perfect wedge of cake.

"Did it say 'Welcome to California'? How sweet—was this your sister?" She tipped the slice onto a napkin and dropped into the seat across from Olivia.

Olivia shook her head.

"No, that's what I initially thought, too, but . . ." She shook her head and then looked at Ellie with a grin on her face. "Okay, I have a story for you. A few weeks ago, before I'd moved into my place, I went to grab dinner at my hotel bar after work. And, well . . ."

Ellie's eyes got bigger and bigger as Olivia went on. When she finally got to the cake, Ellie snatched the note right out of her hand.

"Max Powell sent you this cake? People call him the hot senator."

Olivia grinned.

"Yes, my Google searches have taught me that. I can't believe I didn't recognize him at the bar."

Ellie popped the last bite of cake into her mouth.

"*I* can't believe the hot senator sent you this cake!" She waved the note in the air. "With this note on it!"

She propped the note up against the cake box.

"What did he say when you called him? When are you going to see him again? Where does a senator take a woman out on a date, anyway?"

Olivia pursed her lips.

"I haven't . . . exactly . . . called him yet. I'm still deciding if I'm going to do that."

Ellie frowned at her. Olivia almost laughed—when Ellie, the woman with a perpetual smile on her face, tried to frown, she looked like a little kid playing with facial expressions.

"When you say, 'I'm still deciding if I'm going to do that,' do you mean you're deciding if you're going to call him versus text him, or do you mean you're still deciding if you're going to get in touch with him at all?"

Olivia cut herself another piece of cake.

"The latter. I don't have time for men right now, Ellie! Especially not . . . complicated men."

Ellie dropped her napkin onto the desk.

"Oh, come on. Call the man! Or text him, whatever. This is a really good cake!"

Olivia laughed at that. It was just like Ellie to have her priorities straight.

"It is a really good cake, but what if he sends cakes like this to every woman he has the slightest interest in? I don't want to be just one of Max Powell's conquests."

Ellie picked her cake up again.

"That's an excellent point, and all the more reason to find out. Call him, see if he's trying to woo just some random woman he met at a bar, or if he's trying to woo you, specifically."

Ellie stood up and went to the door.

"But before you do any of that, respond to that email Daphne sent us, would you? She likes you better than me."

Olivia minimized her many tabs open to stories about senator Max Powell and clicked over to her email. Daphne had sent this forty-five minutes ago; she couldn't believe she'd wasted all that time researching a man instead of responding to a potential client.

See, she didn't have time for men. She was

here in L.A. to concentrate on work, not to get "wooed" by anyone. Ellie knew that, what was she even talking about?

But she couldn't just leave senator Max Powell hanging after he'd sent her a cake. He'd been perfectly friendly and not at all creepy; she would be rude to just ignore this gift. Plus, who knows, she might run into him again, and she didn't want to seem like the asshole here.

She picked up her phone to text him.

> Hi Senator—Thanks for the cake, it's delicious. My schedule is pretty booked for the next few weeks, but

No, come on, that sounded laughable. He was a senator; his schedule was likely four times as packed as hers was.

> Hi Senator—Thanks for the cake! But I'm not sure if

No, the exclamation point sent the wrong signal.

> Hi Senator—The cake was very thoughtful, thank you. However

Should she call him Senator? Or Max? He'd signed the card Max, so it seemed overly formal to the point of rudeness to call him Senator after that.

> Hi Max—Thanks for the cake, we all loved it. But I don't know if

"Max" sounded too informal. He was a senator, after all, and she'd only really talked to him that one time. Better to not call him anything.

> Hi, this is Olivia Monroe. Thanks for the cake, it was delicious. I hope all is well with you.

Well, that seemed perfectly appropriate and very cold. She didn't feel that cold toward him.

She sighed. Fine. She'd call him.

Luckily, since it was just after six p.m., he was probably still in a meeting, or at a dinner, or with his staff or something—it would probably go to voice mail. If there was one thing that being a lawyer had taught her, it was how to leave a polite but firm voice mail. That was much easier than a text message.

She tapped out his number on her cell phone and waited for it to ring. She definitely wouldn't have to talk to him; no senator would have his ringer on. And he definitely wouldn't answer a number he didn't know.

"Hello?"

Shit.

"Hello, Max?" Maybe it was a wrong number. It was probably a wrong number—she always did that when she actually had to type a number into her phone.

"Olivia?" His voice was warm, and slightly amused.

Nope. Not a wrong number.

"Um, yeah. Hi. How'd you know it was me?"

He laughed.

"Well, I only give this number out to a handful of people, and everyone else who has it is in my contacts. And you told me you were from Northern California, which made sense with your phone number—you never wanted a New York number?"

He only gave this number out to a handful of people?

"Oh, I thought about getting a New York number on and off, but I'm so glad I never got rid of my Oakland number," she said. "After a while, it was a point of pride for me. Plus, I think there was some part of me that always knew I was going to come home, even in my most insufferable 'New York is the greatest city in the world!' phase. Thank goodness I had the sense to take the California bar right out of law school, or else this whole process would have been a lot harder."

She didn't know why she was babbling on

about her phone number and taking the bar. Why was she even on the phone with a senator in the first place? Not just on the phone, but on his private number. What the hell was going on?

"I had that 'New York is the greatest city in the world' phase, too, in my midtwenties," he said. "The phase ended, but I still love that city. I'm always grateful when I get to go there, though these days my trips there aren't as . . . exciting, let's say, as they used to be."

She grinned.

"I know you think that's a product of your job, and I'm sure it partly is, but I'm here to tell you it's also a product of your age. My twenties were exciting in New York, too, but then I reached that age where I got horrified when someone invited me to something that didn't even start until nine p.m."

Did that make her sound uncool? Oh well, if it did, this man should know right off the bat that she wasn't going to any midnight soirees with him.

"Okay, fine, you've got me there," he said. "Tonight I managed to get my staff to let me get home at five and have dinner alone here in my own house, and I'm thrilled about it."

Oh, so that's why he'd answered the phone when she called. Well, at least she knew his staff wasn't hanging around in the background.

"I understand that so clearly," she said. "When

46

I finally moved into my house here in L.A., that first night I got to have dinner in my own kitchen again, instead of on a hotel bed or in a hotel bar . . . it was 'shower after a ten-hour plane ride' good."

He burst out laughing.

"Okay, now you're speaking my language," he said. "I know very well exactly how wonderful that shower is. But don't you miss Krystal and her perfect martinis?"

Oh God. They'd been on the phone this long already and she hadn't thanked him for the cake yet!

"I do, but speaking of Krystal, thank you for the cake. It's delicious."

"It was my pleasure," he said. "I just wanted to make sure you knew that we do actually have good old-fashioned layer cakes in Los Angeles, even though most dessert menus don't. That bakery is one of my favorites, and they have so many great cakes, I had a hard time deciding which one to send you."

She'd been so distracted by the note she hadn't even bothered to look to see where it had come from. She looked at the box and scribbled down the name of the bakery.

"What were you deciding between?" she asked.

And how had he found the time to do this? Hadn't he had events all day?

"Well," he said. "It was mostly between the

chocolate one that I sent you, and a yellow cake with chocolate frosting, though carrot cake was a real dark horse. But in the end, I decided to go with the first one you'd mentioned at the bar—I figured that was the one you were craving the most."

She couldn't believe he'd remembered the cakes she'd listed at the bar, and in what order.

Was this for real? Was he just making it up that he'd thought about what kind of cake she'd liked the best, when he'd really delegated "send cake to new conquest" to a staffer?

"By the way, I also know some great places for pie, if you're interested in joining me for dinner at one of them."

"Dinner" was just code for a one-night stand, she knew that, but that part she didn't really mind. It was everything else about Max Powell that gave her pause.

Oh the hell with it, Olivia—he sent you a cake, didn't he? Who cares if he placed the call himself or if someone else did; his staffer wasn't there with the two of you at the bar that night to take notes and remember your cake preferences. Plus, remember how hot he is?

But as nice as that was, she was still far too busy to go out with him, and she opened her mouth to tell him so.

"Sure," she said instead. "I'd love to join you for pie."

Chapter Three

✳

Olivia rubbed her hands together as she tried to figure out what to wear to her date with a senator. It had been a while since she'd had some fun, relaxed, no-strings sex, and she deserved this. She'd had a stressful-as-hell few months, with no end in sight. Maybe a fun night with the hot senator was exactly what she needed to give herself a little stress relief.

She had no illusions this would be any more than one night—all she wanted from tonight was a fun romp with someone she found very attractive, and she was certain that's all Max Powell wanted out of her, too. Though she had to give it to him; cake delivery was the best booty call invitation she'd ever received.

She'd given up on real relationships with men a while ago, anyway. Men never really liked her for her, they never made her feel wanted or cared about, and she decided a few years ago that she'd had enough. She'd had casual things with guys since then from time to time, but she'd thrown all of her energy into her career. Which was where it was going to stay.

They were going to some place called Pie 'n Burger, which seemed like a glorified diner—her favorite type of place—though that meant she probably shouldn't wear her favorite heels. She reached for that one pair of jeans that made her butt look fantastic and her favorite red blouse, with one fewer button fastened than usual. She'd noticed Max's quick glimpse toward her cleavage at the bar. Might as well give him a taste of what he was looking for.

When she walked into the restaurant, she looked around for him. The place was bustling and crowded, but she saw him immediately.

"Olivia!"

He came over to her with that big smile on his face. It was far too charming. Even when she'd made fun of him to his face at the bar, that smile had told her he was in on the joke.

"Hi." She smiled back at him. She couldn't help it.

He had his baseball cap from the bar on, and glasses this time. He looked like an off-duty college professor. She noticed for the first time that when he smiled at her, he had a tiny dimple in his chin. Damn it. How was it possible he was even more attractive tonight?

"It's good to see you," he said.

He didn't pull her into a hug, which she'd sort of expected him to, but he did put his hand on her arm and stand very close to her while they waited for their table.

She looked up at him and kept her voice low.

"I have to ask: are the baseball cap and glasses your disguise so you can go out in public without being recognized, like Superman?"

Max grinned at her and moved his hand up and down her arm in a way she could feel all the way to her toes.

"Try them and see," he said.

She reached up with both hands and slid his glasses off, and put them on her own face. She could see perfectly.

He laughed and took them back. The way he slowly pulled them off her made her shiver.

"They look good on you," he said. "The glasses are an extra precaution, but the amazing thing is that I manage to hide in plain sight everywhere in L.A. I don't know if it's just that there are so many people in here who are far more well-known than I am, or that I'm unrecognizable outside of my suit and tie and with my hair all . . ."

"Ken doll–like?" she helpfully supplied.

He sighed and shook his head, but with laughter in his eyes. His lips were full and looked soft, yet firm. How had she not noticed that before?

"Unfortunately, yes, Ken doll–like was exactly what I meant. It's usually much less tamed when I'm off duty." He laughed. "Maybe it's just that I look like Generic White Man Number Five,

51

so I seem familiar to everyone, but not enough so they actually wonder who I am. Sometimes people figure it out after a while, but the baseball hat and/or the glasses help."

Olivia glanced at the hat and shook her head.

"I'm evidence that the hat works—I had no idea who you were when we met at the bar."

Had he known that already? She wasn't sure.

"I wondered about that," he said. "I thought you didn't know, at least at the beginning, but there were a few times you sort of looked at me like you were trying to place me." He laughed. "I'm sorry, is it weird that I remember that?"

Yeah, it was weird, but in a good way. She liked that he'd paid such close attention to her.

"I was trying to place you, but I just assumed you were an actor," she said. "I'm not exactly saying I thought you were Generic White Man Number Five, but . . ."

"But you're not *not* saying that, are you?"

She just grinned at him, and he laughed again.

The host led them to their table, and Max slid his hand from her arm to the small of her back as they walked together. She could feel the warmth of his firm hand through her blouse. Suddenly, she was very glad she was here tonight.

"When did you realize I wasn't an actor?" he asked when they sat down. "Was it at the luncheon yesterday?"

She shook her head.

"No, before that. I got to my room and turned on the TV and . . ."

"And saw my press conference?"

He rested his hand on the table, right near hers. It was warm, strong, and browned by the sun.

"Yes, exactly. Did you watch yourself, too? Isn't that a little . . ."

"Embarrassing? Uncomfortable? Stressful?"

She let herself grin at him.

"I was going to say 'masturbatory,' but those words work as well."

He laughed out loud.

"Okay, yes, that works, too." His cheeks got slightly pink. It was strangely . . . cute? "And yeah, it's that and all of the other things. I've more or less gotten used to watching myself, even though I hate it—it's basically trial by fire when you run for office, because your staff makes you watch yourself, and then they criticize everything you do to make you ultra-aware of your most annoying habits. But I don't do it by choice."

He pushed his sleeves up. She tried not to stare at his forearms.

Tried and failed.

"So that's how you found out who I was," he said. "I'd wondered if it wasn't until you saw me walk up to the podium yesterday afternoon that it clicked."

She shook her head.

"No, but I did wonder if you'd remember me. I was surprised that you did."

He looked at her, and a slow smile dawned over his face.

"Olivia, I promise, you're unforgettable."

A warm glow went through her. She knew this was just his politician charm offensive, but hell if it wasn't working on her.

"Now." He opened his menu. "We should figure out what we're going to order before the waitress comes around again."

She looked at the top of the menu.

"Well, I assumed we would get . . . pie and burgers. Am I correct there?"

Now he rolled his eyes at her.

"Yes, thank you, smart-ass, you are correct there, but the question is what kind of pie? Just a warning: the burgers are good, but the fries need some work. The pies, on the other hand, are great."

After how good that cake was, she believed him. And after the way he looked at her, she was very glad to be here with him right now.

Max put the menu down and smiled at Olivia. He had more fun talking to this woman than to anyone he'd talked to in a long time.

"Okay, I know what burger I want," Olivia said. "But what pie should I get?"

"How do you feel about sharing food?" he asked her.

Before she could answer, he hurried to qualify that question.

"If you don't like to, or we don't know each other well enough, or whatever, that's fine, it's just that . . ."

"I know it's fine." The look on her face said, *I don't care about what you think of me enough to pretend to you.* Well, this woman was certainly bad for his ego.

Or good, maybe, depending on who you talked to.

"But actually, I'm fine with sharing," she said. "I grew up in a very sharing-food kind of family. And plus, I'd rather have lots of things to try than just one."

Oh, thank goodness.

"I did not grow up in a very sharing-food kind of family, but I'm with you on that last thing. I always want to try more stuff on a menu than I have appetite for." He grinned at her. "So I was thinking we could get a few slices of pie and share."

She looked at the list of pies on the menu and then back up at him.

"That depends on what kinds you wanted. I was thinking hard about both the apple and the boysenberry, and then I was also intrigued by the lemon meringue, and then there's the pecan, and . . ."

A woman after his own heart.

"I like all of those," he said. "Unfortunately, there's no strawberry rhubarb here."

She shrugged, which did incredible things to that V in her neckline. This woman got more attractive every time he looked at her.

"We can't have everything."

Just then, the waitress came over to take their order. They both ordered cheeseburgers and fries, with everything.

"We'll go ahead and order dessert now," he said. "We want slices of apple, boysenberry, lemon meringue, pecan, and cherry pie."

The waitress looked around at their booth.

"Anyone else joining you?"

He shook his head and grinned. Olivia covered her face with her hands.

"Nope."

When the waitress walked away, Olivia's head was still in her hands. Finally, she looked up at him. With, he was relieved to see, a grin on her face.

"When I listed all of those pies," she said, "that was just, you know, for discussion, so we could decide which ones to order. That wasn't me saying we had to order them all."

Max liked how, every time Olivia laughed at something he said or did, he felt like it was hard won. Even when it was clear she was laughing at him, like right now.

"I know, but this is your first time here! Plus I want you to be able to accurately tell all of your friends back in New York how much better L.A. is—you can't do that unless you have plenty of evidence."

Olivia brushed her hair back from her face. One curl immediately sprung back. He wanted to lean forward and tuck it behind her ear, but stopped himself.

"That would be a waste of time. There are two kinds of people who live in New York: the ones who know L.A. is better but refuse to move, and the ones who will never acknowledge to their dying day that there's anything good about California. Oh, well, there's the third kind—the ones who are trying to get out. That was me for the past few years. But I never bother to have those arguments about which city is better, partly because the answer is obvious to me, but also because those arguments are pointless and make everyone mad for no reason."

He was pretty sure she'd just insulted him again. Hardly anyone ever did that to his face these days, not even people who strenuously disagreed with him politically.

It was kind of . . . nice?

"I was going to ask why you moved back to California from New York, but I guess that just answered that question. How long did it take you to get back here?"

His big worry with this date tonight had been that he'd have to control the whole conversation himself. That's what had happened the few times he'd gone out on first dates in the past two years—he didn't know if it was because women were intimidated by him now, or because the type of women who were interested in dating a senator thought they should just shut up and let him talk, but whatever it was, those dates were boring as hell. But with Olivia, the conversation was easy; he didn't have to think about it; he could just relax into chatting with her.

"I started really thinking about it almost three years ago—I moved to New York a year after I graduated from law school, and I loved living there, but every time I came to California, it got harder and harder to go back. I decided in earnest about a year ago. I'm sure there's a lot I'll miss about New York, but it feels right to be here in L.A. now."

Oh good, now he could ask her something he'd been wondering about since the luncheon.

"I'm impressed that you've only been here for a month and just opened your firm, and the community center already approached you about joining the board. Doesn't that usually take a while?"

She smirked at him.

"Maybe for some people."

He let out a bark of laughter that made the

tables around them stare. He really liked how cocky she was.

"I liked your speech, by the way," she said. "I don't know if I mentioned that." She had, but he was very happy to hear it again. "And I liked what you said about your criminal justice reform bill."

"Thank you, that means a lot." He knew she—unlike many people who complimented him—wouldn't have done so if she didn't mean it. He reached across the table and touched her hand. It was soft, warm. "The speech itself was mostly my staffer Poppy, so I'll pass along your compliments to her. And the bill is something I've worked really hard on. When I became disenchanted with the way we lock kids up, I spent a lot of time talking to advocates and experts about what we could and should be doing for these kids."

She kept her hand on the table right next to his. Just barely touching.

"That's as unexpected as it is refreshing. We need more politicians to do things like asking experts who have devoted years to thinking and talking about how best to fix problems. It's sad that that's so rare, but I guess it is."

He couldn't tell if that was a backhanded compliment or not, but either way, he'd take it.

"Tell me more about your job," he said. "It must have taken a lot of courage to start your own firm."

She looked proud.

"It did. Though it took a while for me to decide to make that leap. Ellie first brought it up . . . oh God, maybe five years ago? At first it was just a joke, and then it got more serious, but it really wasn't until last year when I finally said yes, I'd do it."

He grinned at her.

"That's definitely the opposite way I make decisions; I'm much more of a split-second kind of guy. What made you finally go for it, after five whole years of thinking about it?"

She opened her eyes wide and shook her head.

"That sounds . . . like a stressful way to live. As for me, so many things finally came to a head." She paused and looked at him for a long moment before continuing. "I was a partner at my old firm, but too often there were white male associates who got far more respect than I did, and the older partners loved to yell at me. I was just sick of it. I was tired of people doubting my ideas and intelligence, tired of just having to take the abuse, tired of working incredibly long days with no time for myself, and very tired of winter in New York. Finally, one day, after holding my rage in at work one too many times, I walked out of the building and called Ellie and told her I was in."

"I'm really sorry you had to go through all of that," he said.

He touched her hand again, and this time she slid her hand into his.

"Thank you," she said. "I appreciate that."

"You're a month into the firm now?" he asked. "How's it been so far? All that you dreamed of?"

He rubbed his thumb back and forth over her hand, and she smiled.

"I'm not really sure quite what I dreamed of, but it's been great so far. Granted, it's been stressful—it's just me and Ellie, and we're doing everything ourselves, from casework and meeting with clients to research to building bookshelves to updating our website to the seemingly endless amount of paperwork the State of California wants from us. But it's incredible to be my own boss, and to do things the way I think they should be done, every single time."

Boy, could he ever relate to that.

"Did you know anything about running your own business before?"

She shook her head.

"Nope, we've both learned on the fly. We both reached out to a lot of other women we knew who have started their own firms and their own businesses, and got a ton of advice, though— thank God for all of them. Some of that advice saved us from making some really bad and expensive mistakes."

She was so animated when she talked about her firm. He liked that.

"You and Ellie have been friends for a long time, right? I bet it's such a change to work with someone you can really trust," he said.

The waitress set their burgers and fries in front of them, but Max ignored the food.

"Oh, it's been great to work with Ellie—the two of us have such different strengths, but we still work really well together. And yes, I trust her implicitly, but we also signed a very detailed contract." She grinned. "That was a very fun day, actually."

Max grinned back at her.

"The true way to any lawyer's heart," he said.

Olivia picked up her burger.

"That's all too accurate," she said.

They were silent for a while as they both dove into their burgers and fries, but he didn't feel the need to rush to fill the silence. The table was just small enough that they kept accidentally touching each other under the table . . . though, after a while, it stopped being an accident, at least on his end.

She was gorgeous, she was smart, and she was funny, but more than anything, she was interesting. He felt like he could talk to her for hours. And holy shit did he want to kiss her.

"You were correct," Olivia said as she put down her burger. "The burgers are great, but the fries need some work."

It wasn't that Max would have liked her less if

she hadn't agreed with his french fry opinions, but . . . well, he was just very relieved she did.

"It's so hard to find a place that has a good burger-and-fry combination—one is almost always significantly better than the other one, and I don't understand why."

Olivia picked up her drink.

"Put *that* on your platform."

They grinned at each other.

"Is your family still in Northern California?" he asked.

"Yeah, my parents and my sister," she said. "They're *thrilled* I'm in L.A. now, let me tell you. You and my sister would get along well—she's also obsessed with both food and politics. She emailed me a long list of all of her favorite places in L.A. before I got here, but I've been so busy I haven't been able to get to them."

She had a tiny dimple in one cheek that only appeared when she smiled really big. How unexpected and charming.

"Now I want to see your sister's list," he said. "That must be weird for you, to be in a new place and needing advice from other people to figure out daily life, after being in New York for so long. I imagine you built a whole life there, with friends and work and everything else." He hated the sad look that came over her face, so he hastened to give her an out. "Sorry if that's too personal, we don't have to talk about this if

63

you don't want to—I was just thinking about it because of how I sometimes feel in DC."

She shook her head.

"No, it's okay, you're right. That makes sense you would feel that way, too—I can only imagine how weird life is for you." She was quiet for a moment. "It was hard to leave a place where I built a whole life to go somewhere brand-new. I do have some friends here, and of course I work with one of my best friends. But she's been living in L.A. for a long time, and she's married, and has a kid, and has her own life here, so . . . it's different, you know?" She shrugged. "Is that how it is for you, too?"

He nodded.

"It is. I've been in DC for . . . I guess just over a year now, but I feel like I barely know the city, and then when I come home, life here has gone on without me. I have a handful of good friends I've known for years, but these days my schedule is so weird I barely see them, and . . . well, it gets lonely."

He hadn't said this out loud to anyone. He'd barely even said it to himself. He didn't know why he'd said it to Olivia, except she looked at him like she was really, truly listening to him.

"Yeah, that sounds hard." She reached her hand back across the table, and it felt natural for him to slide his fingers into hers. "You can't really say,

'Yes, you should book a sitter so we can all have dinner two weeks from Friday,' then two weeks from Friday you're still on an airplane, because you couldn't leave the Senate until some asshole finished spouting his nonsense."

He laughed so hard at that people turned to stare again.

"That's a very accurate way of describing my job."

She grinned at him, then popped another fry in her mouth and made a face.

"I can't stop eating these, even though they're not very good. Kind of like In-N-Out fries—we all know they're terrible, but that doesn't stop me from eating a whole order." She shook her head. "Maybe I just need to find some hobbies, or something." She took a sip of water. "You grew up in L.A., right? Whereabouts?"

He was surprised she didn't know this about him. Most people did.

"I did. In Beverly Hills."

Her eyebrows shot up. She opened her mouth, paused, and then continued.

"I'm impressed that you know the Eastside so well, if you grew up over there."

He shook his head at her.

"We both know that's not what you were going to say. Come on, out with it."

She looked down at her plate, then back up at him with a grin.

"Sorry, was I that obvious? I can't help it, I grew up in the Bay Area in the eighties and nineties, I have a single reaction to hearing that someone grew up in Beverly Hills, and it's—"

"*90210*," they said in unison, and laughed again. He used to hate telling people he grew up in Beverly Hills, but now that his whole background was on the Internet for the world to see, it made it easier.

"Anyway, I don't live there anymore—I went to college at UCLA and have lived all over the L.A. area since then."

"All done here?" The waitress didn't wait for an answer and picked up their plates and swept them away. There was one last bite of burger on his plate he'd wanted. Oh well—they did have five pieces of pie coming.

"UCLA, of course. That explains the hat. I'm disappointed in this poor excuse for a disguise, you know. The same UCLA hat every time, and that's where you actually went to college? Didn't you ever think about something like a Yankees hat, or a USC hat, or something?"

He pulled the cap down over his face.

"Over my dead body."

The waitress came back and slid the five plates of pie on the table.

"Here you go."

Olivia stared at the pie-laden table.

"I can't believe we actually ordered five different kinds of pie, but at least I wore a red shirt instead of a white one." She shook her head. "But I have a feeling this pie will stain no matter what color the shirt."

He pushed the cherry pie toward her.

"Stick with me, kid. One of the first skills they teach you in politician school is how to eat food around other people without spilling—even the messiest food." He handed her a napkin. "Maybe if you're lucky, I'll teach you."

She picked up her fork and grinned at him.

"I might have to take you up on that."

They both dove into the pie, pushing the plates around the table as they alternated bites. She ate with such enjoyment—she would pause and close her eyes after the first bite of each piece, as if she needed to shut the world out to concentrate on it. He wondered if she brought that kind of concentration to everything she did.

He would bet on it.

As they ate, they talked about pies they had known, which led to a discussion of best and worst meals they'd had while traveling, which led to airplane horror stories.

Finally, Olivia put her fork down with a sigh.

"Those were all delicious, but I can't eat another bite." She looked down at her shirt. "I should quit while I'm ahead anyway; I managed to keep this shirt cherry-free, I don't want to push my luck."

When the waitress dropped the bill on the table, Max pulled out his wallet.

"My treat? As a welcome to California?"

Olivia withdrew her hand from her purse and smiled at him.

"Thank you. And thanks for introducing me to this place; you were right about that pie."

He smiled to himself as he tossed bills on the table. He hadn't been at all sure she'd let him pay for dinner. He hoped that meant she liked him some. Because he already knew he liked her a lot.

They walked out to the parking lot, and Olivia pulled her phone out of her purse.

"Well, I should get a car to get me home, so . . ."

Max put his hand on her shoulder.

"You didn't drive? Can I drive you home?"

Please let her say yes.

"I didn't drive, no, because . . . I still haven't bought a car. So yes, I'll take that ride home."

He took an exaggerated step backward.

"Wait. You still don't have a car?" he asked. "And you say you're from California?"

He'd hoped to make her laugh, and he'd succeeded.

"I know, I know, but I've been so busy ever since I got here. I haven't had time to buy one yet."

He led her toward his car.

"That's something a New Yorker would say."

She glared at him, but he was pretty sure he could tell she was smiling behind that.

"It is not," she said. "A New Yorker wouldn't even have a driver's license! They'd just complain about the public transportation here forever." She bit her lip. "And I hate to say this, but they'd have a point."

He opened the passenger door for her, and she got in.

"I hate to cede the point to the New Yorkers, but you're right about that."

They smiled at each other as he closed the door.

Max spread his big, firm hands on the steering wheel, and Olivia couldn't keep her eyes off them. Or her body from remembering every single touch from those hands—when she'd first walked in and he'd put his hand on her arm and then her back; when he'd touched and then briefly held her hand at the table; when he'd handed her napkins and pie and ketchup, and his fingers had lingered for a few extra seconds on hers . . . or had that been her imagination? And then just now, when he'd put his hand on her shoulder, and she'd wanted it to stay there for so much longer.

She smiled to herself. Tonight was going to be good.

"What's your address?" he asked.

She gave it to him, then double-checked in her phone.

"Okay, yes, that's the right address. I still only half know it." She shook her head at herself. "I lived in the same place the entire time I was in New York, so I almost gave you an address that was a few days' drive away."

He smiled at her and pulled out of the parking lot.

"No problem, this is probably a good time of night to start a cross-country drive anyway. No traffic getting out of L.A., so we could probably get to Colorado by morning."

She narrowed her eyes.

"Are you sure about that? How fast do you drive, anyway?"

He threw her a grin.

"Don't you worry. You're very safe with me."

She bit her lip as she glanced sideways at him—that arrogant grin was far too sexy for his own good. Hell, *Max* was far too sexy for his own good. She'd expected to flirt with him a lot tonight, but she hadn't expected to talk to him, with him, that much. He looked right at her when she was talking like she was the only person in the world, and that he was fascinated by what she was saying. And then he asked follow-up questions that made it clear he'd been paying attention! Which in turn made her want to rip his clothes off right there in the restaurant.

That whole focused-attention thing was a politician trick; she knew that. He had some specific professional skills that also happened to be exactly the right way to get into a woman's pants, and he was using that skill for all it was worth.

Well, it was working.

He took his baseball cap off and tossed it in the back seat, and ran his fingers through his hair. She shook her head. She'd been right—perfect tousled waves, even after being under a baseball cap all night.

"Do you like being a senator?" she asked him. "What with the different schedule and the security concerns and the travel and everything else."

Why had she asked him that? Probably because his charm offensive had gotten to her enough that she really wanted to know what he would say.

"That's a hard question to answer," he said after a few moments. "Am I glad I ran and won? Absolutely yes. Is it hard as hell? Harder and more frustrating than I ever imagined it would be. But I think I'm making a difference, which has been my ultimate goal from the beginning. I think—I hope—I'm helping to move the country forward, helping to improve people's lives, here in California and across the country. And I care more about doing a good job than I've ever cared about anything. So . . . I don't quite know if I can say I like my job, exactly; at least, not all of the parts of it. But I'm really honored to be there."

He spoke with so much enthusiasm, so much passion. She hadn't expected that. She'd thought he'd give her a much more politic answer, but that had been an honest one.

"Do you know what I really miss?" he asked.

She shook her head.

"Tell me."

He gestured to the traffic in front of them.

"Driving." He sounded wistful. "Even just sitting alone in L.A. traffic. God, I miss it so much." He laughed. "Sorry, I sound like a poor little rich boy right now, don't I? Complaining that someone else drives me around all the time and I get to relax."

Olivia shook her head again.

"No, I understand what you mean. I always felt that way when I went home from New York and drove my parents' or my sister's car some-where—the time alone with your thoughts driving a car is different than walking down the street, or sitting on a bus, or standing on the subway." She grinned. "And there's absolutely nothing that compares to driving on a California freeway on a sunny day, blasting music with the windows wide open."

He turned and smiled at her.

"Isn't that the truth?"

He glanced down at the GPS and made another left turn.

"Is this your street?"

She nodded. She suddenly couldn't wait to get him inside.

"It's right over there."

She gestured to the small house she'd rented. She'd been determined to live in a real house, after living in an apartment for so long. She no longer had upstairs *or* downstairs neighbors. It was strange and wonderful.

He pulled into her empty driveway and took off his seat belt.

"I'll just walk you to the door."

Oh, okay, sure, he would just "walk her to the door." She smiled to herself. She knew bullshit when she heard it, and that was some bullshit, all right.

As he opened his door, his phone rang, and he pulled it out of his pocket.

"I'm sorry, I thought my phone was on do not disturb, let me just . . ." He glanced at the screen and grimaced. "I'm sorry, I have to take this."

After a minute or so, he jumped out of the car, but left the door open.

"Hey—I'm sorry, I have to run, there's something I have to deal with and it can't wait."

She also knew this kind of bullshit when she heard it.

"Sure, of course," she said, when what she

wanted to do was ask him why the fuck he'd led her on for hours just to blow her off.

She walked up to her front door, expecting him to just jump back in his car and drive away. But instead he walked beside her and waited for her to unlock the door.

"Thanks for tonight, it was great," he said. He patted her on the shoulder and turned to race back to his car.

She walked in the house and barely managed not to slam the door.

Yes, sure, there was a slim possibility that had been an actual emergency. But he'd just patted her on the fucking shoulder and jumped back in his car. Not a kiss on the lips, or even on the cheek, not a lingering glance, not a long clasp of her hand, and definitely not a "let's do this again." Just a pat on the fucking shoulder!

She was pretty sure that had been the Max Powell version of when she'd been on a bad date and had secretly texted a friend to call her with an "emergency."

Why had he even flirted with her all night if he was going to do that? And kept up all the little shoulder touches and back touches and "accidental" brushes of her legs with his, under the table? Was it all just some act?

She dropped her keys in the bowl by her front door and walked into the bathroom to start her bathwater. You know what, this was fine. She could get into the bathtub and read her book and drink a glass of wine and have a nice cozy Saturday night, and that would be better than sex with Max could possibly be.

She knew that was a lie as soon as she thought it.

She pulled her clothes off, wrapped a scarf around her hair, and got in the tub.

Oh God. She could not believe she was sitting here in the bathtub with a glass of wine in her hand feeling sorry for herself after a disappointing end to a date. She felt like a single-woman-in-the-city parody—all she needed was a sheet mask and a box of chocolates to really make it perfect.

She couldn't concentrate on her book, so she leaned over the side of the tub and reached for the stack of magazines she always kept nearby. That glossy pamphlet from the community center luncheon was in this pile, so she flipped through it. While she knew she couldn't spare the money to be on the board, she did want to stay involved with the center. Huh, they had a food pantry and community kitchen there . . . and they were looking for volunteers. Plus, it would only be to her benefit to keep herself and her firm in the forefront of Bruce's mind. He knew everyone in the tech community in L.A., and a referral from him would be gold.

This was a great idea. She'd volunteer at

the food pantry, and get some networking and do-gooding in all at the same time. And tomorrow, she'd do something wild like go for a walk in her new neighborhood. Maybe she'd find that bakery Alexa had told her about. And she was definitely not going to think about Max Powell.

When she got back from the bakery the next morning, a ham-and-cheese croissant in her hand, and a chocolate croissant in her purse for later, there was a vase full of bright spring flowers on her doorstep. She picked them up and stared at them, and then plucked off the note taped to the side of the vase.

> *Sorry I had to run last night—can I get a do-over? I leave for DC this afternoon, but maybe we can see each other again next weekend? I had a great time last night—hope you have a good week.*
> *Max*

Well. Maybe she'd been wrong about that "emergency" after all.

Chapter Four

Max sank down on the couch as soon as he let himself into his DC apartment on Monday night. He was starving, but too tired to search through their fridge for food. Congress had started back up again with a vengeance after their week of recess—he'd been racing from place to place all day, with four overlapping committee meetings, a meeting with some lobbyists, and then all the usual business on the Senate floor he half paid attention to. It must have been equally as busy over on the House side; his roommate and friend, freshman representative Wesley Crawford, wasn't even home yet.

He and Wes had been friends since college. They'd been an unexpected pair, he the rich white kid from Beverly Hills, Wes the Black athlete from the Central Valley, but somehow their friendship had stuck ever since. They'd taken very different paths to get here—Max had gone straight to law school and become a prosecutor, then the L.A. district attorney; Wes had become a teacher, then moved to the school board, and then ran for the open House of Representatives seat in his hometown two years before.

Max had been stunned when Wes suggested they share this apartment, after their disastrous stint as roommates in college. "You're neater now though, right? It's been twenty years," immaculately tidy Wes had said. Max was not neater now, but he promptly hired a cleaning service to come to their apartment once a week to preserve their friendship. Thank goodness for Wes; these past sixteen months in the Senate had been stressful and lonely as it was; it would have been so much worse if he'd come back to this bland, generic, furnished apartment alone every night. At least now he had Wes to vent with whenever either of them needed it.

He wondered what Wes would say about Olivia. Probably make fun of him for sending her the cake, but it had worked, hadn't it? As had the flowers—she'd texted him just after he landed in DC the day before. He'd been so relieved she didn't hold it against him that he'd had to rush away at the end of their date because of breaking news. Times like that he definitely wasn't as big a fan of his job.

Speaking of Olivia, he should text her. He scrolled back through their texts from the past few days.

Thank you for the flowers! Sorry I missed you—was out scouting for a good bakery in my neighborhood, and I think I found one. Haven't tried their cake or pie yet, but the pastries were delicious. A rain check sounds good—next weekend works for me.

You're very welcome, and I'm sorry again I had to run off. I had to just guess on your favorite flowers, I hope there were some you liked in there. I want details about this bakery—maybe you can tell me on Friday night?

Let me check my work schedule, but Friday night should be fine—excited to see what your "normal person" disguise is this time. Different glasses? Different hat? A wig???

He laughed out loud again at the thought of himself in a wig.

I wouldn't know the first thing about where to find a wig, but then I do live in LA, don't I? There must be realistic wigs everywhere. So far I've just relied on glasses/hat/no gel in my hair, but maybe I'll do something wild next time. Stay tuned!

He turned on the TV as he waited for her to text back, and was flipping channels when he heard a key in the door.

"Hi, honey, I'm home!" Max shouted as the door opened. Wes walked in, suit and tie on, natty briefcase over his shoulder, and—bless him—a pizza box in his hand.

"Oh, thank God, I was starving," Max said.

Wes dropped the box on the coffee table and disappeared into his bedroom to change.

"Didn't occur to you to pick up dinner on the way home, did it?" Wes shouted through the crack in his bedroom door.

"I was going to order something!" Max shouted back. Okay, at least he'd been thinking about it.

Max stood up and got plates and napkins (Wes always insisted on this) and brought them to the coffee table. They had a kitchen table, too, but they almost never ate at it.

"Sure you were," Wes said. He came out of his bedroom in sweats and a T-shirt and grabbed two beers out of their fridge.

Wes sat down on the couch and picked up the remote control.

"You're not going to tell me you were attempting to watch preseason baseball when there's basketball on, were you?"

Max sat down at the other end of the couch.

"It's spring training, not 'preseason.' But no,

I was actually looking to see if there was any soccer on."

Wes flipped open the pizza box.

"Hey, thanks again for letting my cousin crash at your place last week when he was stranded in L.A."

Max waved that off.

"It was no big deal; it was only for a night. Nice kid." Max glanced at the pizza. "Broccoli on the pizza? Seriously?"

Wes gave him a stern look.

"You can't work as hard as we both work and not eat vegetables. I should have gotten us a salad, too, but this is better than nothing."

Max's phone buzzed, and he picked it up from the table.

Now I'm already excited for Friday night

Shit, wait a minute—he was only going to get into LAX midday on Friday, if everything went well. He'd better temper her wig expectations. Maybe he could order new glasses or something instead.

Ok don't get too excited—the wig may have to wait until I have extended LA shopping time. This is where being in DC the bulk of the time cramps my style. How's your Monday going?

"*Who* are you texting?" Wes asked him.

Max picked up a slice of pizza and took a bite. Should he tell Wes about Olivia already? He laughed at himself—he hadn't even kissed her yet, and he wanted to tell the world about her.

"Man, do you need to work on your poker face," Wes said when he didn't answer right away. "It's a woman, that's clear enough."

Max shrugged, but he couldn't keep from smiling.

"Yes, it's a woman. Her name is Olivia. Olivia Monroe."

Wes dropped his pizza back on his plate and turned to stare at Max.

"Oh no. She's already a full name with you? You've got it bad. How did this happen? We only had recess for one week!"

Max laughed.

"I know, but it started a few weeks ago. You see, one night there was a water main break in my neighborhood, so I went to a hotel for the night. And at the hotel bar . . ."

Wes covered his eyes.

"No. Oh no. Don't tell me that you, a United States senator, fell for some line from some woman at a hotel bar and took her back to your room, where all of your classified documents live in your electronics. Don't they teach you better than that over in the Senate?"

Max picked up the remote and turned the TV back to spring training baseball.

"This is what you get for thinking so little of me. No, I did not fall for some line from some woman at a bar. I just *met* her at the bar, that's all. And there was no line at all; I'm the one who started talking to her, not the reverse. And . . . we talked for a while, and she was funny, and smart, and interesting, and she kept making fun of me, and . . . it was great. That's all."

Max's phone buzzed again.

> Ok, I won't expect a blond guy to show up at my door Friday then. My Monday is busy—tons of meetings with clients and potential clients. Now on my way to a local bar association thing to network, even though I wish I was on my couch watching bad reality TV

Wes waved his hand at Max's phone.

"That little meeting at the bar was obviously not all, because if it was, why do you have that schmoopy look on your face? Did she take you back to her room after she got you to hit on her at the bar?"

Max rolled his eyes.

"Get your mind out of the gutter. No one went back to anyone's room. I didn't even get her last name—then, anyway. But then—last week when I was back in L.A., I gave a speech at a luncheon. I looked around the room when I was up onstage, and there she was." He held up a hand to forestall Wes's conspiracy theory. "She was not stalking me; she's a lawyer, she just moved to L.A. to start her own firm, and one of the board members of the center has known her for years and invited her to the luncheon."

Wes took the remote back and changed the channel.

"I see. How did you get this poor woman's number, then? Did you fall that hard for her after a chat at a bar and seeing her from across a hotel ballroom?"

Max picked up his phone to text her back.

Good luck! You'll be fantastic.

He looked up from his phone to Wes, and tried to wipe the schmoopy look off of his face. Whatever that meant.

"I remembered the name of her law firm and looked it up." Wes didn't need to know about the cake. "And long story short, we went out Saturday night."

Wes's eyes widened.

"Oh shit. You really are running for president, aren't you?"

Max set his beer down.

"What? No, what are you talking about? How did you get from here to there?"

Wes tore off another slice of pizza.

"Gotta wife up to run for president. Everybody knows that."

Max balled up a napkin and tossed it at him.

"Now you sound like one of those stupid magazines that put both of us on their hottest bachelors in Washington lists. I'm not trying to 'wife up'—I just like her, that's all!"

He wouldn't admit this to Wes, because then Wes would be certain he was going to run for president, but he had been . . . lonely lately for more than just the reasons he'd said to Olivia the other night. He'd been to a lot of fundraisers for other candidates in the past sixteen months, and at many of them, the candidate's spouse was there with them, by their side. He'd wished he had that.

But he hadn't wished it enough to go on a single second date in the past two-plus years. Olivia was different.

"Mmmhmm," Wes said. "How long did this date last, anyway?"

Max sighed.

"Unfortunately, not long enough—Kara called with that leak about the attorney general's announcement, so we had to come up with a statement ASAP. Which sucked, because I had to rush off right when I'd driven Olivia home. But even so, it was one of the most fun nights I've had in . . . well, at least the past two years. I'm going to see her again this weekend, and . . ." He took a deep breath. "She's just great. Smart, funny, thoughtful." He shook his head. "I know it's early, but I can't wait to see her again. I really like her, Wes."

Wes turned to look at him, all trace of mockery on his face gone.

"You really do, don't you? I haven't seen you look like that in years." He punched his friend on the shoulder. "Okay, who is this woman? Let's see." He gestured at Max's phone.

Max sighed and pulled up the tab for Olivia's law firm website.

"This is her," he said, and handed his phone to Wes.

Wes took the phone, stared at the picture for a few seconds, and then looked up at Max with his mouth open.

"Oh. Ohhh, okay. Well, if you are trying to wife up, I approve." He paused for a second. "But."

Max should have known there would be a "but."

"Can I get you to promise me one thing?" Wes asked.

"I'm pretty sure I don't want to do that," Max said.

Wes ignored that.

"Promise me you won't sleep with her yet."

Max opened his mouth to protest, but Wes kept talking. "I know, that's a ridiculous thing for me to say, but just listen. That might force some caution on you. I know how you are—you jump into things, you make decisions in seconds. I don't want you to fall hard for this woman and whisk her off to Vegas on the third date, or worse, have her sell stories about you to the press."

Max had to stop him there.

"That's unfair—yes, okay, some of that is true, but I'm not usually like that with women! I haven't dated anyone in almost three years—not since Lana and I broke up. Plus, I'm not in the habit of spilling my guts to people. I don't know why you think I need caution here!"

Wes held up a hand.

"Sure, but you do jump into things quickly, and while most of the time your split-second decisions turn out well—that decision to run for Senate sure worked out—you and I both know the times when they haven't. Remember Death Valley?"

Max grabbed another piece of pizza.

"I get us stranded in the desert *one time* twenty years ago, and I have to hear about it for the rest of my life, huh?"

"I'm just saying—you haven't changed that much in those twenty years," Wes said. "Remember when you lost it on the attorney general on CNN last fall?"

Max sighed. That moment had gained him a lot of press, and a lot of cheers from people on his side, but it hadn't particularly helped his criminal justice reform bill.

"Don't remind me. But I don't see what one thing has to do with the other. I've only gone on a handful of boring first dates since Lana, and the first time I meet someone I actually like, you want to throw cold water all over it?"

Wes dropped his hand on Max's shoulder.

"I'm not trying to be a dick, but everything is a little more high risk for you now. And if you saw the look on your face when you talked about her . . . I just want you to be careful, that's all. And for her sake, I'm sure you don't want to get photographed leaving her house some morning and have her put on blast as the new girlfriend of the hottest bachelor in DC before either of you is ready for that."

Max sighed and leaned his head back against the couch.

"Damn it. That's an actual good reason. I hate it when you're right. Okay, fine, I promise. Thanks for the buzzkill."

Wes grinned at him.

"Anytime, man, anytime."

Wednesday afternoon, Olivia sat at her desk and looked from her silent computer to her silent phone and back. She hadn't gotten an email since eleven a.m., or a text message since just after noon. She couldn't remember the last time this had happened in her working life. Maybe in her first few months as an associate, before she'd passed the bar?

Monday and Tuesday had been much the same. She'd had calls with one of their handful of clients, and one call with a potential client, and she had done lots of networking, but it wasn't at all the amount of work she'd been used to. Or expected.

Yes, yes, it was still the early days. And sure, she was still occupied doing some of the seemingly unending administrative setup for the new firm, but now that she and Ellie were mostly done with that, the silence was starting to terrify her. She was already tired of lying to people that their new firm was "soooo busy" like she'd said in an email to a former colleague today. But she knew she had to fake it till she made it, so fake it she would do.

But . . . how long would she have to fake it? Had this all been a huge mistake? Did this silence mean their firm was going to fail? She had a lot of money saved up—she'd been thinking about getting out of the big-firm life for a while now, and she'd tried to save as much as possible—so she wasn't worried she wouldn't be able to pay her rent or would have to give up on the firm in the short term. She had enough to support herself for at least the next two years, if necessary . . . but if it were necessary, that would mean she had failed.

Honestly, if she still had to rely on her savings by early next year, she'd have to give up, realize she couldn't cut it, and go crawling back to a big law firm.

It was different for Ellie—Ellie relished her newfound work-life balance, and she seemed to have no worries at all about how quiet everything was right now. Ellie could pick her kid up from school, go to teacher conferences without having to balance the needs of clients and demanding senior partners, and have dinner with her family every night. And Ellie had a husband to fall back on, one who made a substantial salary of his own. She didn't have to support herself or worry that she might have to cash in her 401(k) if this venture of theirs didn't work. Olivia didn't resent Ellie for any of that, and she didn't doubt her passion for their firm, but it was just fact.

On her date with Max, she'd had to pretend she was successful, confident, and oh so busy. The whole time he'd asked about their firm, she'd held back her anxiety and fear and doubt, and put on her Proud Businesswoman/Boss Lady hat. And while she *was* proud of herself and her firm, she was also terrified.

What could she do now, this afternoon, to make this firm a success? She'd networked her ass off at the bar association on Monday night. But there wasn't anything else going on tonight that she could find, for either lawyers or small businesses.

Hmmm. She flicked through a bunch of the tabs she had open on her computer. That wasn't until next week, that was invitation only, that one cost too much . . . oh, wait. The food pantry! One of their volunteer times was Wednesday night at six. Perfect.

At exactly 5:55 p.m., Olivia jumped out of the car in front of the community center and thanked the driver. She looked down at her outfit and made a face; she was in slim black pants, a silk blouse, and pointy black flats, which probably wasn't the best outfit for volunteering. This had been her work uniform when she lived in New York—there it was perfect: almost always work appropriate, easy to dress up with a blazer and heels—but here in L.A. it seemed way too dressy for almost everything she did.

She walked into the building and followed the signs to the food pantry.

"Hi," she said to the person at the door. "I'm here to volunteer. I'm Olivia Monroe."

The woman at the door grinned and shook her hand.

"Hi, Olivia Monroe, I'm Jamila Carter. I'm the coordinator here. Welcome. Since this is your first time, I'll show you around and get you ready to start."

Olivia liked the looks of Jamila—somewhere in her late twenties, with long braids piled up into a huge bun on top of her head and a clipboard in her hand. Olivia instinctively trusted someone holding a clipboard.

"Is it that obvious that it's my first time?" Olivia asked as they walked into the kitchen. "I should have worn something different, but I kind of came on the spur of the moment."

Jamila laughed and shook her head.

"Your outfit is fine." She stopped and looked Olivia over. "Well, okay, I see what you mean, but we'll give you an apron. It wasn't that; it's that I've worked here since the beginning, so I kind of recognize everyone at this point. How did you find out about us?"

Olivia looked around the large, busy kitchen and was suddenly very glad she'd come tonight.

"I moved to L.A. pretty recently—I just started my own law firm here—and one of the board members brought me to the luncheon last week. I don't live that far away, so I thought I'd help out." She looked around. "This place is a lot bigger than I expected."

Jamila set her clipboard down on the counter.

"This is the cafeteria from when this building was an elementary school. The food pantry started here on a much smaller scale when the community center first opened, just as a place for people to leave donations for community members in need, and we still have that. But after a while we all saw the need for meals for our elderly and homebound members, and I asked around to see if we could get larger-scale food donations to cook with. One thing led to another, and about a year ago we started this community kitchen and meal delivery service as a part of the food pantry."

Olivia looked around the room. Everything looked clean and organized, with big piles of produce in stacks. Other volunteers—mostly older Black women, but lots of other ages and ethnicities, too—came in and put on aprons and said hi to Jamila.

"This is great. So you've been here from the beginning?"

Jamila waved at someone who'd just walked in.

"I have, and we've really grown. We started off with just a volunteer event on Friday nights once a month—at first, we really didn't know what we were doing, and just sort of made big vats of soup or whatever based around our donations that week. Now we're here twice weekly; on our Wednesday and Friday nights, we bring in volunteers to make complete, wholesome meals for members of our community who can't get outside or cook for themselves easily. On Thursdays and Saturdays we have other sets of volunteers who do our deliveries. We try to make enough food each night for thirty to forty people, though our goal is to increase that to a hundred by the end of this year."

Olivia hadn't quite realized—despite Jamila's mention of an apron—that she'd be cooking tonight.

"That's an impressive goal," she said. "To go from making thirty to forty meals to a hundred."

Olivia really hoped they would give her very clear instructions with this whole cooking thing; that had never been her strong suit. She looked around at the ingredients set out at the different stations.

"How do you figure out what to make from week to week?"

Jamila smiled.

"That's where I come in—I've worked as a cook in restaurants for a while. I've figured out a lot of recipes that work with some of our most frequent food donations, and that our community members will like."

"Wow," Olivia said. "That's impressive. I bet that was a real challenge. They're lucky to have you."

Jamila handed her an apron.

"Well thank you, but I'm lucky to have this place, too. It feels good to give back, yes, but I feel like I'm getting a lot in return." She stopped and bit her lip. "I'm sorry, I'm going on and on about this—I can talk about this place for hours."

Olivia shook her head.

"No problem. Where do we start?"

Jamila led her over to one of the counters.

"Okay, on a scale of one to ten, how good of a cook are you? With one being, like, you can barely open a can and heat up the food inside, and ten at, say, you're a restaurant chef. Be honest, no judgment."

Olivia laughed.

"Probably somewhere around a three? Maybe a four, in a pinch? I can definitely open up cans of food and heat them up, but I don't quite know the difference between what it means to sauté something or braise it."

Jamila steered her in front of a big bowl.

"Okay, perfect—tonight we're making turkey meatballs with mashed potatoes and sautéed spinach. I'm going to put you on meatball duty; no chopping or sautéing involved, you're just going to mix together a bunch of ingredients and then roll it all into meatballs. How does that sound?"

Olivia laughed to herself. This was definitely not what she thought she'd be doing tonight when she woke up this morning.

"That sounds great," she said.

Two hours later, Olivia's feet hurt from standing in the same place for hours in her far-too-pointy shoes, her hands were ice cold from rolling what felt like millions of meatballs, and her eyes stung from all of the onions that the woman next to her had chopped. But when she looked at the forty sealed containers of meatballs, potatoes, and spinach, she felt like she'd really accomplished something.

"Great work tonight, team," Jamila said as they moved the containers from the counters to the refrigerators.

Olivia dropped her apron in the spot where all the other volunteers dropped theirs, took off her gloves, and washed her hands.

"Thanks for coming tonight, Olivia," Jamila said as Olivia dried her hands.

"It was my pleasure," Olivia said. And she meant it, too.

"I hope we'll see you again?" Jamila raised an eyebrow at her.

Olivia nodded and pulled her phone out of her purse.

"Absolutely. I'll try for next Wednesday."

She went to order a car, but Jamila stopped her.

"Do you need a ride home?"

Olivia looked up at her.

"I do, but I'm probably out of your way—are you sure?"

Jamila shrugged.

"I've gotten too many rides from other people in my life to care about going a little while out of my way. Give me a second to lock up."

As they drove off, Jamila asked the question she'd known was coming.

"Is your car in the shop?"

Olivia shook her head. Everyone in L.A. seemed to believe it was unthinkable to not have a car.

"I haven't bought a car yet. I know, I know, everyone gives me that look. I'll get to it eventually, I promise."

Jamila laughed.

"I would hope so. I mean, I know there are people in L.A. who don't have cars; it just makes life a lot more difficult, that's all."

Yeah, she'd realized that in this past month.

"I know—I need to do it sooner rather than later."

Jamila glanced at the GPS and got on the freeway.

"Well, if you need help, let me know—car buying is one of my best skills. I've helped a bunch of friends."

Olivia relaxed into the passenger seat.

"I've never done it before, so I might take you up on that."

Jamila grinned at her.

"Just let me know. How are you liking L.A.? Settling in well? I'm sorry the dating scene here is . . . what it is. I've heard it's much better in New York."

Olivia couldn't help but smile. She hadn't gone on a date in her last year and a half in New York, and somehow she'd met someone almost as soon as she'd landed in L.A.

"Wait a second. What's that smile? Are you dating someone already?" Jamila asked in an outraged tone.

Olivia laughed.

" 'Dating' is probably the wrong word, let's put it that way," she said.

Jamila grinned.

"Even better, honestly. All the good stuff, none of the drama."

That was an excellent way to put it.

"Indeed," Olivia said.

She smiled out the car window. She was definitely looking forward to her date with Max on Friday night.

Chapter Five

Max pulled into Olivia's driveway, grabbed the flowers from his front seat, and walked up to her door. More flowers were probably too much for a second date, but he'd walked by a flower shop that day and had bought them on impulse. He hoped she liked them.

Olivia swung open the door. God, she looked incredible tonight.

"Hi," she said.

He smiled at her.

"Hi to you, too." He held up the flowers. "You didn't tell me what your favorites were, so I just sort of guessed."

She took them from him and beckoned him into the house.

"These are beautiful, thank you. Let me put these in some water and we can go."

He followed her through the hallway and into the big, bright kitchen.

"For someone who doesn't cook, you got a house with a great kitchen."

She laughed and took a tall, narrow pitcher out from a cabinet.

"I know—isn't it a waste? It might make me want to cook more, though. Ellie looked at houses for me, and she loved this one so I grabbed it, but she cooks a lot more than I do."

He watched her fill the pitcher up with water and arrange the flowers in it. He might have to bring her an actual vase next time.

"I can't believe you haven't gotten a car yet," he said as they got in. "That's very un-California of you, you know."

She put her seat belt on and set her bag in her lap. Whenever she didn't smile at something he said, he was afraid he'd made her mad. Oh God, had he gotten that used to yes-men around him who laughed at everything he said?

"I know," she said. "But it seems like such an ordeal. There are so many choices. Domestic or foreign? Normal or electric or hybrid? Sedan? Sports car? SUV? And that's all before I have to do that thing where I go to the dealership and test-drive it and deal with all the sexism from a dealer and negotiate the price or whatever. It's all exhausting." She looked over at him, and her face relaxed into a smile. "I know, you're rolling your eyes at me—you spent all week dealing with national security secrets and actual significant problems for humanity, and I'm sitting here whining about how hard it is to buy a car."

He put his hand on her shoulder for a second as he turned around to back out of her driveway. He didn't need to do that; he had a backup camera, he could see perfectly well to get onto the street. But she didn't seem to mind.

"Trust me, I'm definitely not rolling my eyes at you," he said. "It makes sense that something in your personal life would fall to the bottom of the to-do list. That's often how it is for me, anyway." Though the idea of taking that much time and energy to make a decision like that was foreign to him. He would have just stopped at the first dealership he saw and bought whatever looked good to him. That was exactly what he'd done the last time he'd bought a car, as a matter of fact.

He decided to change the subject, since the car thing seemed to stress her out.

"Speaking of work, how's the new firm going?"

She moved her bag to the floor, then back to her lap.

"Well, really well. Lots of meetings with potential clients, and we've gotten some work from one of the clients I used to work with in my old firm, so that's great. And Ellie and I have done a ton of networking this week, so we hope that'll bear fruit soon."

He turned to smile at her as they waited for a light.

"Oh, that's great news. I know a few people who have started their own firms, and the beginning is always stressful, but it seems like you've hit the ground running."

She nodded.

"It seems like it. And I had a really great time volunteering at the community center's food pantry this week. Well, it's both a food pantry and community kitchen; do you know their model?"

He shook his head.

"I don't. Tell me about it."

She spent the rest of their drive to the movie theater doing just that, and he was captivated the whole time. Olivia seemed to really care about the place and the work they did, after only one time there. It made him like her even more, this enthusiasm and joy for a project that was built to help people who needed it.

"Speaking of," she said. "I saw you on TV the other night, talking about the need to improve the food stamps program. I liked what you said."

He tried not to smile too big.

"You saw that? Thanks for watching."

That had been some good timing on his part. It probably helped that he actually cared about that issue.

"Do you like that part of the job? The TV, and all of that? It's one thing to mess up in front of a judge, and another to mess up live, in front of millions of people."

He laughed.

"Thanks, now I'm sure I'll have that going through my head the next time I'm on TV. But actually, yeah, I do like that part, and it helps that

I'm good at it." He winced. "Does that sound arrogant? I don't mean it that way . . . well, only partly, I guess. But in the past year or so I've had to be honest with myself about what I'm good at in this job and what I'm not good at—I'm good at TV spots, speeches, and talking to constituents, and it helps that I enjoy doing all of that."

She looked at him sideways.

"And what are you not good at?"

He laughed again.

"I guess I walked right into that one, didn't I? I'm less good at all of the politicking on Capitol Hill, the trading favors and using coded language and being passive-aggressive—I hate all of that, but I feel like I'm going to have to learn how to do a better job of it in order to get anything done in the Senate."

He was probably being too honest with Olivia, but he couldn't help it. She'd asked him a real question; he wanted to give her a real answer.

"Why did you run for Senate in the first place?" she asked.

He shrugged.

"I'm an arrogant asshole who thought I could handle it?"

They both laughed.

"I'm sure that's true, but why else?" she asked.

He pulled into the movie theater parking space and turned off the car before he answered.

"I wanted to make a difference. I know, it

sounds so trite. But it felt like . . . I had a charmed life, you know? I was born rich, I grew up in fucking Beverly Hills, life came easy to me. I didn't understand that for a long time, but once I did, I realized it was all a waste unless I used my abilities and my privilege to help other people. I was a prosecutor first, and that's when I really saw how much pain and sorrow there is out there in the world. And I got really sick of putting people in prison—people who didn't deserve it, or who had gone through so much in their lives. And I knew the only way to really fix things was to change the laws in the first place."

He looked at her for a second and then looked away. That might have been a little too much honesty. But it was hard not to tell Olivia the truth, when she looked at him like she really cared about what he said. Like she cared about him. He told most of the world the glib, easy answer, but somehow he couldn't do that to her.

Ah. This was why Wes was so concerned.

Granted, he hadn't told Olivia the entire truth—this was still the flattering version of his life story. He still wanted her to like him, after all.

"And now I'm in a job where I wear fake glasses to go out on a date—I hope you like these." He pulled a pair of new glasses out of the glove compartment and slid them on, and was relieved to see her smile. He grabbed his UCLA cap from the back seat and put it on, too.

He wanted to reach for her hand, but it seemed too early for that. He compromised, and put his hand on her back as they walked toward the theater.

"Anyway, I hope this movie is funny—after the week I've had, I could use a few laughs." He looked over at her. "I'm glad we could do this. It's really great to see you again."

Olivia smiled at him, and moved closer to him as they walked.

"I'm glad, too."

Max seemed different tonight, and Olivia couldn't figure out why. Maybe it was their second date, so they knew each other a little better? Maybe it was the texts they'd been exchanging all week, which had gotten progressively more friendly and relaxed over the course of the week? Maybe it was his mood, just off the plane from DC? Whatever it was, she liked it. He seemed more human.

She'd been especially surprised by his heartfelt outburst about his job on their way here. She'd wanted to ask him more questions about that, but he seemed a little embarrassed, so she decided to hold off. But everything he said about his job made her respect him more.

She shook her head at herself. What was she doing? She didn't need to like and respect this guy! Sure, yes, it was nice, since she'd likely be voting for him for reelection in about four years, but this movie was just a preamble to sex later that night, and then they'd never see each other again. Liking him too much was a waste of time!

Max scanned the tickets from his phone, and they found their seats inside the movie theater. This was one of those new theaters with reserved seats and big comfortable chairs, and when they sat down, they grinned at each other.

"Can you believe we put up with those old, narrow movie theater chairs for so long?" Max said to her.

"You read my mind," she said as she reclined her chair. "These are great."

He reclined his chair to meet hers, and handed her the popcorn.

"Don't let me eat so much popcorn I ruin my dinner," he said.

She laughed.

"If you were that hungry, we could have stopped on the way here. Or gotten you your own popcorn."

He shook his head.

"I'm actually not that hungry—I ate so many of those cookies they give you on the plane, but it's easy to eat an enormous amount of popcorn without even thinking about it."

When the trailers started, Olivia relaxed into her chair. She barely cared what was on the screen; it was just nice to be out, in this comfortable chair, with Max next to her. Their arms touched as they lay on the armrests, and it felt soothing. Comforting. For just a moment, she could believe that someday her career and life would be in order again. She moved her hand just a tiny bit closer to his, and he immediately wove his fingers together with hers. She had a sudden instinct to pull her hand away—this felt too . . . boyfriend-like. She didn't want a boyfriend, and she especially didn't want someone like Max Powell for a boyfriend. He was too high profile, too full of himself, too high maintenance for her. And she was sure he didn't want someone like her for a girlfriend. But she couldn't bring herself to let go of his hand. So they watched the rest of the movie like that, hand in hand.

She forced herself to let go of his hand when the credits started.

"What did you think?" he asked her as they walked to the car.

"Oh, I liked it," she said. "It wasn't great film-making or anything, but I was entertained from beginning to end and didn't look at the time once. That's all I ask for in a movie."

Granted, she didn't know if the reason she didn't look at the time was because of the movie or because she'd been with him, but she wasn't going to tell him that.

"Right there with you." He opened the car door

for her. "Any thoughts on where, or what, you want to eat?"

She was suddenly starving.

"Somewhere we don't have to wait for hours—lunch feels like forever ago."

He nodded as he drove out of the parking lot.

"Agreed—maybe it was because they kept eating in that movie."

They tossed around restaurant ideas as they drove in the general direction of her place, until she saw a sign up ahead.

"Can you believe I haven't been to In-N-Out since I've been back to California?"

He immediately threw on his blinker, just like she knew he would.

"Are you serious? That feels sacrilegious. Let's go."

He started to pull into a parking spot, but she stopped him.

"No, let's go through the drive-through—it's probably packed inside. We can eat at my place."

He put his hand on hers.

"Olivia Monroe, you're the most brilliant woman I've ever met."

She laughed at him, but damn was this man getting to her. Every time he looked at her, she wanted him to touch her. Every time he touched her, she wanted it to last longer. And now, he was coming back to her place, to touch her, she hoped, for a very long time.

She stopped herself. *No, Olivia, don't build it up too much—sure you haven't had sex for months, but you haven't even kissed this guy. Just because he has a good head of hair and a sexy smile doesn't mean he knows what to do with his body . . . or yours.* Okay, but it had the *potential* to be good, didn't it? He paid attention when she talked, and he clearly liked looking at her. That was honestly half the battle for most men—if he could listen when she said *Yes, no, right there, YES,* he had the advantage over about eighty percent of men.

Maybe ninety.

When they got back to her place, Olivia led him to the kitchen, and picked up the bottle of red wine on her kitchen counter.

"Wine? I have white wine in the fridge if you want that. I'm not sure which one goes better with In-N-Out, though."

His eyes lingered on her, and her whole body tingled.

"Whichever one you're having," he said.

She took two wineglasses down from the cabinet and opened the red wine. He didn't jump to try to open it for her, thank God. She enjoyed it when men opened doors for her and all of that, but too often men tried to take over every damn thing from women in the interest of "chivalry," and Olivia hated that. She poured two glasses, and led him into the living room.

"Let's sit in here," she said. "It's more comfortable than the kitchen stools at the counter, and I don't have a kitchen table yet."

He followed her into the living room with the food and sat down next to her on the couch. Very close to her on the couch.

"A car, a kitchen table, what else do you still have to buy?"

She laughed as she took their food out of the bags.

"Oh, probably a million things. A new wardrobe, for that matter—all of my clothes are too dark and too formal for L.A. I think the only time I've seen anyone in a suit since I got here was that luncheon, and that was only you and a handful of other lawyers."

He squeezed out ketchup for both of them and picked up a fry.

"Has it been hard? The transition?" he asked.

Yes, much harder than she'd expected.

"Not really," she said. "Maybe at some point it will be, but for now, it's all a new adventure, you know? And it's a relief to be back in California."

She took a bite of her burger so she wouldn't be able to answer any more questions, and maybe he got the hint, because so did he.

"Ahh, that hit the spot," he said when he finished his burger. "I haven't been in months and it was just what I was in the mood for. Thank you for suggesting it."

He took a sip of wine and smiled at her over his wineglass, and she felt that electricity between them again. She must be really attracted to this man, because usually right after she finished a cheeseburger was when she felt the least sexy possible, but for some reason, being with Max Powell was the exception.

"Okay, so, list of things Olivia still has to do in L.A.: buy a car, buy a kitchen table, buy a whole new wardrobe. Anything else?"

Olivia picked up her wineglass and took another sip as Max looked down at her. Had he gotten even closer to her on the couch, or was it just her imagination?

"Oh, I'm sure there are so many more things. Go to the beach—I haven't done that once since I've moved back. I've always wanted to go to the Getty museum and have never been. Oh, and Disneyland—I've always loved it there, but I haven't been in a long time. I know it's super touristy, but I've never gone up to see the Hollywood sign—the problem is I feel like you have to hike to do that, and I definitely don't have hiking clothes. Or, like . . . a hiking mentality. Or . . ."

Max plucked her wineglass out of her fingers and set it down on the table. The look in his eyes made her feel breathless.

"I have one more thing to put on your list. But you can check it off anytime you want." He trailed his fingers along her jaw and drew her even closer to him.

"Oh? What's that?" She hadn't meant to whisper, but then she hadn't expected him to make her tremble. She put her hand on his knee. God, why did it feel so good to touch him?

He leaned in, inch by inch, until their lips were a hairsbreadth apart.

"Kiss me," he said.

And she did.

His lips were soft and gentle . . . at first. But after a few moments of light, tender kisses, he slid his hands into her hair and pulled her hard against him. She threw herself into the kiss, kissing him harder, deeper. She could tell he liked it, so she did it again, until he pulled her on top of him so she was straddling him. Now she could *really* tell he liked it. He leaned down to kiss her neck—this man had good instincts, God did she love being kissed there. She took the opportunity to run her fingers through his thick hair, and felt him sigh and then kiss her harder.

She reached down and tugged his shirt out of his jeans, and ran her hands up and down his back. He pulled her head back down to his and kissed her hard, but as they kissed, he reached around and took her hands in his.

Did he not want her to touch him there? Or touch him at all? No, she was on his lap right now, he clearly liked it when she touched him and kissed him, but as tactful as it had been he'd definitely removed her hands from his back.

She pulled away and looked at him. He certainly *looked* like he was enjoying himself. All flushed, with swollen lips and unfocused eyes.

"Do you want to move to my bedroom?" she asked, just as he said, "I should probably go."

As soon as Olivia realized what he'd said, equal amounts of rage and humiliation rushed over her.

"I see," she said.

She scrambled off his lap and tugged her dress down.

He touched her arm, but she pulled away and stood up.

"I think you're right," she said. "You should probably go."

Was this somehow fun for him? Had last time not been an emergency, but instead just a way for him to get off on leading her on?

"No, wait, Olivia . . ." He sighed. "I should have done this earlier, but you're so . . . well, I got carried away. This isn't . . . I really . . ." He stopped and closed his eyes for a second and then looked at her. "I did this all wrong, but can you let me explain?"

All she wanted was to pick him up bodily and throw him out her front door, but (a) she didn't think she was strong enough for that, and (b) she was pretty sure that was a federal offense. Honestly, right now, (a) was the more significant issue for her. *Note to self: take some weight lifting classes.*

But as she glared at him, her rage faded. Slightly. He looked so contrite, so eager to say whatever it was he wanted to say. She still felt like this was a trick, that the politician in him was going to come out and give her some bullshit speech he'd given a million other women. But he'd asked if he could explain, without just launching straight into his "I don't want to sleep with you" stump speech, and maybe that was part of the act, but it was just enough for her.

She sat back down on the corner of the couch and pointed to the opposite corner.

"Sit there. You have exactly three minutes." She dug her phone out of her pocket and opened the timer. "Starting . . . now."

Max sat down where she'd pointed.

"I just thought maybe we should get to know each other better, that's all," he said.

Olivia rolled her eyes and stood back up.

"I lied, you don't get three minutes after all. That's seriously all you can do? Didn't you just tell me you were good at talking to people? I get it, you're not interested, and this whole night was some bullshit, but you don't have to keep bullshitting me just to protect your reputation or whatever. Trust me, I won't tell anyone about this."

Max leapt off the couch and reached for

her hand, but stopped just short of grabbing it.

"No, I swear, that's not it, that's the opposite of it. I'm really not lying, I do want to get to know you better, but . . ."

This man clearly thought she was as gullible as every other woman he'd done this to. That whole listening-to-her-and-taking-her-seriously thing had just been an act.

Max looked at the undoubtedly skeptical expression on her face and stopped.

"You're not buying this, are you?" he asked.

She shook her head. Why had she even given him a chance to "explain" anyway?

"Okay, okay." He took a deep breath. "The real story is that . . . shit, I only had three minutes and it's probably closer to two now so I'm going to rush through this, but the short version is I really like you. That's why I want to get to know you better. I like you so much that . . . oh God, it's so embarrassing to tell you this, but I should have figured out something else to say in advance and I didn't and I'm wasting my minutes, and I think you probably won't believe anything but the truth right now so I just have to say it: I told a friend of mine—a congressman, he's my roommate in DC, anyway that's not important—I told him about you, and he made me promise not to sleep with you yet."

Olivia dropped back down on the couch.

"He what?"

That was definitely not the bullshit answer she'd thought she was going to get.

"I know, I know." Max sighed and sat next to her. "We've been friends for a long time, he knows me well, and when I told him that I really liked you and I thought we might be able to have something real, he said . . ."

Olivia held up a hand to stop him. This was . . . not what she'd expected to hear. It was not what she'd expected of Max at all, as a matter of fact.

"You really like me? You told him we might . . . I didn't think . . . We met at a bar! I thought this whole thing was just a prelude to get me into bed! Are you looking for a *girlfriend?*"

He looked down, his cheeks pink.

"Yeah, actually. I mean, I wasn't exactly actively looking—I wasn't scouting the bar that night for girlfriend material, if that's what you mean. But yeah, that's something I want to have in my life."

She'd been sure he just wanted a fling. One night, maybe a few more, nothing serious.

"Anyway, when I met you, I was immediately interested. I went back to the bar the next day to look for you, but Krystal said you were gone."

"You did?"

The timer went off. Olivia picked up her phone and silenced it.

"I did," he said. "That's one reason why I was

so happy to see you at the luncheon. I don't just send cakes to anyone, you know!"

All Olivia could do was stare at him. This night was not going the way she'd expected. On so many fronts.

"As I think I've mentioned, I have a tendency to be kind of impulsive sometimes," he said. "And so I thought—Wes thought—I shouldn't get in too deep, too fast. But if that's not what you're looking for, if you're not interested in me like that, I get it."

He stood up, but Olivia reached for his hand and pulled him back down.

"I wasn't saying that . . . I mean, I wasn't *not* saying that . . . I'm just surprised, that's all. I didn't realize . . ." She threw her hands in the air. "I just thought you were trying to get into my pants! Which, if it wasn't clear, you were succeeding at!"

Max dropped his face into his hands again.

"Please, don't remind me, or I'll lose all of my willpower here." Then he looked straight into her eyes. "Not that I don't want to get into your pants, because good God do I ever. As I assume you noticed."

Olivia smirked at him. She *had* noticed, as a matter of fact, but when he pulled away, she'd sort of forgotten all about that.

He grinned back at her, and then his smile faded.

"If this isn't what you want, I completely understand, and no hard feelings. It's especially tricky because of my job—I don't know if you want to sign up to be a senator's girlfriend. And hell, I don't even know if you're interested in me like that." He paused and looked at her. Shit, she'd sort of forgotten about that part. She was only really thinking about the Max in front of her, not the senator part of him.

"Anyway, I'm not asking you for anything huge now, or any sort of commitment or anything like that. But I am telling you that I like you a hell of a lot, Olivia Monroe. I like everything about you, I like spending time with you, I like laughing with you, especially when you're laughing at me, I like eating pie with you, and I really, really liked kissing you. Do you . . . will you give me a chance?"

Olivia looked at him for a long beat. His hair was still tousled from their kisses, his shirt had a lipstick smear on it, and his eyes were the puppiest of puppy dog eyes. Damn it, how could he give her those eyes and still look so sexy?

"Can I think about this?" she asked. "I didn't expect any of this, and I'm just . . . I need to think."

He leaned over and kissed her softly on the lips before he stood up.

"I understand," he said. "But I'm going to hold next Saturday night for you. Just in case."

When she closed the front door behind him, she could still feel the pressure of his lips against hers.

She had a hell of a lot to think about.

Chapter Six

Olivia got to work on Monday morning and walked straight into Ellie's office.

"If this is about the Dewan case, I just sent you an email about it," Ellie said, without looking up from her computer.

Olivia dropped two cups of coffee on Ellie's desk, one for each of them. This was probably at least Ellie's fourth cup of coffee. Ellie always got to work at the crack of dawn so she could hang out with her kid after work; Olivia was happy to check email from bed, roll into the office closer to ten, and stay late. It made them a good pair, especially since neither of them judged the other for her schedule.

"I saw the email while I was on the bus and responded, that's not what this is about." She dropped down into the chair on the other side of Ellie's desk. "Finish what you're doing; I need your full attention for this."

Ellie looked at Olivia for the first time since she'd walked into the room. That mischievous look of glee Olivia remembered from law school came over her face.

"Ooooh, I like the sound of that. Okay, hold on just one second."

Olivia had thought about Max's bombshell all weekend as she tried to get work done while she sat on the same couch where she'd almost pulled off his clothes. Finally, she'd given up and left the house to go for a walk. She was so turned upside down by their conversation and the thoughts swirling around in her brain that when she'd walked by a gym, she wandered inside and joined it. It was probably just the glittery pink sign outside that got her.

It was more like two minutes than one second, but finally, Ellie hit save and turned around.

"Okay." She took a sip of coffee and opened her eyes wide. "What story do you have for me?"

Olivia took a deep breath.

"I went out with . . . Max again this weekend."

Ellie put down her coffee.

"And then what? What's wrong? What did that man do to you? Do I have to go kill a member of Congress?"

Ellie might actually do it, too, all while in her string of pearls and perfect blowout.

Olivia laughed and shook her head.

"No, no, nothing like that. It's just that . . . Ellie, he wants to *date* me."

Ellie looked at her quizzically.

"Um, yeah, I sort of assumed so, since this was your second date and all."

Olivia shook her head.

"I just thought he wanted to sleep with me! I thought he just wanted a fun little fling and then we could both go on our own merry ways, but no. He doesn't want a fling! He wants a girl-friend! More specifically, he wants *me* to be his girlfriend! Maybe not immediately, but, like . . . at some point."

A broad grin spread across Ellie's face.

"And?"

Olivia threw up her hands.

"And??? Ellie, I don't know what to do with this! I am not senator girlfriend material; you have to be all poised and blond—no offense to present company, obviously—and smiling and characterless for that. Hell, I'm not even Max Powell girlfriend material, forget the senator part! I'm not thin enough, my butt is far too big, hell, my hair is far too big for men like him! Plus, I don't have time to be dating someone right now! I just moved here, I need to devote myself to making this firm a success, and . . . I don't know, buying a car, and learning L.A. geography, and whatever else. I don't want to be a girlfriend!"

Ellie nodded, a little too forcefully.

"Sounds like someone is protesting a little too much, don't you think? What's wrong with being a girlfriend?"

Olivia ignored Ellie's first question and stopped to think about the second.

"I was in too many relationships in my late twenties and early thirties with men who got mad at me for how much I was working, or required so much of my time to sympathize with them about their mean lady boss or tuck them into bed when they had a man cold or whatever. And worse, they never really cared about me, even though I didn't want to admit that to myself. I just couldn't do it anymore, especially not when I was trying to make partner. And even after I made partner, I still had to prove myself at the firm, so I just never wanted to have to choose."

Ellie folded her hands together.

"And now, you don't have to prove yourself to anyone anymore. And despite what you said about how you don't have time, I know just as well as you do that you do indeed have time. Date the man, unless he's totally unattractive or a pompous asshole. And I've seen pictures, I know he's not the former; and if he was the latter, we wouldn't even be having this conversation."

Good point, Ellie, but . . .

"He isn't a pompous asshole YET, you mean. So far he's smart and funny and hot and listens to me, but that all seems far too good to be true. *Max* seems far too good to be true, Ellie! Men like him always have this vision in their head of who they think I am and what they want me to be and why they want to date me, and then they get to know me better and decide I'm too loud, or too intimidating, or too ambitious. They don't want the real Olivia. He must be bullshitting me about all of this. He's a politician, after all; they're good at that. I know his whole sunny, positive, golden-retriever-fighting-for-justice thing can't last! And what if he really is thinking about running for president like people are saying? In that case, he's definitely not to be trusted: there's no way a candidate for president would want a Black woman with natural hair and big hips on his arm!"

She'd been perfectly happy about the idea of a fun little fling, and Max had to ruin it all.

Ellie nodded.

"Mmmhmm, sure. Then why are we having this conversation again?"

Another good point for Ellie, damn her.

"Because I was so stunned when he said he wanted to date me that I said I'd think about it! He said he'd hold Saturday night for me, and I said I'd let him know by then. And now I have to figure out what I'm going to let him know!"

Ellie's smile widened.

"So you're thinking about it. You wouldn't be thinking about if you didn't like him."

She was thinking about it. She was thinking about it too much, as a matter of fact.

"Yeah, I'm thinking about it. I shouldn't be, I should have just said no right away. But . . .

he was a *very* good kisser. And he's a lot more interesting and smart than I expected him to be. Fine, yes, I like him. And, I don't know, he seems to really like me."

It was more than that, but she wasn't sure if she could explain it to Ellie. Somehow, she felt connected to him, which seemed ridiculous. But even from that first interaction at the bar, they'd been on the same wavelength. She'd thought it was just attraction, the same kind she felt with plenty of other guys she'd had flings with. Now she didn't know anymore.

Plus, no man had done this kind of full-court press on her in a long time. She had to admit she really enjoyed it.

Ellie just sat there and looked at her silently as Olivia thought through all of this. Finally, she put down her coffee.

"Olivia. You know the only reason you walked in here was because you wanted me to tell you to go out with him, so go out with him! What do you have to lose?"

What did she have to lose? So much: her control over her own life, her freedom, her focused concentration on her work, her ability to do whatever she wanted whenever she wanted without consulting someone else or worrying about anyone else's work calendar or schedule or finances or desire to pick up and go to Portugal for a weekend. That's what she had to lose.

Fine, even though she'd never actually picked up and gone to Portugal for a weekend.

Plus, what if she actually got attached to Max? Despite what he'd said, she didn't think there was any way it could lead to anything serious. Sure, he said he wanted a girlfriend, but he probably actually only wanted someone to have regular Saturday night plans with whenever he was in Los Angeles, someone who would drop everything and hang out with him at ten at night after events and let him vent about his stressful career and applaud him when he was on national TV, maybe text him a few times throughout the week, and that was it. And that was all well and good, but what if his stupid charm made her fall for him?

Ellie pointed a finger at her.

"Come on. Out with it."

Olivia sighed, and said what had been in the back of her head all weekend.

"What if I end up actually liking him? Really liking him, I mean. If that happens, I have so much to lose, Ellie! What if he gets me to like him and then he gets to know me better and doesn't like me anymore, which is what always fucking happens? I didn't move out to L.A. to get my heart broken."

Olivia knew she didn't have to say anything more; Ellie knew all the details of the other times her heart had been broken.

"Do you remember what you said to me when you and That Asshole broke up?" Ellie asked, after a few moments.

Olivia loved how Ellie refused to even use her ex's name.

"I said a lot of things to you then—which thing do you mean?"

Ellie picked up her coffee cup.

"You said that he never made you feel wanted, and you couldn't do this again until a man made you feel like he wanted you, all of you. Well?"

She'd completely forgotten that she'd said that. But it was true then. And was still true now.

"Max does make me feel wanted," she said slowly. "At least, so far he does. He's made his interest in me clear, since the very beginning. But it's not just that: he listens when I talk, really listens, he always looks at me like he's so focused on me and glad to be with me, and . . . did I tell you he went back to the hotel bar to look for me after that first night? But it's still early, that doesn't—"

Ellie cut her off.

"Then I believe you have your answer, don't you? And look, I know it's still early, and I know you don't want to risk anything here, but sometimes the only way to get something good is to take a few risks."

Easier said than done. She loved Ellie, but married people gave such glib dating advice sometimes. Plus, didn't Ellie remember she hated taking risks?

"I'd say remembering your favorite cake after a quick conversation—then sending it to you—says the man wants you all right," Ellie said, that smug-married smile still on her face.

The problem was, as much as Olivia wanted to argue that point, she couldn't. She still marveled that Max had done that.

"Sure, fine. But . . . maybe he's just good at that kind of stuff, and it's not about me."

Ellie smiled at her.

"Only one way to find out."

Max got back to his office late Wednesday afternoon after three interminable committee meetings in a row. Four members of his staff followed him into his private office, and he waved them all back out.

"Give me ten minutes to catch up on things; decide among yourselves on who goes first. You all get the next hour, but divvy it up responsibly."

He shut the door before they could argue with him, and immediately pulled his personal phone out of his briefcase. Did he have a text from Olivia? He scrolled through the texts that had come in, looking for her name, but nothing.

Not to be arrogant, but there were a hell of a lot of women out there who would jump at the chance to be his girlfriend. Hundreds! Maybe thousands!

Okay, that was pretty fucking arrogant, and also absolutely untrue. But there were at least a few! Why was it that the one person he'd met in the past two years whom he couldn't stop thinking about was not in that number?

Olivia had seemed all in on him on Friday night, until she very much wasn't. He winced at the memory of that night—he really should have figured out a plan in advance. The look on her face when he'd said the word "girlfriend" . . . well, he hadn't expected that.

He sighed and spent the rest of his ten minutes of silence playing a game on his phone, his one real guilty pleasure. At exactly ten minutes, he threw his door back open.

"Okay, who goes first?"

As he'd known would happen, Kara, his chief of staff, walked into the room. Kara had been by his side for three years now; he'd hired her to run his campaign for Senate in the early days, and he'd managed to convince her to come to DC with him after he won. Everyone had told him it was a bad idea to make your campaign chief of staff your Senate chief of staff, but he didn't listen; he'd known from the first time he met her that he and Kara would work well together. And he'd been right not to listen—she did a great job steering his ship, and any bad decision he'd made so far in the Senate was his fault, not hers.

"You're in a bad mood today, sir—were the hearings as boring from inside the room as they seemed on TV?"

He laughed. This was also why he liked working with Kara; she could come right out and say he was in a bad mood. All of his other staffers were too polite and formal with him; he still wasn't used to it.

"Even more so, if possible," he said. "Sorry for snapping at everyone, it's been a long week."

Kara shook her head.

"Sir, it's Wednesday."

In his first year in the Senate, he'd tried to break Kara of her habit of calling him "sir," but to no avail. She'd told him that he was just as worthy of respect as all the older senators were, and she wasn't going to let anyone think he wasn't, down to what she called him. He'd given up, but it still felt weird to him. Wes was one of the only people in this whole city who called him by his first name.

He sat down at his desk and picked up a pen.

"Okay, what's on the agenda?"

Kara looked down at her notebook.

"You asked me to check in with my contacts with leadership about your criminal justice reform bill, and . . . it's not great news. Unfortunately—"

He sighed.

"In an election year, when some of the people

who would vote for the bill are fighting tooth and nail for their seats, we don't want to give their opponents ammunition," he finished her sentence. "Is that it?"

They both knew he was quoting her own words back to her. She'd said that to him months ago, when he'd told her he wanted to push this bill now, this year. She'd tried to get him to wait until the following January. But he hadn't listened.

"That's certainly part of it, sir," she said, her eyes firmly on her notepad. Kara never said "I told you so," even when he knew she must be dying to.

He let out a deep sigh. He knew what Kara wasn't actually saying out loud was that his bill was close to dead. Damn it.

"I'm not going to give up on this, I'm sure you already know that."

Kara stood up.

"I did already know that, as a matter of fact." She grinned at him. "That's why I work for you."

After three more meetings with his staffers, Max gathered up his papers to walk home. It was already dark, and he was suddenly depressed. About being in this dark, cold, lonely city; about having this difficult, stressful, pointless job, where personalities and conflicts and elections and money mattered more than helping people; about not having anyone to talk to about any of that.

He picked up his phone, but no, Olivia hadn't texted. Instead he texted Wes, whom he hadn't seen since the week before, because of their terrible schedules.

> Heading home now, and look at me, I'm going to order the pizza this time. What kind do you want?

He walked out of his office and waved to his staff members who were still there. As he left the building, he looked back down at his phone, willing Olivia to contact him, right now, tonight, to turn this day around.

Just then, a text flashed across his screen.

Was this it? Did he finally have magical powers? If so, maybe there was hope for his criminal justice reform bill.

Nope, not Olivia.

> Beat you to it; a pizza—and a SALAD— should arrive right when you do. But you can pick up more beer on the way home, we're almost out.

Damn it. There went the one victory he thought he'd get today.

He took the food out of the hands of the delivery guy as he walked into their apartment building, and opened their apartment door to find Wes on the couch in his sweatpants.

"Here's the food and the beer." He tossed everything on the table.

Wes looked up at him and narrowed his eyes.

"No 'Hi, honey, I'm home'? No complaints about the salad? What happened to you? Where's Normal Max tonight?"

Max sat down and flipped open the pizza box.

"Normal Max has been beaten down by the machinery of the United States Senate, that's where Normal Max went. Kara thinks my criminal justice reform bill is on life support. That's confidential, of course."

Wes patted him on the shoulder.

"Oh man, that sucks," he said. "But the machinery of the United States Senate has beaten you down before, and I haven't seen you like this since . . . What else is wrong?" His eyes widened and he held up a finger. "The girl! I haven't seen you since last week—what happened with the girl?"

Max shrugged and looked away. Damn Wes for knowing him so well.

"I told her how I felt, and that—fuck you for making me do this, by the way—that we couldn't have sex, which . . . well, never mind. Anyway, she seemed taken aback, and said she'd 'think about it.' But that was Friday night, and I haven't heard from her since then. I think I lost my chance with her. I never should have listened to you."

Wes dropped his head in his hands.

"I didn't tell you to *tell* her that; good God, Powell! I thought you were a better politician than that."

Yes, well, so had he.

"I didn't make a plan! I just blurted it all out! This is why I have people write my speeches and talking points for anything important; I've always been bad at shit like this when I don't prepare! Anyway, that's what happened with the girl."

Wes closed his eyes and shook his head.

"Okay, well, there's nothing we can do about that now. That was Friday night—have you texted her since then?"

Thanks for the reminder.

"I texted her on Sunday from the plane, just saying to have a good week. She said, 'Thanks, you, too!' and that was it."

Wes pushed the container of salad over to him.

"Please eat some of this and come to your senses. That was Sunday, today is Wednesday. What are you waiting for? We're too old for those games about when you should text a woman and when you shouldn't. You like this woman, that's obvious—don't whine about it to me. Text her!"

As much as Max hated to admit it, Wes was probably right. Well, not about the salad.

"I was trying to give her space!" he said. "But you might be right. Plus, she'll definitely tell me to go away if she doesn't want to hear from me; she's that type."

Wes grinned.

"I like her even more now."

Max rolled his eyes and pulled out his phone.

> How's your week going? Any more thoughts on Saturday? Maybe we could tick off some more of the items on your to-do in LA list?

There. That was friendly and breezy but still interested. He hoped.

He pressed send, and immediately realized exactly why he hadn't done this earlier. Because now, it was going to be even worse waiting for her to text back.

"Satisfied?" he said to Wes.

Wes dished out some of the salad into a bowl and took a very pointed bite.

"About that, at least. Now eat some damn vegetables; we both need some in this godforsaken town."

Just as Wes got up to go to the bathroom, Max's phone buzzed.

> Thanks for giving me time to think about it—Saturday sounds great. Maybe the Getty?

Max smiled, for maybe the first time that day. Finally, something went right.

Chapter Seven

Max wished he could spend all day Saturday with Olivia, but he had an event that afternoon to honor one of his old teachers who was about to retire. So he'd suggested they head up to the Getty in the late afternoon to see the art and walk around, and then they could picnic outside at sunset. As soon as Olivia agreed, he ordered a bunch of picnic supplies from his local, exorbitantly priced grocery store—they were supposed to have great pie, so he ordered one of those, too. He hoped the pie lived up to the rumors.

Max slapped on a name tag from the front table when he walked into the event, and was immediately surrounded by people. He hadn't brought any of his staff along with him today, because this felt more like a personal event than a political one, but now he suddenly appreciated everything they did for him. He shook what felt like hundreds of hands, tried to remember what everyone said to him, and took all their business cards with no idea of what to do with them. He laughed at himself—he'd gotten so used to having one to four extra brains working on his behalf at all times, it was like he didn't remember how to do all this himself. This was probably a good exercise to go through every so often, just so he didn't get too soft.

Finally, he made his way over to Ms. Sussman and gave her a hug.

"Congratulations on forty years as a teacher, and on your retirement," he said. "Best teacher I ever had, even though you sent me to the principal's office far too many times."

She blushed and hugged him back. And then scolded him gently, as he'd expected.

"Now, Maxwell," she said. Ms. Sussman was one of only two people in the world who called him Maxwell; the other was his grandmother. "That only happened twice, and I'm sure you agree with me that you deserved it both times."

He grinned.

"I absolutely did," he said.

Max chatted with her for a while, until another of her former students came up to them. They'd had this event for her outside of school hours because so many of her former students wanted to come. She'd worked at his private high school early in her career, and then twenty years ago she'd surprised everyone by moving to a public school in East L.A., and had been there ever since.

Soon, her daughter brought him up to the

microphone for one of a handful of speeches. He talked about how much she'd taught him, most of which was about how to be a good person and how to treat other people well, told a self-deprecating story about himself that made people laugh, told one of his favorite stories about Ms. Sussman that made people cry, and managed to weave in his passion for criminal justice reform, especially as it related to kids. When he walked down from the podium, he was proud of that speech.

At the end of the event, Ms. Sussman brought him around to meet some of her more recent former students. He went around the circle and shook hands with all of them, but one of them looked so familiar. Why couldn't he place him?

"Great speech, Senator," they all said, and he smiled.

He knew this kid. Who was he? He glanced down at the name tag to see if that would help. Mateo Ortega.

Oh. It all came back to him now.

Mateo's brother Antonio had been a defendant, early in Max's career as a prosecutor. He'd stolen stuff from a store, and knocked someone down on his way out. Max, full of his own importance, had thrown the book at the kid.

He'd spent years regretting that. He still did. After he spent a few years prosecuting that kid and some of the others like him, and saw what his actions did to their lives, his feelings about the criminal justice system had fundamentally changed. He'd consulted advocates—many of whom he still consulted on a regular basis—changed his entire process, and after he'd become the district attorney, had changed policies in the office to try to keep kids, and everyone else, out of jail and prison as much as possible.

But none of that had helped Antonio, who'd been incarcerated for two years because of Max.

On the way out of the event, Max caught up with Mateo in the parking lot.

"Hey, Mateo," he said. "How's your brother?"

Mateo barely glanced at him.

"Okay, I guess. I mean, I don't really know. He's back inside. Supposed to get out again in a few years, with good behavior and all."

Fuck.

"Oh," Max said. He pulled a card out of his pocket. "I'm very sorry to hear that. Well, if you ever need anything, or if he does, or you're looking for a job in government, or anything . . . call my office, okay?"

Mateo took the card and dropped it in his pocket, still without looking at Max.

"Yeah, sure. I'll get right on that."

Max didn't blame the kid for his rudeness; hell, it had probably taken all of Mateo's self-control to not punch Max in the face. And Max would have deserved it.

He drove home on autopilot. He wished he hadn't seen Mateo. He wished he didn't have such good memories for faces and names. A normal person wouldn't have seen a twentysomething who had been a preteen the last time he'd seen him and remember either the face or the name; why couldn't he be a normal person? Then he wouldn't be thinking about Antonio and his family right now. He'd instead just drive back home and remember how he'd brought tears to Ms. Sussman's eyes with his speech, the laughter of the crowd, and that one baby who had the fattest cheeks he'd ever seen. He'd drive home and look forward to seeing Olivia later . . . fuck. Fuck, he'd almost forgotten his date with Olivia. He had to pull himself together and out of this funk before he got to her house.

By the time he got back to his house, changed out of his suit and into jeans, collected all of the food into a tote bag, and drove back down to Olivia's place, he'd gotten more of a hold on himself. For the rest of this night, he just had to forget that he'd seen Mateo, forget about all of this. He could do that—he'd done a fundraiser the day he and his last girlfriend broke up, and had made a floor speech the day after his grandfather died, and each time he'd shut his emotions away, put his big politician smile and his big politician voice on, and aced it each time. He could ace this, too.

He knocked on Olivia's door, and made sure a big smile was on his face when she opened it.

"Hey! Ready to go?"

She gave him a slightly weird look, but he brushed it off. Olivia always looked at him like she didn't quite know what to make of him, but she kept going out with him anyway, didn't she?

"Almost," she said. "Come in for a second while I grab a sweater? It's warm now, but I want to be prepared for after the sun goes down."

Max nodded and followed her into the house. She walked through the kitchen and into her bedroom, and he stood just outside the doorway while she looked through her dresser drawers.

"I'm really excited that you're going to get to see the Getty!" he said. "You know, not only does it have a wonderful art exhibit, but it has some of the best views in all of Los Angeles. You don't want to miss the sunset there! Also, fun fact: did you know that a number of the former curators were investigated for trafficking in stolen antiquities?"

She walked out of her bedroom, heavy gray cardigan in hand, and gave him that look again.

"Are you okay? You're acting strange."

Apparently he wasn't acing this yet.

He shook his head.

"No, no, everything's great! Just excited for tonight." He shot another big smile at her.

She shrugged, then walked into the kitchen.

"We can bring wine, right? I know you said you were taking care of the picnic supplies, but I bought this bottle of wine today; I thought it would be fun to bring it."

He took the bottle of wine from her and set it back down on the counter.

"Unfortunately we can't, but we can buy wine there. Whether you can bring wine to a location often has to do with the way their liquor license is set up, but sometimes it's just about wanting to drive more wine and beer sales of their own."

Olivia steered him into the living room and sat down on the couch.

"Okay. What's going on? I know I don't know you all that well, but you don't seem like yourself."

How could she see right through him like this?

He started to shake his head again, and she stopped him.

"Please don't say 'Everything's great!' again in that weird voice, or spout another fun fact at me. You're not on TV right now, you know. You don't have to tell me what's up, but . . . is something wrong?"

He sat down on the couch next to her and took a deep breath.

"Do you know, I can't remember the last time someone asked me that," he said.

She put her hand on his shoulder. It felt really

nice. Comforting. No one had comforted him in a really long time.

"I'm guessing that means the answer is yes. Do . . . do you want to talk about it? We don't have to rush off to the Getty just yet, you know."

He looked at his watch.

"We do if we want to get to see any of the art before sunset. Sunset is at sevenish, and by the time we get there, and park and everything, it'll be—"

She moved her hand down his arm and covered up his watch.

"We don't have to go to the Getty tonight. It's not going anywhere, we can go another time."

Something in him thrilled at her implication that there would be another time, that they had a future together. But he still wanted to push on, to not admit defeat.

"Oh, but I know you wanted to go up there, and I have all this stuff for the picnic in the car. Don't worry about me, I'm fine!" He flashed a bright smile at her and stood up.

She stayed on the couch.

"You're doing it again. It's okay if you don't want to tell me what's up, but don't pretend to me, okay?"

He dropped back down next to her.

"I'm sorry. It's just been . . . a tough day today, for some unexpected reasons. I didn't want to burden you with all of that."

She slid her hand in his.

"I have an idea. How about you go back to the car and get all of that picnic stuff, and bring it right in here, and I can open up that bottle of wine without having to pay for it, and we can sit here and have our picnic and relax." Her eyes twinkled at him. "Plus, your hair still has that Ken doll look; you might get recognized at the Getty."

He brushed his hand over his stiff hair, and shook his head.

"I can't believe I forgot about that. You sure that's okay?" he asked.

She stood up.

"I'll open the wine right now."

He went out to the car for the picnic supplies, and by the time he got back inside, she'd moved the coffee table to the far side of the living room and had spread a big blanket out on the floor, with the bottle of wine and two glasses in the middle of it.

"See what a good picnic we can have indoors?" she said when he came inside.

He dropped the bag down onto the blanket and unloaded it.

"And we don't have to worry about the wind coming up and blowing the blanket away, or ants," she said. She uncorked the wine bottle and poured wine for both of them.

"*And* we can use actual wineglasses instead of

plastic," he said. He touched his glass to hers.

She set to unwrapping all the food he'd brought.

"Ooh, you got some good stuff. I'm going to pretend I don't see that pie until later, but I'm very excited about it. And this cheese looks oozy and perfect. I'm starving."

He tore off an end of the baguette and handed it to her.

"Me, too."

He hadn't realized that until now.

She looked at him, and her expression softened.

"When did you eat last?" she asked. "Do they feed you at those things?"

When had he eaten last? That half a bagel he'd downed for breakfast while he read a stack of memos and briefing papers.

"Technically, yes, there's usually food at these things—there was today. But the problem—and the thing I still forget, even though I've been in this job for going on two years now—is that even when there's food I almost never get the opportunity to actually eat it." He laughed. "Today wasn't so bad, because the food was just things like sandwiches and vegetables and dip, but a few months ago I went to something in the Central Valley and there was all of this amazing Mexican food and I kept putting food on a plate and taking one bite and then having to shake someone's hand or take a picture with someone else and my plate would disappear and I would get a new one and it would happen all over again. I think I gave up after my fifth plate and just made my staff go out to an enormous Mexican meal with me after we left."

Olivia handed him a piece of baguette, covered in that good, oozy cheese.

"Here, eat this. I can't have a senator faint from hunger in my living room. That feels like a felony of some sort."

He looked away from her and pretended to check the bag to make sure he hadn't forgotten anything. He'd briefly forgotten why they were here on her living room floor instead of on their way to the Getty, but those jokey words of hers brought everything back.

He cleared his throat.

"I . . . the reason I was upset this afternoon . . ." He put his wineglass down and rubbed his temples. "It's kind of a long story, we don't have to go into all of that."

She touched his arm gently.

"You don't have to tell me if you don't want to, but I don't mind long stories."

He looked into her eyes and could tell she meant it.

"Okay." He took a deep breath. "You know I was a prosecutor before I was in the Senate, right? Well, I had this mentor early in my career, a family friend; he was the whole reason I became a prosecutor in the first place. He was an old-school prosecutor, very hard-line, all about safety and how kids especially need to learn what they did was wrong, and I listened to him. Far too much. People talk about prosecutorial discretion; well, at first, mine went in the 'more jail, more punishment' direction. This isn't a defense, but I floated through most of my life as a privileged trust fund kid, not really paying attention to politics and all of the bad things that could happen to people—sure, I volunteered some in school, but I guess I bought into that whole 'they didn't work hard enough' bullshit." He sighed. "That job made me wake up. After a few years in, and a few years of seeing the hard situations these kids lived in, and the racism they dealt with every day, and listening to advocates who somehow never gave up on me, I realized how much I didn't want to keep being that kind of prosecutor. Hell, that I didn't want to be that kind of person. Throwing kids behind bars could, and often did, ruin their futures and cause so much harm to their families. I was the one causing that harm. I came very close to quitting my job then."

He looked at the floor. He still remembered how angry at himself he'd been then, how he'd realized how wrong he'd been, how much pain he'd caused.

"Why didn't you?" Olivia asked.

He looked at her, for the first time since he'd

started this story. She was giving him that look again, like she really cared about the answer. Like she really cared about him.

"My friend Wes. I called him and told him I was going to quit and why, and he yelled at me." Max smiled to himself. "I'd never heard him like that. He told me he was glad I'd finally woken up, but what a damn waste it would be if I woke up just in time to hand over the job to another clueless trust fund baby. He said we needed good prosecutors, that those kids needed me, now more than ever." He looked down. "Until then, I think I really believed I deserved everything I got in life. That job made me realize . . . so much. About everything. Among other things, I still can't believe my eyes were so closed to the way racism infects every part of the criminal justice system. There were just so many little things that I just didn't see. Or worse, ignored." He shook his head. "I listened to Wes. I stayed at that job, eventually I even became the DA. I've worked hard for years now to help kids like the defendants I saw, so they can change their lives, and stay in school, and so one mistake won't follow them forever."

He looked down at his piece of baguette covered in cheese. He'd somehow lost his appetite.

"But?" Olivia said.

He sighed.

"But today, at the event this afternoon, I saw

a kid there. He's not a kid anymore, he must be in his early twenties now. His brother was one of those defendants who I worked hard to toss in jail in those early years of my career. The kid seems like he's doing well, but when I asked him about his brother, he told me he's back inside." He shook his head. "And that's my fault. All of it. I could have helped his brother. He wasn't a bad kid; most of them aren't. I could have gotten him into programs to rehabilitate him, made it easy to wipe his record, gotten him back to school, to his family, to people and places that keep kids—and the adults they become—out of prison. But I did the opposite, and here we are."

Mateo would never call his office, he knew that. He wished there was something he could do for him and his family. Especially since he wasn't accomplishing what he wanted to in the Senate.

"And I guess it hit me particularly hard today, because my criminal justice reform bill—one of the whole reasons I ran for Senate in the first place—has a really hard road ahead. I have such a big list of things I want to change. Mandatory minimums, policing, bail, funding for public defenders, the way we try children, and so much more. I know, it's all ambitious, but I thought I could start big, and at least get some of that passed. But none of it? It just feels like . . . nothing I do in this job matters. Like nothing is going to change."

Now that he'd started, it was like he couldn't stop talking.

"I was really hopeful about the bill when I first announced it—I got a ton of press attention, I was on all of the TV shows, and people kept saying how important criminal justice reform is, blah blah blah. I know people bring up bills just to use as talking points—hell, I've done it, too—but with this one, I really wanted to make some real change. And there have been some strides, in the past few years, but I guess there's a limit to how much change people can really handle. How much good they really want to do."

Olivia rubbed his arm gently, up and down. The expression on her face was softer than he'd ever seen it.

"That bill was the whole reason you ran for the Senate?" she asked.

He nodded.

"Well, criminal justice reform in general." He laughed. "I didn't even think I'd win. I jumped into the race on a lark when the Senate seat came open. I just hoped it would raise my statewide profile enough so that when it came time to run for governor a few years later, I'd have a real shot. And then, strangely, everything just kept going my way."

Olivia poured more wine into both of their glasses.

"Do you regret it? Running for the Senate, I mean."

He thought about that question for a long time before he answered.

"No," he finally said. "No, I don't regret it. Not even on my worst days, the days I'm frustrated at the world and every other member of Congress, and it's midnight and I'm in my boring Washington apartment. Even then, I want to scream and rant at everything wrong with the government, but I want to make it better, and I think right where I am is exactly the place I should be." He looked at her and smiled. "Thank you for making me realize that."

Olivia stared down at the bright red blanket she'd pulled out of her linen closet to turn into their picnic blanket. She'd assumed Max had run into an ex, or had gotten a call from someone in his family, or had to fire someone on his staff, or something else stressful but easy. For something like that, she could listen to his story, pat him on the shoulder, sympathize with him, tell him he'd done the right thing (if, indeed, he had), and then they'd eat pie and hopefully make out.

But this was different. This wasn't what she'd expected.

Should she tell him . . . no, definitely not. There was no point. Plus, tonight had been heavy enough as it was.

Strangely, though, it had been heavy in a good way. She'd enjoyed going out with banter-y, fun, hot-boy Max the past few times she'd seen him; she'd looked forward to doing it again tonight. But tonight she had serious, thoughtful, introspective Max. She might like him even better now.

A lot better, actually.

"Thank you for telling me that," she said. "And for not blowing me off when I asked you if something was wrong."

He smiled at her.

"Thank you for asking," he said.

She looked at him, and the look in his eyes was so warm, so grateful, she had to look away.

"Okay," she said. "Here's what I propose. We sit here and eat our food and drink our wine and watch a really dumb movie on my brand-new TV there, and then we eat that entire pie, and then maybe we'll drink more wine." And maybe after that they'd make out, but she hoped that part didn't need to be said. "Does that sound like a good way to recover from today?"

He smiled at her.

"Just you, here with me, is a way to recover from today. Thank you for being here." He moved closer to her. "This would have been a depressing, lonely night without you. I'm really glad to be here."

He stroked his finger across her cheek, and then

pulled her chin up toward his. He kissed her on the lips, gently, tenderly, but still with so much power. Olivia lost herself in that kiss. She put her hand on his cheek and felt his stubble there from his long day. Everything in her wanted to speed him up, to unbutton those last buttons of his shirt, to move his hands to where she wanted them, but she let him lead the way, and kept the kiss just as slow and gentle as he wanted it.

Finally, he pulled back and stroked her hair.

"I'm really glad to be here," he said again.

"I'm really glad you're here," she said.

She touched his cheek, then traced her fingers over his dark eyebrows. She marveled at his long, curly eyelashes. Life was so unfair.

"How'd you get this scar?" she asked, her finger on his left eyebrow.

He laughed.

"Back when I was still an assistant DA, I was out at a bar one weekend with some friends, and some people near us got in a fight. I, very stupidly, jumped in to break it up, and got hit with a broken beer bottle. I probably should have gotten stitches, but once everything died down, I just wanted to relax and see the end of the game. I had a black eye for like a week afterward." He kissed her softly. "Most people don't even notice it anymore."

She leaned her head against his shoulder while he picked up the remote and flipped among all of the possible streaming services for a silly movie for them to watch. For the next hour, they sat there together, her head on his shoulder, his arm around her, snacking, drinking wine, occasionally giggling softly at the movie, until he pressed pause.

"Are you ready for pie?" he asked her.

"I was arrested when I was a teenager," she said.

He stopped halfway through leaning over to get the pie, and sat back down.

She hadn't meant to say it. And she definitely hadn't meant to blurt it out like that. She hadn't meant to tell him this at all. She almost never told people about her arrest; not because she was ashamed of it, but because it always made them look at her differently, and she hated that.

"Do you want to tell me about it?" he asked.

She nodded slowly.

"It was stupid, just one of those teen things. There was this guy I liked, and he wanted to break into the school one weekend night just to prove he could, and I thought if I went along with the group, maybe he'd like me back, so I did. We got caught, of course, and we all got arrested. It was . . . terrible." She flashed back to that moment the police had come in, that call she'd had to make to her parents, the look in her baby sister's eyes the next morning. "It ended up okay—community service, it got wiped from my record, et cetera, and I'm fine about it now, I have been for a long time, but it was really awful at the time, and for a while later."

She rarely thought about that year anymore. She told her story occasionally, but it was more of a recitation at this point, an uplifting little story about survival and triumph. She never touched on the actual hard parts; how she'd disappointed her family, how she'd disappointed herself, how she'd worried about her future, so much so that it made her sick to her stomach for months on end.

"Anyway, in the grand scheme of things it was just a blip, and I was fine, and it's not something I think or talk about much. The few times I've told people about it, they often get weird—fascinated in a creepy way, or all condescendingly proud of me. Sometimes I've talked about it when I've volunteered with kids and teenagers, and once a few years ago I alluded to it at a city council meeting to help my sister out, but I don't tell a lot of people about it anymore. But I thought . . . I guess I just thought I wanted to tell you."

He took her hand.

"You didn't have to tell me, but I'm really glad you did."

She kissed him this time. She kept her kiss soft and slow, but as she drew him closer to her, his kiss, his touch, got more passionate. His hands roamed around her body, and my God did they feel good. She didn't let herself touch him below the shoulders until his hands were on her thighs; then she sighed happily and moved her hands down his chest. She slid her hands up underneath his shirt.

"Can I?" she whispered in his ear.

He nibbled at her neck as his hands moved up and down her body again.

"Mmmhmm."

She pushed his shirt up and over his head, and gave herself up to stroking his chest as they kissed. His chest hair was springy under her fingers; it delighted her. She couldn't stop touching him, kissing him. By the way he kissed her harder, he felt the same way. She trailed her hands down to his waist, and lower. His hands slid up under her dress.

This felt too good. She pulled away from him.

He reached for her again.

"We don't have to stop," he said.

She wanted to listen to him so much, but she knew she couldn't.

"It's been an emotional day for you, and as much as I want to take you at your word right now, it feels like it's a better idea to chill out a little, eat some of that pie, and watch the rest of this movie."

He sighed.

"You're probably right about that." He reached for the pie again, but this time he turned around with a grin on his face. A very sexy grin.

"I have a better idea than pie."

She scrunched her nose at him.

"Better than pie? How is that—"

Before she could finish her sentence, he pushed up her dress and knelt at her feet.

She looked at him in disbelief. Was he really going to do what she thought he was going to do?

"Max, you've had a long day, you don't have to . . ."

Why the hell was she arguing with him about this? What was wrong with her? She shut her mouth and let him guide her legs open.

He knelt at her feet and pushed her legs further apart.

"I know I don't have to, but I really, really want to."

Well, if he put it like that.

He tiptoed his fingers up the inside of her thighs, and she giggled.

"Any more objections?"

She folded her arms behind her head and smiled down at him.

"Not a one."

He slid first one finger inside her, then a second. She leaned her head back and closed her eyes. God, the way he touched her, she couldn't get enough of it.

He spent a while exploring her with his fingers, touching her in slow circles that felt so good she could hardly bear it. And then, thank God, she felt his tongue against that spot where she most wanted him. Finally, she screamed, and dropped her hands by her sides.

He sat up, disheveled and grinning.

She sat up, too, and smiled at him.

"Now do I get some pie, so I can decide if that was actually better?"

Max let out a bark of laughter and stood up.

"Oh, Olivia. I like you so much."

The smile fell from her face as he cut their pie. She liked him so much, too. Oh no.

Chapter Eight

✳

Olivia fell in line with Jamila on the way out to her car on Wednesday night. In the past few weeks, it had become a routine that Jamila would drive her home after her volunteer shift. It had been another productive evening: this time they'd made forty servings of lasagna, with roasted carrots as a side. Olivia couldn't believe how proud she felt at the end of the night when she saw the sealed packages, all lined up in the fridge and ready to be delivered the next day. It felt amazing, like this was a real accomplishment—no matter what else she'd done today, she'd done one tangible thing to help people.

Not only that, but she felt a real sense of community here. Some of the other regular volunteers had been working at the food pantry since it had started, and after she showed up the second time, they'd taken her under their wing. They'd laughed at her—but in a kind way—when she asked questions, they'd taught her to chop and dice, and they always oohed and aahed over her outfit when she walked in on Wednesday nights. She felt like she was part of something; that there were people who embraced her, and whom she embraced right back. Many of them were from the neighborhood and so they knew some of the recipients of the meals well, which almost made it feel like they were cooking for family. Olivia wondered what they would think of Max.

Max hadn't pressed her to make any grand commitment to him before he'd left her place late Saturday night, and they'd texted more or less the same amount this week as they had in the previous weeks. But something had changed between them after the confidences they'd exchanged that night.

Why had she told him about her arrest? Their whole conversation had been about him, not her; it wasn't like she would have been lying to him if she hadn't told him anything. She'd woken up that night at four a.m. and spent an hour mad at herself for that. But when she woke up the next morning, she had a text from Max waiting there on her phone, and somehow she wasn't angry anymore.

No, now the problem was that she was mostly scared. She'd meant for this to be a casual, easy, low-key thing to keep her busy while her firm was slow, but the amount of space Max took up in her head was neither casual nor low-key. And she had no idea what to do about it.

She knew one thing: if they slept together, it would absolutely not be casual. Which sucked—

she just wanted to have some really fucking great sex with that really fucking hot guy who kept touching her like that and kissing her like that and, oh God, *looking* at her like that. But that was the problem—there would be nothing casual about the sex with anyone who looked at her like that.

Oh no. How did she look at *him?*

She needed to stop thinking about him. She was acting like some sort of lovesick puppy.

"Sooo, tonight was interesting," she said to Jamila when they got in the car. "I'm glad we had all of the manpower, but . . ."

Jamila looked at her sideways.

"But how did those frat guys hear about us? I have no idea! One of them called me yesterday and asked if they could bring a group of ten, which I didn't think was actually going to happen but I said sure, and then they brought a group of twenty. Must have been some sort of community service requirement from school."

Olivia tossed her bag on the floor.

"Yeah, when I walked in, I thought maybe I was in the wrong place! But hey, I'll take it." That reminded her. "Do we ever get high school groups out to help? I used to do a lot of volunteering with teens—now that my work schedule isn't as packed, I need to find a way to do that again."

She'd thrown herself into that kind of work in

her early years in New York, but then her job had taken over most of her life. Maybe now she'd have more time to do it again.

"Not as often as I'd like," Jamila said. "I need to work on that; I've been wanting to find a way to get teens in the community more involved. Sometimes they do the delivering with their parents, but that's not enough." She laughed. "Speaking of that, our new friends from tonight are going to do a bunch of delivering for us tomorrow and next week!"

Olivia turned up the music.

"Wow, they all have cars?"

Jamila laughed at her.

"This is Los Angeles, Olivia—a lot of people here have cars."

"I know, I need to get one. But it's a big decision! And I've never actually bought a car before, so I'm intimidated by the whole going-to-a-dealership-for-it part."

Jamila turned to her with a wide smile on her face.

"What are you doing tomorrow at lunch-time?"

Olivia desperately wished she had a client meeting, or a conference call, or something.

"Nothing specific, but I have work to do." She didn't want to ask, but she had to. "Why?"

Jamila flashed a huge smile at her.

"Because I'm going to pick you up from work,

and I'm going to take you to buy a car, that's why."

Olivia argued with her, but somehow the next day at 12:15, she got into Jamila's car.

"Seriously, if you have better things to do on this beautiful Los Angeles day, you don't have to spend the afternoon helping me buy a car," Olivia said.

Jamila waved her words aside.

"Thanks for making me feel like a loser since I actually don't have anything better to do on this beautiful Los Angeles afternoon." She made a face at Olivia, and they both laughed. "Okay, what kind of car are we buying today?"

As soon as they walked into the dealership, a tall, thin salesman with a big smile on his face greeted them.

"Can I help you two today?" He looked back and forth between Olivia and Jamila. "Let me guess . . . sisters?"

Olivia looked at Jamila and grinned. Sure, why not.

Jamila nodded and smiled at the salesman.

"Hi . . . Brad," Jamila said. Oh right, he was wearing a name tag. "My sister and I here would love to test-drive a few cars, if you have them on the lot?"

Two hours later, after four test drives—one car twice—some negotiation, and a whole lot of signing of papers, Brad handed Olivia a key.

"Congratulations on your new car, Ms. Monroe," he said.

Olivia and Jamila grinned at each other as they walked out of the dealership.

"I'm taking you to happy hour for that," Olivia said. "Isn't there a good Mexican place nearby?"

Olivia pulled into a parking space by the restaurant after circling the block only four or five times. She made it to a table before Jamila did, so she pulled her phone out of her bag. She had to tell Max about her car. They'd texted a few times already today, but she hadn't told him she was going to actually buy a car. Partly because she hadn't really believed it herself.

Guess what I did today?

Just then, Jamila dropped down into the seat across from her. Olivia pushed a menu toward her friend.

"I shouldn't drink anything if I have to drive that car home; I'm too paranoid," Olivia said as they looked over the menu. "But you should have something if you want. I'm definitely getting a plate of nachos as big as my head."

Jamila shook her head.

"Oh, thanks, but I don't drink. You should come back here sometime when you're not driving— the margaritas are supposed to be great. And the nachos are fantastic."

After they ordered food, Jamila cleared her throat.

"Before you started your own firm, did you work in a different law firm for a while?"

Olivia nodded.

"For the bulk of my career, so . . . what, twelve or thirteen years. Why?"

Olivia geared herself up to give law school advice—that's where questions like this usually led.

"Did you have to deal with people—mostly men—not listening to you, or your ideas? Or pretending they'd come up with your ideas themselves?"

Olivia laughed.

"Every single fucking day, more or less. That was one of the reasons I started my own firm." She took a sip of the agua fresca the waitress dropped down in front of her. "Why, do you have to deal with that at the community center?"

Jamila's eyebrows went sky high.

"Every single fucking day!" They both laughed. "I mean, that's a slight exaggeration, but for instance—I got involved with the center really early on because I grew up in that neighborhood and was excited there was a new community center. And when I suggested a meal delivery service to the executive director, he blew me off. For months, he blew me off! And then all of a sudden I find out he went to the board and told them his amazing idea about what to do with the cafeteria we weren't using, and the board got all excited, and I wanted to throw things."

Olivia nodded.

"Yeah, that sounds about right. And you feel like an asshole complaining about it, since it's happening, isn't it, and it's doing good in the community, isn't it? But—"

"But I'm still so bitter! Exactly!" Jamila said. "And you know how yesterday we were talking about getting more teens involved in our work? Well, I had a great idea while I was driving home: you know how people always say the best time to get teenagers talking to you about what's really going on with them is while you're in the car? What if we paired up teens and our adult volunteers to do deliveries, in a sort of stealth mentorship program? It would get the kids more involved in the community and the center, and over the course of the weeks and months, they'd get to know the other volunteers, and have someone else to get advice from and rely on."

Olivia could feel a huge grin spreading across her face.

"I love this idea."

Jamila grinned back at her.

"Good, because I love it too—thank you for inspiring it. But . . ."

"But you're worried that if you tell your boss, he won't give you the credit for it. Again."

Jamila nodded.

"Exactly. And don't get me wrong, I really love this job, and for the most part I get to have a lot of free rein, and I feel really proud of the work we do. But he takes all the credit for it! Over and over again! I'm sorry for ranting about this, you're a volunteer, but I just saw the board meeting minutes, and it goes over all of the meals we've made and given out over the last quarter, and congratulates him, again, for his great idea! Olivia, I'm so mad I could spit."

Olivia wished she were surprised.

"What I would do—" She stopped herself. "I'm sorry, like the older sibling I am, I have the habit of giving advice whether someone asks for it or not. Do you want advice? I promise, it won't hurt my feelings if you say no, you just needed to vent over some nachos."

Jamila shook her head.

"No, I'd love your advice, actually. That's partly why I brought it up. You always seem so . . . put together and no-nonsense. Like you wouldn't stand that shit for a minute."

Olivia sighed. She was glad she seemed like that, at least.

"Thanks, but sadly, I've had to stand it, many times. Especially early in my career, when I felt blindsided by it, and had no idea what to do other than just sit there. But my biggest piece of advice is very lawyerly—do everything in writing. And shout yourself to the heavens. Email him your ideas, your successes, your numbers, and be as bold as hell in claiming them for yourself. And this is the key: cc board members on those emails. Especially the one you're going to send about this teen program, because I love it. Hell, feel free to cc me on that email too! Basically, you need to make it impossible for him to keep pretending you have nothing to do with this, and even more impossible for the board to be clueless."

Jamila nodded slowly.

"That sounds . . . smart, but really scary."

The waitress put their nachos in front of them, and Olivia picked up a cheese-laden chip.

"Oh, it's definitely scary, especially at first. It gets a lot better with practice, though. Feel free to send me any draft emails, if you want me to look them over before you send them. I've gotten very good at this in the past six or seven years." She took a bite of the chip, and reached for another one. "It'll be good payback for your help in buying that car—maybe even better than these nachos."

Jamila spooned salsa over a chip.

"I'll definitely take you up on that. Thanks. Thanks a lot."

Olivia smiled at her.

"My pleasure. We shouldn't all have to reinvent the wheel every time, you know?"

Olivia hated that this all-too-familiar thing was

happening to Jamila, but it made her feel good that Jamila had asked for her advice. Especially since the whole car-buying process, and her anxiety over it, had made her feel vulnerable. She was glad both she and Jamila had shared with each other.

Maybe she'd made a real new friend here in L.A.

"Okay, and can I ask you another question?" Jamila put down her chip. "Where do you get all of those great button-down tops? I can never find ones that fit my chest; but yours all fit perfectly!"

Olivia laughed.

"I couldn't, either, for years. Then finally I just gave up and bought one two sizes too big—which was hard enough to find—and got it tailored. It was so perfect I got like ten more."

Just as Jamila got up to go to the bathroom, Olivia felt her phone buzz in her pocket.

Don't keep me in suspense!

She grinned, and sent Max the picture of her and the car that Jamila had taken right before they left the dealership.

I bought this!

Just as he sent back a flurry of exclamation points and applause emojis, Jamila sat back down. Olivia slid her phone into her pocket.

Jamila grinned at her.

"Sooo, things are going well with that guy?"

Shit, Olivia had forgotten that she'd told Jamila anything about Max, if only vaguely.

"It's . . . complicated. But . . . yes, I guess so."

Jamila laughed.

"That smile on your face as you looked at your phone was more than 'I guess so.' "

Olivia covered her face with her hands. Apparently she had her answer about how she looked at Max.

"Okay, you got me. Yes, it's going well, it's just that . . ." She put her hands back down on the table and looked at Jamila. "When we first started—and actually, when I first told you about him—I thought it was going to be a casual thing and probably wouldn't last very long. But . . ." She took a deep breath. "It's possible I was wrong about that. And I wasn't really prepared for something like this." She laughed. "I don't know why I say that in the past tense; I'm *not* really prepared for something like this."

Jamila looked at her like she was a brand-new species.

"What do you have to prepare for? Can't you just keep dating?"

It sounded so easy when Jamila said it like that.

"That's sort of what we've been doing, but . . ."

It was too early—both in her friendship with Jamila and her relationship with Max—to tell Jamila who Max was, so she couldn't tell her the whole story, even though she desperately wanted to. "I don't know if you've noticed this about me, but I'm not that much of a 'go with the flow' kind of person."

Jamila laughed at her again.

"Oh, really, the woman who took two months to buy a car isn't a 'go with the flow' kind of person? I never would have guessed."

Olivia couldn't help but laugh.

"I'm just saying," Jamila said as she picked up a chip, "any guy who makes you smile like that is worth getting out of your comfort zone a little."

Her other friends, or her sister, would tell her she wasn't acting like herself, that they hadn't seen her so into a guy in a long time, and blah blah blah. But Jamila didn't know her well enough for that, so she just cheered her on. It was kind of nice to have a new friend.

"You might be right," she finally said.

She texted Max back as soon as she got into her car.

Can't wait to show you the car in person this weekend! That hike you mentioned sounds good, but please remember that I've spent the last ten years living in New

York, where there are no hills, and be gentle on me. See you Saturday.

She looked down at her phone and smiled.

Max couldn't stop thinking about Olivia as he got ready for their hike on Saturday. Obviously, Olivia was gorgeous and brilliant, but there was more to it than that. Maybe it was just that she challenged him in a way no one had in a while. She forced him to earn her respect, and whenever she smiled or laughed or nodded at something he said, he felt like he'd won something. But she was also so warm and caring, under that perpetually suspicious look on her face—the way she'd noticed something was wrong last weekend was proof of that. He felt such a connection with her already. If he was honest with himself, he'd felt that since the very first night at the bar.

She was the only person he'd felt this easy with, this comfortable with, this happy with, in as long as he could remember. He could open up to her in a way he couldn't, and didn't, to almost anyone other than Wes. Sure, he could be impulsive in his actions, but he rarely let himself be anything other than the public version of Max Powell with other people. Why didn't he mind doing that around Olivia? Maybe because she'd been the only person in years who had looked past his whole senator persona and asked if he was okay. She'd recognized he was a person in there, that he had feelings underneath his senator facade.

He had to admit it to himself: he was falling for her, and the more time he spent with her and the more he thought about her, the harder and faster he fell. And no, that wasn't taking it slow, but you know what—fuck taking it slow. Slow was a waste of time; he was thirty-nine years old, he knew his own mind, he knew what he wanted. He'd known Olivia for two whole months now. That was plenty of time for him to know how he felt about her.

Was that enough time for her, though? He hoped to find out.

Olivia got to his house at two on Saturday afternoon, and he threw open his door and pulled her inside.

"Are you ready to go?" she asked as she walked in. "You know I'm still not sure about this whole hiking thing." She was wearing leggings, sneakers, a black T-shirt, and a very doubtful look on her face.

God, he'd missed her.

Before she could step farther into his house, he wrapped his arms around her.

"You are a sight for sore eyes," he said as he pulled her against him.

"Why, you're tired of all of the suits in Washington and you're thrilled to see some yoga pants?" she said as she snuggled against him.

He ran his hands up and down her body and grinned at her.

"I'm thrilled to see you, full stop, but the yoga pants are a bonus, I'm not going to lie."

He leaned down to kiss her, just as she slid her hands into his hair and pulled him to her. He kissed her hard, like he'd been dreaming about doing all week. She kissed him back just as hard, he hoped for the same reason. They stood there for a while, kissing, touching, not saying anything, but he felt—he hoped—they communicated a lot all the same.

"If you still want to go on that hike, we should probably go at some point," she said in his ear. "Though, if you'd rather go on a nice, civilized, I don't know, winery tour or something, I'd be happy to be spontaneous for once."

He laughed and pulled away.

"If you really don't want to go on a hike, we can totally change our plans," he said. "But I did get that cheese you liked so much last week."

She walked ahead of him into his kitchen.

"Then, by all means, let's hike."

He picked up the backpack full of food, water, and ice packs, and gestured toward the door.

"All ready," he said. "And I can't wait to admire that new car of yours. Do you want to take it, instead of mine?" He didn't say this to her, but he had a feeling a few local reporters recognized his car, and the last thing he wanted was to get photographed while out with her.

She slung her backpack over one shoulder.

"Sure, but can you drive? I'm getting used to the car, and I think I even like it, but driving in hilly areas and places where I don't know where I'm going stresses me out. And I know it'll make me even more stressed if you're there in the car, judging my driving."

"I won't be judging your driving!" he said with a laugh.

She unlocked the car and got into the passenger side.

"I'm sure you're telling the truth, but I would still *feel* like you were judging me, no matter what."

He tossed his backpack in the back seat and got in the driver's side. After a comically long amount of time, they figured out how to adjust the driver's seat for his longer legs, and he drove them in the direction of Griffith Observatory.

When they got there, they pulled into the back corner of the almost full parking lot.

"I guess this whole 'hiking' thing is very popular here in L.A.," Olivia said.

He strapped his backpack on and adjusted his hat so it shaded—and mostly covered—his face.

"It just means that if you faint from exposure, there will be plenty of people around to carry you to safety."

She glared at him.

"Is that your idea of a joke?"

He grinned at her.

"Oh, you know it was funny."

She finally let a smile break through.

"Fine, it was a little funny."

He leaned down to kiss her, but took a step back before he did. Right, they were in public. He'd almost forgotten.

Olivia pulled her hair back into a low ponytail and put a black baseball cap on.

They hiked along the easy version of the trail for a few miles. He slowed his stride to match her shorter one, and let himself relax, for the first time in weeks. They walked side by side, and didn't hold hands, but were so close they may as well have been. Their fingers brushed from time to time as they walked along, and it felt so good to be this close to her, after a whole week of being away. Every so often, he would turn to look at her, and just marvel that he'd found someone like her. Sometimes she would catch him and smile at him, and he would smile back. They didn't talk about anything hard, just the perfect spring weather, her adventures at the community center this week, and the guy who'd gotten incredibly drunk on his flight on the way home and had been escorted off the plane when they'd landed. Once they could see it, they stopped to take pictures of the Hollywood sign. And the whole way, he was so happy to be here, in one of his favorite places, with her.

After a while, he pointed to a big tree up ahead.

"Want to dive into these snacks?"

Olivia grinned.

"I thought you'd never ask." She looked out at the view and shook her head. "I have to acknowledge that this hasn't been as bad as I thought it would be. Even kind of . . . nice."

That felt like the biggest compliment he'd ever received.

"I like you so much," he said. He didn't mean to say it, it had just come out.

She turned to look at him, surprise and . . . was that pleasure on her face?

"Why, because I grudgingly admitted that nature can be okay sometimes?"

He laughed out loud as he dropped his backpack under the tree.

"That, and for other reasons, too." He looked down. He really should tie his shoe. "You know. I don't think I ever thanked you for last week. I needed a quiet night—and to be able to talk to someone—more than I realized."

Olivia sat down, and he sat down next to her.

"You're welcome," she said. "I was glad I could help." She smirked at him. "Though . . . you did say thank you, in your own way."

He blushed. That move of his might have

violated some part of his pledge to Wes, but he hadn't been able to resist.

"I did, didn't I?" he said.

She unscrewed her water bottle and took a sip.

"How was this week?" she asked. "I saw you on TV the other night talking criminal justice reform." She grinned. "I should say, I saw you changing the subject to talk about it when you were actually on to talk about the scandal of the day."

She'd watched him on TV? He smiled, then sighed.

"Thanks for watching. And yes, I'm good at turning the topic and making it look like it was the host's idea—it's one of my real strengths." He took the cheese out of his backpack and handed it to her. "I'm going to fight for my bill no matter what, even if leadership wants me to shut up about it. I'm still so pissed that they aren't moving it forward. Maybe if I keep bringing it up, reporters will ask my colleagues questions about it. Maybe that's all I can hope for."

He hadn't realized how bitter he still was about this until he'd started talking.

Olivia shook her head.

"No, there must be something else you can do." She held up a hand to stop him from interrupting her. "Not about the bill, you know more than I do on that. But there must be something else you can do to help the kids and their families. If the goal is to help them, I'm sure there are other ways to do that. What are they?"

He sat up straight. God, she was right. That was the question he needed to ask.

"Of course there are. I've been so laser focused on my bill that I haven't considered anything else." He took off his hat so he could see her better. "My staff has tried to get me to concentrate more on some of the other things I can do—education, job-training programs, housing—and I support all of that, but I threw my whole everything behind this bill. I guess . . . I don't want to think this way, but putting my energy elsewhere seems like admitting defeat." He sighed. "And I guess my politician ego couldn't let go of what a major victory this would be. I told myself it would be a victory for the people, and it would. But it would be a big one for me, too."

Olivia nodded.

"I completely understand that. But what if you frame it as throwing energy at *additional* options, but don't give up on your bill yet? Keep fighting for your bill, but make this a new thing. Make this a new thing: about education, or health care, or housing, or some bullshit about 'the American family' or something. Talk to a bunch of teachers and parents and make sure you talk to the kids, too. Hell, go on a listening tour of town halls across California, focused on communities that don't usually get heard, or youth, or whatever, to get ideas for how to help."

He dropped his water bottle onto the blanket. Thank goodness he'd put the top on first.

"I love this idea! Town halls across California, in marginalized communities. It's perfect. I'm going to text my chief of staff about this right now." He pulled his phone out of his pocket.

Olivia laughed.

"That poor woman, getting texts from you with random ideas on a Saturday."

Max looked up from his phone and shrugged.

"Luckily she's used to me by now. But also luckily, I don't have any reception up here, so I can't send it yet. Hold on: let me just note this down so I can send it later."

He typed busily with his thumbs for a few minutes, then put his phone away.

"Sorry about that." He touched her cheek, just for a second. "Thank you—for the idea, and for making me feel less discouraged about everything. And I'm sorry, we've been talking about me a lot, haven't we? How are you? How is the firm going, still super busy?"

Olivia made herself smile big, like she always did when she got this question, and nodded.

"Oh yeah, really busy. I'm lucky I got away all afternoon today." Suddenly, her lies felt like ashes on her tongue. She just couldn't do it anymore. Not with Max. "No. Wait. I'm sorry, none of that is true. It's not that busy at all, and I'm really worried about it."

Max looked confused.

"Wait, what do you mean? I thought you've been wildly busy since you started?"

She shook her head.

"No," she said again. "I know I told you that. I lied to you. I'm sorry. They say you're supposed to fake it till you make it, and I've been faking it too much. We keep networking and reaching out to potential clients but we aren't getting as much interest as I'd hoped. We have some clients, and we've done some pitches, but not enough, and I'm so stressed about it. I knew this would be hard, but I guess I didn't realize how hard it would be on me." She finally turned to look at him. "I didn't mean to lie to you about this, but I'm just so anxious about it and scared that I made the biggest mistake of my life and that we're not going to make this a success, and I'll have to . . . anyway, I'm sorry."

All her lies and anxieties came spilling out, until she forced herself to stop talking. What did Max think of her now?

She didn't realize she cared so much about that—and about him—until this moment. In retrospect, she should have known when she agreed to go with him on a hike, of all things. And she really should have known when she went shopping for new athleisure for said hike—she, Olivia Monroe, who had said she'd never be one of those L.A. people who bought fancy yoga pants! She looked down at her brand-new $100 yoga pants and laughed at herself—these certainly did make her ass look great, at least.

How did Max manage to get her to spill her guts to him, just by sitting there next to her, with that open look on his face? He'd thought she was this successful lawyer; how would he feel now that he knew she wasn't?

He nudged her.

"Hey," he said softly. She turned to look at him. "It's okay. I understand."

The look in his eyes was so kind, it made her want to cry.

"You do?" she asked.

He nodded.

"I do. This all must be really hard on you." He put his arm around her and pulled her close. She knew they shouldn't be touching in public, but she was so grateful for his embrace that she ignored that.

"It is," she said. "Especially since I know I'm good at this, I know Ellie is too, and I know we make a great team. And it was hard enough to get clients to have faith in me when I was in New York, and then I had the full backing of a big law firm."

He patted her hair softly as he dropped his arm.

"Starting your own business is never easy, but I can only imagine how much harder it is when you're a Black woman and have to deal with racism and sexism on top of everything else," he said.

She took a long breath. What a relief for him to acknowledge that.

"I have full confidence in you that you'll make it, by the way," he said.

She squeezed his hand, then let go.

"Thank you. It means a lot to hear you say that." She closed her eyes for a second, then looked back up at him. "Max, I have to know. You say you really like me, but is this the kind of thing you do a lot? Like, the cake, and all of that?"

He turned his whole body to face her, a very sweet smile on his face.

"No, I've never sent a cake before to try to get a woman to go out with me."

That was a nice answer, but that wasn't quite what she'd meant.

"Thank you for saying that, but I guess what I meant was . . ." Shit, how should she phrase this?

"If what you meant was, do I go around picking up women in bars on a regular basis, the answer is no," he said. "And if what you meant was, do I go around going on dates with women and telling them I like them a lot, the answer is also no. I sent you that cake on an impulse, because you'd disappeared from my life after I saw you in that hotel bar, and when you reappeared, it felt like magic, and I refused to let you go again. And every moment I've been with you since then has told me that impulse was correct."

"Oh," she said. There he was again, making her feel wanted. More than anyone else ever had.

"I, um. I'm really glad you sent me that cake," she said. "And I'm really glad to be here with you. I like you a lot, too."

A wide, bright, joyful smile spread across Max's face.

"You do?" he asked.

She'd tried so hard to fight it, but she couldn't anymore.

"I do," she said. Everything about Max was unexpected, and Olivia had never liked the unexpected. But somehow, she couldn't get enough of Max.

He picked up the cheese and crackers and put them back into his backpack.

"Great. Then how about we go back to my house and take our clothes off?"

She laughed out loud.

"I thought you'd never ask."

Chapter Nine

✳

It took a great deal of self-control for Max not to drive back to his house like a bat out of hell. Only two things stopped him: (1) he did not want the headlines that would come if he was stopped for speeding; and (2) he was driving Olivia's brand-new car, and if he did anything to risk it, she might murder him before he got the chance to have sex with her.

"I just want to be clear on this," he said on the drive back to his house. "Are we, like, together together now?"

Even while driving, he could tell she was laughing at, not with, him.

" 'Together together?' Is that some sort of official designation, Senator?"

He slid his hand onto her thigh and forced himself to keep his eyes on the road.

"You know what I mean."

She put her hand on top of his.

"Yeah, I guess I do. And yeah, I guess we are. But . . ." She took a deep breath. "I'm not quite ready to publicly be senator Maxwell Stewart Powell's girlfriend, if that's okay. I mean, I at least have to get a haircut, and some new lipstick, before I have to be in paparazzi pictures."

He laughed.

"I'm not famous enough for paparazzi pictures." He turned his hand over and squeezed hers. "But I know what you mean; it's early for all of that."

She'd turned it into a joke, but he understood. They had really only just started; he didn't want to invite the rest of the world into their relationship yet, either.

"Plus," she went on, "your staff will probably freak out if they find out you're dating someone who got arrested as a teenager."

He laughed and touched her cheek.

"Number one, your records are sealed, no one has to know about that. And number two, I know at least three people on my staff who have been arrested much more recently, so they have no grounds to complain."

They got to his house after a much longer drive than he wanted it to be. As soon as he closed the door behind them, he reached for Olivia.

He kissed her, and kissed her, and kissed her. All of the kisses he'd wanted to give her while they were on the hike, while she'd given him advice and confessed about her own anxieties, he gave her now, again and again and again.

And then, suddenly, kissing her wasn't enough.

He took her hand and led her into his living

room, and fell down with her on the couch while they laughed together. And then, finally, he reached for the bottom of her shirt, that T-shirt that was so snug, that shirt that had been driving him wild all day.

"I feel like I've been waiting forever for this," she said.

He leaned forward to kiss her again, just for that.

"Good God, it's been a nightmare," he said.

She ran her fingers from his temple to his chin.

"This whole waiting thing was your idea, you know."

He shook his head.

"Don't remind me, especially right now. I feel like the stupidest person in Congress, and that's saying something."

He tugged off her shirt, and then sat back to stare.

"Holy shit, Olivia."

She smiled wickedly at him.

"Hmmmm?"

He couldn't take his eyes off her.

"If I had known all day that you were wearing this underneath that shirt, I might have aborted the whole 'hike' idea and never even left the house."

Her bra was the sexiest thing he'd seen in months, with the exception of the woman wearing it. It was hot-pink sheer lace, and he couldn't decide if he wanted to rip it right off her body or to have her keep it on as long as possible.

"It's not the kind of bra you're supposed to wear on hikes, but I had to draw the line somewhere," she said.

"My God, you're amazing," he said. He reached for her again, and let his thumbs dance over her dark nipples.

"Do you like that?" he asked.

Her eyes closed halfway, and she nodded.

"I like it a lot," she said.

He kept touching her, sometimes gently, sometimes roughly, to see how she responded, what made her bite her lip, or moan, or toss her head back. After he felt like he'd driven them both to the breaking point, he sat up and pulled her pants off.

"You have matching panties?" he almost shouted.

She laughed out loud.

"Look, I wasn't *sure* it was going to happen today, but a girl can hope, can't she?"

He reached for her hands and pulled her upright.

"That's it. The couch is all well and good for some things, but right now, I need you in my bed."

She tossed her head—and her ass—as she walked ahead of him toward the stairs.

"And what do you propose to do while we're in there, hmm?"

He walked behind her up the stairs and blessed his good fortune.

"Well," he said as he joined her at the top of the stairs. "First, I'm going to rip those panties right off of you. Then I'm going to make you come so hard you're gasping for air. And then I'm going to fuck you until neither of us can remember our names. Does that sound good to you?"

She reached for his fly and unzipped his pants.

"Mmm, that sounds excellent, but can I suggest a slight change in the agenda?"

She didn't wait for his answer before she pulled his pants down.

"The thing is," she said as she pushed his underwear to join his pants on the floor, "I've been waiting to see this for quite some time." She wrapped her hand around his hard cock. "And, as I anticipated, it doesn't disappoint. So, if you could just . . . give me a moment here."

She pushed him against the wall, right outside his bedroom door, and sank to her knees. Then she looked up at him and smiled.

"Is that all right with you?"

He'd lost all ability to speak. The sight of her there, in that hot-as-hell lingerie, her lips less than an inch from his cock . . . he was surprised he was still standing.

But she was clearly waiting for some sort of signal from him, so finally he nodded. Seconds later, her tongue darted out of her mouth and licked the tip of his cock. He closed his eyes but immediately opened them again. He had to keep watching her.

First she licked him from the tip to the base, then she wrapped her hand around his cock and sucked him into her mouth.

Holy shit, she was so fucking good at this. He wanted to tell her that, he wanted to say something, but all he could do was stare at her and enjoy the hell out of this.

It felt so good—her lips around him, the friction of her hand and of her tongue, her other hand gripping his ass—he knew he wasn't going to last long. He closed his eyes to try to hold himself together, but then he felt the scrape of her teeth against him, and he knew he was done.

He collapsed on the floor next to her after he came, and when he could open his eyes again, she was smiling down at him.

"We haven't even made it to the bedroom yet," he said.

She smiled again and reached for his hand to pull him up.

"I think it's time, don't you?"

Olivia couldn't help herself from a little swagger as she pulled Max into his bedroom, both of them giggling like teenagers. He had clearly enjoyed the hell out of that blow job, but the weird thing was, she'd enjoyed giving it to him almost as much as he'd enjoyed getting it. She usually could take or leave giving blow jobs—men were often gross and smelly, they always tried to push your head in one direction or another, which just made you feel like a blow-up doll, and they were rarely appropriately appreciative, and instead just seemed to think of blow jobs as their due.

But it had been different with Max. It was only because of the way he'd looked at her on the couch and again on the way up the stairs that she'd done it at all. She couldn't remember anyone ever looking at her like that—with awe and excitement, like he'd unwrapped a present he'd wanted for years. When they got to the top of the stairs and he was still looking at her like that, she had to pull his pants off; she couldn't help herself.

They tumbled together into his bed and turned to look at each other, both with big grins on their faces. It felt strange and impossible and completely right that she was here with him.

He pulled her against his chest, and they lay there for a while together. It had been a long time since she was this happy, this comfortable, lying like this in a man's arms. She hadn't realized how much she missed this feeling.

Or maybe she felt that way now because she was with Max. Maybe she just missed every moment she hadn't spent with him.

She trailed her hand over his springy dark chest

hair and then back down. He laughed and flipped her over before she could get where she was going.

"I'm going to need a little more recovery time than that, you know. I'm thirty-nine, after all."

She smiled up at him.

"I think I remember you saying something a few minutes ago about what we were going to do in here—Senator Powell, do you fulfill your campaign promises?"

He hooked his thumbs around her panties, and with one quick tug, they were off her body and thrown across the room.

"Absolutely I do," he said. Then he slid down her body and proceeded to make her come so hard she was gasping for air.

When she had—sort of—recovered, she reached down for that excellent dick again.

"Ahhh, here we are," she said as her hand closed around it.

"Here we are indeed." He kissed her greedily, like he couldn't get enough of her. Dear God, she felt like she was being tricked, like she was in a dream. Not just how good they were together in bed—that was a delight, of course. But the way he looked at her, the way he touched her, the way he treated her, was like nothing she'd ever experienced. Like he felt lucky to be with her. She could get addicted to this.

"Hold on one second." He let go of her and

rolled over to the other side of his bed. He opened a drawer of his nightstand and then fumbled with a box. She sat up with a grin.

"New box?" she asked.

He looked sideways at her and shrugged.

"I bought it after our first date. My old ones had all expired, and I was . . . well, I was hopeful."

She dropped back down onto the bed while he pulled a condom out of the box. After that night, she thought he hadn't been interested in her at all, and meanwhile he was out there buying condoms with her in mind. This was one of the few times she was very happy to have been wrong.

It took him only a few seconds to get the condom out of the box and on.

"I like the way you watch me do that," he said.

She ran her hands up and down his chest, his back, and let them come to rest on his butt.

"I liked the way you watched me, too," she said.

Suddenly, there was no time for talking, just kissing, and touching, and stroking, and sucking. At long last, he slid between her legs, then paused and looked down at her.

"Please," she asked.

He pushed inside her, and she gasped.

"Did I hurt you?" he asked.

To the contrary.

"No, no, it just felt so good."

He grinned.

"Thank God."

And then he did the same thing again, but harder, and again, and again. Her gasps and his moans were the only sounds in the room. It felt so good, she wanted this to go on forever; it felt too good, so good she almost couldn't handle it. Then he reached his hand down between them to touch her in exactly the place he knew she wanted to be touched, and she pressed her mouth into his shoulder so she wouldn't scream. He went faster and faster, and then collapsed on top of her.

"Holy shit," he said as he rolled to the side and pulled her against him.

"Mmmhmm," was all she could respond. After a few seconds, she looked up at him.

"If all hikes end like that, I wish I'd gotten into hiking years ago," she said.

He laughed and then gave her a look that made her dizzy.

"You make me so happy, Olivia Monroe," he said, right before he kissed her again.

Chapter Ten

Max poked his head into Kara's office when he got in on Monday morning.

"Hey, do you have a minute to chat? I want to talk to you about something."

Kara followed him into his office.

"Anything wrong, sir?"

He flicked the lights on and sat down behind his desk, coffee in hand. After . . . everything that had happened between him and Olivia after the hike, he ended up never sending that text to Kara, so he'd decided to wait to talk to her in person.

"No, no, nothing's wrong, the opposite. I had an idea over the weekend. Well, actually, it wasn't my idea—I was talking to a friend about the criminal justice reform bill and it was their idea."

Not for the first time, he wanted to tell Kara about Olivia. Partly so he'd be able to actually give her credit for this idea, but also because Olivia was becoming a bigger and bigger part of his life, and it felt absurd that Kara didn't know about her. Kara had been by his side for three years now—he either saw or talked to her almost every day, and the days they didn't talk, they texted or emailed. She knew everything about him, almost. Except for this.

But no, he couldn't tell her yet. It would be completely inappropriate for him to tell someone who worked for him about his new relationship. Besides, it wasn't like this was the kind of thing they talked about; all he knew about her personal life was that she'd once brought her girlfriend to the office holiday party. He hoped he'd get to tell Kara about Olivia eventually, but that would be when he and Olivia were ready to go public, and they weren't there yet. No matter how great things had been over the weekend (and they'd been really, phenomenally great)—that wasn't in the plan for the immediate future.

"What was the idea, sir?" Kara asked.

Right, the idea.

"So I know you've been gently telling me for a while that the bill might not go anywhere. Well, my friend reminded me of something you and others here have also been trying to tell me: I can keep fighting for the bill, but I can do other things to help the cause of criminal justice reform. What if we had town halls in marginalized communities all around California—to find out what people most care about, to figure out other ways to help them, and so they know we're listening to them and working for them, instead of just trying to fight a possibly losing battle? We might even try to get state legislators involved, see if we can change some California law in the process."

Kara nodded slowly.

"Hmm. I like this idea, sir." She flipped open her notebook and scrawled a few lines. "It'll take a lot of work—from both the DC and local staffs, but I think everyone will be excited about it."

Max rubbed his hands together. He couldn't wait to tell Olivia this.

"Fantastic," he said. "Maybe the first one could be in a few weeks? I could do one every Friday afternoon for the next few months!"

Kara laughed out loud.

"Excuse me, sir. I'm sorry, but no. A few weeks? This will take a great deal of planning and coordination; it'll take closer to a few months for us to do this right."

Sometimes he was happy that he had a staff who would tell it to him like it was and not jump to satisfy his every whim, even if those whims were ridiculous. But when they laughed at him like this . . . okay, fine, he was still happy about it, just less happy.

"Right, I didn't think about that," he said.

Kara flipped through her calendar.

"Plus, your schedule is pretty packed for the next few months, what with it being an election year and all. You have at least one fundraiser almost every week until I don't know when."

This was the problem with having someone on

your staff whose literal job it was to schedule your time—he had no idea what was on his calendar from week to week.

"Nobody in Congress wants to vote for my bill, but they still want me at their fundraisers, huh?" he asked.

Kara looked up at him, a wry smile on her face.

"You know how this town works—you get a lot of headlines and buzz, so whether or not they want to vote for your bill, they still want you to make speeches to get people to throw dollars toward their campaigns."

Kara made another note, then looked up at him.

"However, we could make this into a plan for the August recess. There will be lots of places that will be thrilled to have you, and some members of Congress, or Democratic challengers, who will be very happy to be on board."

Kara stood up, notebook in one hand and calendar in the other.

"Let me call Andy, and then he can talk to the district offices and we'll see if we can come up with a timetable." She paused at his office door. "Good idea, sir. Please thank your friend for me."

Max pulled out his phone to text Olivia as soon as Kara had closed the door behind her.

Chief of staff loves the town halls idea— told me to thank you for her. So thank

you, from both me and her. Wish I could
thank you in person right now, though.

Not for the first time, he wished Washington,
DC, and L.A. were closer together. If only he
could see Olivia again tonight.

"What have I gotten myself into?"

All week, as Olivia had done client work,
written pitches for clients the firm hoped to get,
and gone to lunches and coffees with law school
friends and former colleagues to try to drum
up business, that phrase had been drumming
through her head. But not about the firm—about
Max. How had she committed herself to him?
And how did she miss him this goddamn much?
Their weekend together had been so perfect, and
she hated that because of the time difference
and his job, all they had time for this week was
occasional texts and a few quick phone calls.

And then she was furious at herself for missing
him that much. And liking him that much. She'd
caught herself daydreaming about his eyelashes
in the middle of the workday, like some lovesick
teenager. His eyelashes! He kept saying—and
acting as if—he liked her that much, too, but this
all just seemed far too good to be true.

The worst part was, she knew she desperately
wanted it to be true. She wanted Max to be the
caring, thoughtful, interesting man he seemed to

be. She wanted the opportunity to get to know that man better. She wanted his desire for her, his interest in her, to be real. But she was still afraid she couldn't trust any of it.

"Ready for bowling?" Max asked as Olivia opened her front door on Friday night.

She stepped outside.

"As ready as I'll ever be. I haven't gone bowling in years. We'll see how this goes."

He gestured down the street.

"I'm parked a few houses down—I don't want anyone to recognize my car in your driveway. I'm sorry, I should have thought of that before."

"Oh, that makes sense." She was glad he'd thought about it now. "Thanks."

They got in the car and he reached for her, then pulled back.

"I'm sorry, I forgot. I can't kiss you here; I should have come inside for a few minutes. And I've been wanting to kiss you so much all week."

She put her hand on his knee.

"We'll have plenty of time after bowling. Or"—she raised an eyebrow at him—"we could go back inside."

He grinned at her, and put his hand over hers.

"If we do that, we're never leaving. And you know, I like bowling, but . . ."

She squeezed his hand.

"Look how impatient you are. Don't get me wrong, I like it, but we can wait."

Plus, she had her own reasons for wanting to go bowling tonight.

He drove them out to a place he'd found online that was supposed to have pub food that was actually good and beer in a bar attached to the bowling alley, and where you could reserve lanes in advance.

"Thank you for finding this place—I'm glad we're not going to have to wait forever for a lane," she said.

He laughed.

"I'm glad I found this place, too, or else I wouldn't have suggested bowling at all. I loathe having to wait for things. I know maybe that makes me a privileged jerk; sometimes I make myself wait in line for brunch, just to prove I still can, but I hate every second of it."

Olivia laughed.

"I hate it, too. That first weekend after I got here, I went to one of those places for brunch that I see all over Instagram, and I had to wait for an hour and a half! The food was good, but I'm not sure if there's any food worth waiting an hour and a half for on a Sunday morning."

"Thank God you feel that way," he said.

He put on his fake glasses before they got out of the car. She still hadn't seen him in that blond wig, but the glasses, plus his tousled hair and plain T-shirt, really did make him look different from the Senator Powell she saw on TV.

Their lane was flanked by teenagers' birthday parties. The teens had obviously been there for a while and were already rowdy, which was perfect. Teens wouldn't pay attention to the two of them, bless them.

Max picked up a bowling ball with three fingers, while Olivia tried out one ball, then another.

"I don't even remember what I'm looking for here—what are these supposed to feel like?"

He picked up one of the balls she put down.

"You want it heavy enough so it can spin down the lane and knock over all of the pins but not so heavy you have trouble tossing it."

She picked up a silver glittery ball and smiled.

"I think this is the one."

Max went back to the first one he'd picked up.

"Are you just saying that because it's sparkly?"

She grinned at him.

"So what if I am? A woman's got to have some flair if she has to wear shoes like this, okay?"

He laughed and shook his head.

"Let's order some food now, I'm starving. You can press the buttons right here and they bring it to you."

They ordered loaded nachos and beer to start, and someone brought over their beer as Max and Olivia were setting up the scoring on the screen.

"How long has it been since the last time you were bowling, again?" Max asked her as she moved her glittery bowling ball from one hand to another.

She pursed her lips.

"Oh, let me see . . . at least seven years, it must be? The last time was for my friend Justine's thirtieth birthday, and she must be thirty-seven or even thirty-eight by now? So we'll see how this goes, I guess."

He looked both kind and a touch condescending, just as she'd expected.

"Do you want to go first, or do you want me to go first?" he asked.

She put her finger to her lips as she considered that.

"You go first. Show me what I'm supposed to do so I remember."

He nodded and took a sip of his beer.

"Okay—you put your three fingers in the ball like this," he said, demonstrating. "Then you start from back here, and take a few not-quite-running steps, toss your arm back, and let the ball loose down the lane."

His ball went flying down the lane, and it knocked down about half the pins. Olivia nodded slowly.

"Good job, look, you got—what, five of the little sticks down."

He laughed.

"Pins, and I'm kind of rusty, but thanks. I also haven't done this for a while, though for me it was less than two years ago. Right after I got elected, actually. We had a little bowling alley victory party for the campaign staff. Though that night I drank a lot more beer and hugged a lot more people than pins I knocked down. Here, I get one more try before it's your turn."

He picked up his ball again and threw it down the lane; three pins fell that time.

"I used to be better at this, I promise," he said as he walked back to join Olivia.

She stood up and patted him on the shoulder.

"You seem pretty good at it to me." She picked up her sparkly bowling ball and walked toward the lane. Max stood to the side to watch her with a smile on his face.

"You do it like this, right?" She took a few quick steps forward, swung her arm back, and released her ball straight down the middle of the lane. It flew all the way down and, *SMACK*, knocked all ten pins over in seconds. Max's mouth dropped open.

Olivia threw her arms in the air.

"I've still got it!"

She turned to Max with a cocky grin and saw realization dawn over his face.

"You . . . you were conning me!" he said. "With that whole 'oh, big, strong man, how do you hold a bowling ball' act. Weren't you?"

Her grin got bigger.

"I couldn't help myself! Plus, I haven't gone

bowling in years, so I wasn't sure if I'd still be good at it, but turns out I am."

He stared at her without saying anything.

She sighed inwardly. She knew this was how he'd react. That's why she'd done it.

She hadn't initially meant to pretend to Max that she didn't know much about bowling. It wasn't like she'd been testing him—well, not exactly. But she knew all too well that men didn't like it when you beat them at something. She learned that at a very young age when she beat Chris Riley in the spelling bee in third grade and he didn't want to be her friend anymore. For a long time after that, she'd lost to boys on purpose, until one time when she lost a prize she really wanted to win, to a boy who didn't even like her in the first place. Since then she'd played to win in everything she did, which, yes, had made her lose out on a few relationships, but at least she'd never lost her self-respect.

So when Max suggested bowling, she'd known she might beat him. And despite how great he was last week, despite how much he said he liked her and respected her, she knew that with men, like and respect only went so far. And so for the first time in a very long time, she'd thought about finding a way to back out of playing a game with a man so she wouldn't have to face losing Max. But she knew she'd always wonder how Max would react if she beat him. So instead, she challenged herself to play to win, and to win big, to win with swagger, just so she'd know, once and for all, that Max Powell was just like all of the other guys.

"Are you mad about this?" she asked. "Because, oh man, if you can't handle—"

"I'm falling in love with you," he cut in. "I was trying not to even admit it to myself, much less to you, but I can't help it. I know it's too soon, I shouldn't have said this, but you can't kick my ass at bowling like that and do a touchdown dance with that look on your face and expect me not to fall in love with you on the spot."

Now it was her turn to stare at him, speechless.

He was falling in love with her? Not despite her ambition, but because of it? It was the triumphant, victorious look on her face when she'd beat him in bowling that made him realize it?

"I—" she said, and then stopped. She hated how Max's face lit up and then fell when she didn't finish the sentence, but she had no idea what to say.

"I don't want you to feel like you have to say something back," he said. "I didn't mean to say all of that just now, obviously. Or maybe not obviously, I don't know, we still don't know each other all that well, which might make everything I just said sound ridiculous, but—"

"It didn't sound ridiculous," she said in a quiet voice.

His eyes drilled into hers, and a smile slowly dawned over his face.

"Good," he said. "Now, let's talk about something else. Um, how's the firm going? Unless you don't want to talk about that, that might still be stressful, um, how's the food pantry, did you go there this week?"

She took a sip of beer and tried to pull her mind away from what Max had just said.

"The firm is going . . . okay. Ellie and I are both working every avenue to get business, which is all we can do, and the handful of clients we have seem to like our work a lot, which is key. We've gotten a few small projects lately, and that's promising. I'm still anxious about it, though. I just wish we had one more big client; then maybe I could take a deep breath." She picked up a nacho. "And yeah, I did go to the food pantry this week. I'm really glad I started going there—I think Jamila, the woman who runs it, and I are becoming actual friends, which is great. I told you about her; she's the one who helped me get the car. And she had this really great idea for getting teens more involved with their work."

For the rest of their time in the bowling alley, they drank beer, ate nachos, and talked about everything but the thing they were both thinking about. She told him about Jamila's idea, and the birthday cake they'd had for one of the other regular volunteers that week; he told her about the protest signs he'd seen that week that had almost made him laugh out loud on national television. And every time they made eye contact, they both looked away, like if their eyes met for more than a few seconds, they'd have to stop talking and laughing and pretending that everything between them hadn't completely changed in the past hour.

They finished the game—Olivia won handily, though Max had gotten a lot better over the course of the game—and Max touched Olivia's hand.

"You ready to take off? Or do you want to hang out here some more?"

She shook her head.

"Let's go. I have no cake at home, or even pie, but I do have ice cream, if that tempts you?"

Max grinned at her.

"You are very good at tempting me, Olivia Monroe."

They got in his car in the parking lot and were both quiet as they drove back to her house. Then, just as they got off the freeway, Max cleared his throat.

"I meant everything I said back there. In case you were wondering."

Olivia turned to look at him.

"I thought you did."

After all of her doubts over the last week, somehow she hadn't doubted that for a moment.

"Oh. Okay. I just wanted to make sure."

She couldn't stop thinking about what he'd said. It had been spontaneous and heartfelt and like nothing she'd ever experienced before. She'd had men fall in love with her before—or at least, tell her they had. And she'd fallen in love, too. But she'd always felt like she had to hide parts of herself with all of those men: her ambition, her enthusiasm, her body. Sometimes all of the above. But for someone to really see her, to want her, to love her, the true Olivia, like Max did . . . it all felt brand-new. She had no idea how to respond.

"I don't want you to think . . . You took me by surprise, that's all. I didn't realize . . . well, any of that."

Max reached over and took her hand.

"I know I caught you off guard. But I'm glad you know now." He grinned at her. "How about we go back to your house, eat some ice cream, make out like those teenagers around us were all doing, and finally, at long last, I can let you drag me back to your bedroom. Does that sound good?"

She slid her hand into his. That was exactly what she needed right now.

"That sounds great."

Chapter Eleven

*

A few weeks later, Max glanced through his calendar during his regular Tuesday lunchtime meeting with Kara. Everything looked normal, except for the weekend. There must be some mistake.

"Why am I on flights to and from San Francisco on Friday and Sunday? Was that some mistake?"

Kara gave him that look he hated, the one he always tried to avoid getting. The "why am I working for this man when I'm so much smarter than him?" look.

"Because, sir, you have two events this weekend in the Bay Area, remember? Friday afternoon right after you get in you have a meeting with a group of teachers and students in Oakland, then that dinner with the tech people, and Saturday night you're doing the big party fundraiser in San Francisco."

Kara was right, she was so much smarter than him. How the hell had he managed to forget this? He and Wes had even had conversations about it—Wes was going to be at the fundraiser, too. But this would mean he'd spend the entire weekend away from L.A. Which would mean he would have two whole weeks away from Olivia.

"Shit. Yeah, now I remember." What if he flew down to L.A. after the fundraiser on Saturday night, and then back to DC from there on Sunday afternoon? That was, if there was a flight late enough Saturday night from San Francisco to L.A., and if the fundraiser didn't go too long for him to get on that flight, and if Olivia didn't mind that he'd get to her house after midnight on a Saturday night and fly out again twelve hours later. But he couldn't make a plan like that without telling his staff *why* he needed a twelve-hour detour to L.A.

"Is something wrong, sir?" Kara asked him.

He shook his head.

"Nothing's wrong. I just completely forgot I wasn't going to be in L.A. this weekend. I left my good pair of running shoes at my house, and I was looking forward to picking them up."

He *had* left his good pair of running shoes at his house, but he almost always left them in L.A.

"Oh, we can get someone in the L.A. office to pick them up and send them to meet you in the Bay Area, that's easy."

He brushed that away.

"Don't worry about it, I'm sure the L.A. staff has better things to do than pick up my shoes. I should just order another pair to leave here in

DC anyway. Okay, what else do we need to talk about?"

They ran through the rest of his schedule for the week, but the whole time he could feel the emptiness in the pit of his stomach. He wasn't going to get to see Olivia this weekend. He pretended he was looking up something else and flipped through his calendar, and realized he'd seen her at least once a week for the past three months. He only wished it had been more.

The past few weeks they'd spent as much time together as possible. He almost always had at least one event to attend while he was in L.A. for the weekend, often more, but other than that, he was with her almost the whole time. They'd been at her place and at his, at the movies and at the beach, and one rainy Saturday night when they were both in bad moods, he'd ditched his previous idea for a date, told her to put on all the rain gear she had, and drove them out to Anaheim for four glorious hours at Disneyland, where the rain cleared up just in time for the fireworks. They got in the car afterward, soaking wet and freezing cold and both smiling from ear to ear.

He'd kept waiting for her to respond in some way to what he'd said that night at the bowling alley, but she hadn't. Their night at Disneyland had been the perfect time for it—they'd held hands on the roller coasters, they'd walked around with huge smiles on their faces, they'd stood, arms wrapped around each other, during the fireworks, and he'd known the entire time that he was no longer falling in love with her—he'd fallen completely. But she hadn't said anything, so he didn't bring it up again.

Did she feel the same way? He had no idea. He tried to be mature about this, to not feel hurt, but he couldn't help it. Sometimes he just wanted to say "I love you, Olivia! Do you love me?" When he'd shown up at her house wearing a red wig, she laughed so hard she'd cried, and then she looked at him with this tender, loving look in her eyes, and he was sure she was going to say it. She hadn't, but that look from her gave him hope.

It felt like a physical ache, how much he missed her, how much he would miss her even more in the days to come, how much it would suck to get on that long flight back to California on Friday morning and know he wouldn't see Olivia at the other side of it.

He tried to shake it off. This wasn't a big deal. He'd see her the following week; it would be fine.

When Kara left his office, he put his head down to try to read through his stack of briefing papers for the hearings the next day, but he couldn't concentrate on them. The whole reason he and Lana had broken up, shortly before he announced his run for the Senate, was because he'd been so busy he hadn't made time for her, and he'd realized he hadn't cared enough to make time for her. He couldn't conceive of not making time for Olivia. He pulled his personal phone out of his bag.

> Bad news—completely forgot I'm not coming to LA this weekend. I'm in the Bay Area all weekend. A school event, a dinner, and huge fundraiser I can't believe I forgot about

Wait. He had an idea just as he sent that.

> Hey—want to come with me? I could do my events, you could see your family, and in between, we could see each other

He dropped his phone in his pocket and bit his lip. Would she go for this? He hoped so.
A few hours later she texted back.

> Hahaha that sounds delightful but you know it's impossible

As soon as his meeting was over, he texted back.

> Why is it impossible? You told me you were overdue for a weekend at home— you can have that! See your sister, go

to your old favorite burrito places, and spend the nights with me

Plus, otherwise, we won't get to see each other until next weekend

After only a few minutes, she texted back.

Let me think about it. Talk to you later?

He knew Olivia well enough by now to know she never made a snap decision, but God, that part of her frustrated him. He wanted her to be excited, say yes, say she loved him, and not have to stop and think about it every time.

He would just have to convince her, that was all.

Olivia could not believe she'd let Max talk her into coming to the Bay Area this weekend. She still hadn't told her family about Max, and there was no way she'd make it through the weekend without telling at least her sister. But as soon as she walked out onto the pavement at the Oakland airport and took a deep breath, she felt her shoulders relax. Sometimes, it was just really fucking good to go home.

She still felt conflicted about her decision to move to L.A. instead of the Bay Area. It made perfect sense business-wise: there were already a lot of firms that did what they did in the Bay Area and fewer in L.A., their handful of anchor clients was mostly based in Southern California, and, most important, Ellie was already settled in L.A. with her family.

But even though she'd lived away from the Bay Area for a long time now, it was still home, in the way New York had never been and L.A. wasn't yet. Her whole family was here, and even though her mom drove her up the wall half the time, the rest of the time her mom was making her crack up, cooking her favorite foods, or bragging about her. And she always had fun with her sister.

That was probably why she'd finally said yes to Max. After all, Olivia had barely seen her sister since she'd moved back to California.

At first she hadn't told Alexa about Max because she knew Alexa would have a lot of questions, and Olivia knew she didn't have the answers. Plus, she didn't want to get her sister all excited for nothing, and she knew Alexa would be excited about this. But if Olivia was going to stay with Max in his hotel room this weekend, and not in her sister's guest room, she would definitely have to tell Alexa about him.

Just then, Alexa pulled up in front of her. She jumped out of her car and grinned at Olivia.

"Is that all you brought for the whole weekend?"

Olivia pulled her little sister into an enormous hug.

"It's a deceptively large bag—looks like a briefcase, but I can fit a weekend's worth of clothes in it. Plus, I know if I buy anything and need to bring it back, I can steal one of your many tote bags."

They smiled at each other as Olivia tossed her bag into the back seat of Alexa's car.

"Good to have you home. I'm a terrible little sister for not coming down to visit you yet— just give me the best weekend to come and I'm there."

Olivia relaxed into the front seat of the car.

"You're not terrible, but we'll sit down with our calendars while I'm here and figure out a time. I'm just glad you were free this weekend for this last-minute visit."

Alexa glanced at her as they drove out of the airport.

"Speaking of, that was unlike you. I've never known you to do a last-minute anything, unless it was for someone else, whether it's a celebration or some sort of a crisis." She raised her eyebrows. "What friend are you in town for this weekend?"

Damn her sister for knowing her too well.

"Um. So, actually . . . it's not exactly . . . there's something . . ."

Damn it, why was she struggling with this so much?

Alexa laughed.

"See, I knew it. What is it?"

Olivia took a deep breath.

"I'm dating someone. He's in town this week-end for . . . work, so I thought I'd kill two birds with one stone and get to see you and him, too."

Alexa squealed, just as Olivia knew she would.

"Livie! That's so exciting! Who is he? How'd you meet? How long has this been going on? I can't believe you've been holding out on me, I need all the details."

Olivia was glad her sister had to concentrate on the busy road in front of them and couldn't see her face.

"So. Well. As to how we met. The thing is . . . you remember? When I first got to L.A., and I called you from my hotel, because I met this guy at the bar, and he turned out to be—"

"YOU'RE DATING MAX POWELL? SENATOR MAX POWELL? ARE YOU SERIOUS?"

Alexa yelled so loud Olivia was sure half of Oakland heard her.

"I'm serious, and it's . . ."

Alexa didn't stop yelling.

"I CANNOT BELIEVE MY SISTER IS DATING MAX POWELL, HOLY FUCKING SHIT, NOT ONLY IS HE A SENATOR, BUT HE'S HOT AS HELL."

Olivia held up a hand.

"Alexa! You're married!"

Alexa glared at her.

"I may be married, but I'm not dead! Hold on, I can't have this conversation while I'm driving."

She pulled into the parking lot of a Dollar store and turned off the car.

"Okay." She took off her seat belt and turned to face Olivia. "Someone finally kept a secret from me. Now, tell me everything."

Olivia shook her head and laughed. And then she told her. Everything.

"He told you he loved you?" Alexa yelled. "And? What did you say? Do you love him?"

Olivia didn't meet her sister's eyes.

"He said he was falling in love with me, not that he loves me."

Alexa brushed that aside.

"That's a distinction without a difference. Answer the question."

Why had she let her sister go to law school, damn it?

"I . . . I didn't say anything. That was around a month ago, and I still haven't said anything." She dropped her head in her hands at the expression on her sister's face. "I know, I know. I KNOW. But even he acknowledged that it was early, you know! And you know I need time to make my mind up about these things! He said he didn't need me to say anything back, but . . ." She looked at her sister, a tiny smile on her face. "I might. Soon."

Alexa threw her arms around her.

"Oh, Liv, I'm so happy for you!"

Olivia let her smile get bigger.

"I'm still not ready to say . . . that, but, Lex, I really like him. More than I've liked anyone in a long time. I've been hesitant, not just in telling you, but in everything about him. It was just . . . it all seemed too good to be true, everything about him did. I think I'm starting to believe it's all actually true."

It felt scary to say that. But over the past few weeks, she'd finally let herself think it.

"Even though it's hard for me to really . . . let go in that way."

Alexa nodded.

"I get that. It was hard for me, too. Even after Drew moved up here and everything. It was hard to really trust him. Trust *us*. I'd had so many bad experiences before, I guess I started to believe that kind of love wasn't for me—that no one would fall in love with me. So when Drew did, it took me a while to really believe it."

Olivia looked at her little sister. She'd had no idea.

"That sounds . . . familiar." She laughed. "It's weird, but he gets me in a way no one has really seemed to. And the more he sees the real me, the more he seems to like me, which is pretty incredible—I can talk to him about work, or volunteering, or how much I love using power tools, or things I'm worried about, and where other men wouldn't like all of those sides of me, or get bored, or talk down to me, he listens, really listens and wants to know more. The two of us are very different—he's sort of an idealist, while I'm the conventional one, which is funny enough in itself—but it feels like we complement each other?" She bit her lip. "Things feel good." She let herself smile. "Really good. I'm not sure I knew things could feel this good, actually." She shook her head. "Oh God, I hate that I said that out loud, I feel like I'm jinxing things, but . . ."

Alexa shook a finger at her.

"No such thing. But . . . I do have another question. Who else knows about you two? And . . . are you ready for what might happen if and when it's not secret anymore?"

Leave it to her sister to ask the hard questions.

"I know, it's going to be a big whole thing when we get there, but I'm not going to worry about that yet. And in answer to your other question, only Ellie knows."

Alexa started the car and smiled.

"You said when, you know."

Olivia put her seat belt back on and raised her eyebrows at her sister.

"What do you mean, when?"

Alexa smiled.

" 'When we get there.' Not 'if.' 'When.' I like it."

Olivia opened her mouth to protest. Then she closed it without saying anything. Alexa drove on, a smug look on her face.

Before they walked into Alexa's house, Alexa nudged her.

"Can I tell Drew about this? He won't tell anyone, I promise."

Olivia laughed.

"Yes, of course you can tell him, but no one else. And definitely not Mom and Dad, not yet!"

Drew had Olivia's favorite Chinese takeout waiting for her, so they all sat down to eat. And then Olivia told an edited version of her Max story, this time to Drew, whose eyes just got wider and wider.

Right when Olivia finished, Alexa dropped her chopsticks.

"Oh my God. I just realized something. You said he's in town for a fundraiser?" A wide smile spread across her face. "I'm pretty sure that the mayor of Berkeley—and his chief of staff—will be at that same fundraiser tomorrow night."

Olivia dropped her head onto the table, barely missing the chow fun.

"Oh no. Oh no oh no. Is this some sort of anxiety dream? My little sister is going to be at the party with my boyfriend tomorrow and I can't go?"

Alexa looked gleeful.

"Don't worry. I'll be good. I promise."

Drew stood up to go into the kitchen.

"Hold on. I think we need more wine for this conversation. I'll be right back."

Alexa jumped up.

"Oh, wait, I know just the bottle, I'll help you find it."

While they were gone, Olivia checked her phone, which she hadn't done since she'd gotten in Alexa's car.

> At dinner with these tech dudes; almost done, thank god, they're so annoying. Can't wait to see you soon. I hope you're having fun with your sister!

She looked up from her phone to find her little sister pointing and laughing at her. It felt like she was back in high school.

"What are you laughing at?" she said to Alexa.

"Oh, nothing," Alexa said, with that same smug look she'd gotten since she was a toddler and was telling on her older sister. "It's just that gooey look on your face makes it very clear who you just got a text from."

It was even more annoying when her sister was right.

"I don't . . ." She was about to say "I don't

know what you're talking about," like she would have said twenty years ago, but realized that was ridiculous. They both knew exactly what Alexa was talking about. So instead she just let her smile get as gooey as she wanted it to. "He says he's almost done with his dinner and hopes we're having fun."

Alexa's whole face softened.

"Oh, that's so nice."

Olivia sighed and dropped her phone on the table.

"He *is* so nice, that's the problem with him, Lex! He's so nice! He's smart! He's generous! He's attractive! He's rich! He's funny! He's perfect!" Now she rolled her eyes at herself. "Okay, fine, that's an exaggeration, but you know what I mean. What happened to me?"

Alexa put her hands down on the table.

"Are you telling me that in the three or whatever months you've been dating this man, you haven't discovered any of his flaws?"

Olivia took the glass of wine Drew handed her.

"No, it's even worse—I've seen plenty of his flaws! He's hotheaded, he's impulsive, he has an enormous ego! He's used to the whole world doing his bidding, in a way he doesn't even realize; he's incredibly privileged, which he sort of realizes, but not anywhere to the degree he needs to. Also, I don't think I've ever seen him eat a vegetable. And his shoes are all just impossibly ugly. He has these old brown suede shoes he wore one day straight from the airplane and I realized he was on the actual Senate floor with those things on and I wanted to throw them in the garbage immediately, but I don't think we're at a place yet where I can do that. But the bad part is, I know all of that, and I *still* get that fucking gooey look on my face when he texts me! I can tell I get it! I try not to get it! But the goo just spreads over my face and I can't make it stop!"

Now Alexa and Drew were laughing so hard they couldn't speak, and Olivia joined in.

"I know this all sounds so stupid," she said as soon as they all recovered.

Drew shook his head.

"It doesn't sound stupid at all. It sounds exactly like how I felt when I met this one." He poked her sister in the arm. "At least you're being more mature about it than I was, and you're not pretending you're not falling for him." He reached across the table and pushed her phone toward her. "Text him back. Tell him we're almost done with dinner and you'll be on your way to the hotel soon."

She picked up the phone and smiled at him.

"I'm glad my sister married you."

Drew reached for Alexa's hand.

"I'm glad your sister married me, too," he said.

"What hotel is your senator boyfriend staying at?"

Olivia grinned.

"The Fairmont."

Chapter Twelve

Olivia walked into the hotel lobby and checked her texts for Max's room number.

Just getting on the elevator!

She got off the elevator without incident and walked down the hall to his room. But before she could even knock on the door of room 1624, the door swung open.

"There you are." Max grabbed her arm and pulled her inside.

"Here I am," she said as they wrapped their arms around each other.

"I missed you so much." He traced her face with his fingertips, like he was memorizing it.

"I missed you, too," she said. She ran her fingers through his hair. It was slightly longer than normal—he usually got a haircut from the same guy in L.A. every three weeks on Saturday mornings, and tomorrow was his regular haircut day, so it would have to wait until next weekend. It felt ridiculous, and wonderful, that she knew that.

"It feels like it's been forever since I've seen you," he said. He pulled her silk blouse out from where it was tucked into her jeans and unbuttoned the first button.

"It was only a week ago," she said. Why did she still always go breathless when he touched her like this?

He nodded and unbuttoned two more buttons.

"I know. But I spent two days thinking I would have to go two weeks without seeing you. I can't even tell you how much I missed you those days." He dropped a gentle kiss on her lips as he unbuttoned another button. "It made me realize a week is my limit."

Maybe that was why she'd missed him so much this week, too.

"Did you have fun with your sister?" he asked as he stroked her cheek.

She smiled as he kissed her earlobe.

"I did. I finally told her about us, and she freaked out. And . . ." Damn it, she had to tell him this part when he wasn't distracted. "Max, wait, hold on a second."

He pulled back a few inches but kept hold of her waist.

"Why, is something wrong?"

She shook her head.

"Not wrong, exactly, but I should warn you— my sister's boss is going to be at that fundraiser tomorrow night. Which means . . ."

He dropped his head on her shoulder.

"Which means your sister is going to be at the fundraiser, too. And you're not."

She ran her fingers through his hair again. She liked it a little too long like this.

"Exactly. Sorry to spring this on you at the last minute. She's very nice!"

He stood up straight and laughed.

"Oh, I'm sure she's very nice, just like you are, and a shark, just like you are, too."

Well, Olivia couldn't disagree with that.

"It'll be fine! Though I wish I could be there to see this." She kissed him on the cheek. "How was the event today? And the dinner tonight?" she asked him.

He reached for her buttons again.

"Great, and very boring, in that order. But that last part doesn't matter, because I have you with me right now. I'll tell you all about both after."

She raised her eyebrows at him.

"After what?" she asked.

He unbuttoned her last button.

"After I pull your clothes off, throw you onto that big bed over there, and have my way with you for hours, woman who asks silly questions."

He unzipped her jeans and pushed them over her hips onto the floor as she giggled. Then he bent down and threw her over his shoulder, which only made her giggle harder.

"Oh my God, what are you doing? If you throw

out your back because of me and you're out of commission for weeks, I'm going to feel so guilty!"

He walked across the room with a few strides and tossed her onto the huge bed. She laid back on the pillows and smiled at him as he pulled his own clothes off and dropped them to the floor.

"It would be worth it," he said as he landed on the bed next to her. "It's too fun to surprise you to restrain myself just for fear of my aging back."

Olivia turned to look at him, and before he could move, she pushed him down, flipped over, and knelt over him.

"Now it's my turn." She smiled down at him, and at the surprised—and aroused—look on his face.

She kissed him hard, and he kissed her back just as hard. All of her longing and frustration and confusion and joy about him came out in that kiss. He was everything she wanted, he was everything she wasn't sure she could have, he was everything she was unsure about, he was everything that made her happy.

"You're so fucking incredible," he said as he reached around to unclasp her bra. "Sometimes I don't believe you're real."

He pulled her bra off and caressed her breasts in just the way she loved. He'd figured that out so fast.

"Likewise," she said as he slid down so he could suck her nipples into his mouth. When she felt the gentle scrape of his teeth against her nipple, she moaned, and then caught herself.

"Oh shit," she said in a whisper. "Do we have to be quiet? Do the people on either side of you know who you are?"

He pulled back, but kept her nipples between his fingers.

"I don't think they do, but . . . just to be safe, we should probably be quiet." He grinned. "I guess I should have thought of that before throwing you on the bed, huh?" He danced his tongue around one breast while he squeezed the other. She held her lips together so she wouldn't cry out.

"Thank goodness this bed has so many pillows for me to scream into," she said.

He pulled her underwear down with one hand, and she kicked them onto the floor.

"I'm going to make it my goal for you to need all of those pillows," he said. He slid a finger inside of her, hard, and she gasped. His thumb moved in first slow, then fast circles, with his other hand still squeezing her nipples. Dear God, it felt incredible.

Then, suddenly, it wasn't enough. She reached down to stroke the hard length of him, and it was his turn to gasp.

"I need you inside me now." Sure enough, he'd

left a pile of condoms on the bedside table. She grabbed one and opened it. "I knew you'd be prepared."

"I was waiting for you for a while, okay? I didn't want to waste time!"

She grinned and slid the condom on him and then lowered herself until he was poised just at her entrance. He rose up to meet her, pushed himself inside of her, and soon they were moving in sync, so fast and so hard she could barely breathe, she could barely think, she could only feel. And then everything felt so good that she could hardly move, but she had to keep moving and moving until there were fireworks behind her eyes and she smashed a pillow to her face to scream into it.

No wonder she'd missed him so much. Had anything ever felt this good? Had anything ever felt so right? She collapsed on top of him, and he wrapped his arms around her.

"You're the best thing that's ever happened to me," he whispered in her ear.

Why did that make her feel even better than the sex had?

The next day, after a lazy breakfast in bed and some enthusiastic postbreakfast exercise, Max reached over and tickled Olivia.

"What are we going to do for the rest of the day?" he asked.

She looked back at him with a slow, satisfied smile.

"I thought you were booked with senator stuff all day," she said.

He reached for his phone and pulled up his calendar.

"Not until midafternoon—I'm doing some local news interviews and then the fundraiser, but I'm free before that."

She pulled his arm around her and rested her head on his chest.

"I was going to head over to Berkeley this afternoon to get a mani/pedi with my sister, so it looks like our free time coincides. What do you want to do?"

He brushed her hair back and kissed her fore-head.

"Weeell, we could stay here all day."

"I knew you were going to say that." He could hear the smile in her voice. "Any other ideas?"

"Hmmmm. Ooh! Yes!" He squeezed her hand. "I've taken you to some of my favorite L.A. places—how about you do the same for some of your Bay Area spots? It's only ten a.m., so we have a few hours before I have to get back here to change and turn into a senator again."

She sat up and turned to look at him with that smile he loved so much, the one where he could see the tiny dimple in her cheek.

"What a great idea." Her smile got wider. "And

I know exactly where I'm going to take you."

Forty-five minutes later, they stood facing each other on a squeaky BART train. Olivia smiled up at him, a wicked expression on her face.

"When's the last time you were on public transportation, hmm?" she asked him in a low voice.

Embarrassingly, he had to think about that.

"It's got to have been at least . . . five years, maybe? Probably more. Oh God, that's terrible, but I always drive everywhere in L.A. anyway, so it must have been some time when I was up here or somewhere else for a conference."

Olivia laughed at him.

"Well, at least you look like you're blending in."

He looked down at himself and shook his head. He didn't have any of his fake glasses or his baseball hats with him on this trip, so he'd had to improvise so he wouldn't get recognized. Jeans, T-shirt, and one of the tech company branded vests he'd been given at the dinner last night. With that, plus his unshaven face, he hoped he could pass as a tech bro.

They got off at Fruitvale Station in Oakland and walked around for a while until they reached a taco truck with a long, noisy line.

"Here we are!" Olivia parked them at the end of the line. "Best tacos in the Bay Area. Maybe all of California."

"That's a bold statement, don't you think?" Max asked her.

She nodded.

"Oh, very bold, and obviously there are some incredible tacos in L.A., which which is why it's debatable, but you'll see when you have them how good they are."

He put his arm around her as they waited in line.

"I guess I will. But I thought you didn't like places you had to stand in line to eat?"

She brushed that off.

"Taco trucks are different, you know that."

He didn't argue with her. Right now, he couldn't think of a place he'd rather be than standing here with her, in the sunshine, with nowhere he had to be for hours.

He leaned down and kissed her cheek.

"This was a great idea," he said.

They'd been standing there for about ten minutes, inching closer and closer to the tacos, when Olivia felt Max stand up straight.

And then, very slowly, he leaned over to whisper in her ear.

"I just realized that I know the woman standing right behind us. She's a reporter with the *San Francisco Chronicle*, she's interviewed me a few times. I don't quite look like my senator self today, but . . ."

Olivia froze, and then nodded slowly.

"Okay. Um, do you want to go?"

Max looked at her like she'd asked him if the sky looked green.

"And deny myself the chance to have the best tacos in the Bay Area, maybe all of California? Are you kidding me?" He pressed his lips together and paused for a moment. "But do you want to go? We can if you want to."

She thought about that for a minute. The smart thing to do would be to leave right now, so the reporter didn't recognize Max and blow their secret. Especially because the two of them had been standing there hand in hand for the past ten minutes; it would be pretty obvious to anyone who saw them that they were together. They never did that when they were out in public together in L.A., but somehow in the Bay Area, away from their regular lives, it felt like they could do whatever they wanted. And she didn't want to stop. She shook her head.

"We came all this way. And the tacos smell so good." She put her hand on his stubbly cheek. She kind of liked him all scruffy like this. "Don't you have an embarrassing cousin who lives in the Bay Area anyway? Peter, right? He works in advertising or something?"

He kissed her on the cheek and smiled at her.

"Mmm, yes, yes I do, thanks for reminding me."

Max kept his back to the reporter for the next five minutes until they got to the front of the line, and Olivia kept trying to remember to call him Peter, which just made them both giggle. Max ordered two of everything on the menu, which she'd known he would do before they even discussed it, and they claimed a corner of a picnic table.

"Are we going to take the tacos to go, or eat here and tough it out?" Max asked her.

She grinned at him.

"We've come this far, haven't we?"

He reached for her hand and held on tight.

"I'm so glad we have," he said.

She looked into his warm, kind, mischievous eyes.

"Me, too," she said.

Max felt that usual burst of adrenaline as he strode into the hotel and toward the ballroom for the fundraiser. He loved this part of his job. He gave a damn good speech, and he knew it, and he knew he was going to do it tonight, too. He turned to grin at his two staff members who were there with him, and then sighed. Georgia and Zachary were both great at their jobs, but he wished he had Olivia next to him tonight instead.

That morning and afternoon together had been so fun and relaxed, he'd wished it didn't have to end. She'd looked so happy when they finished their pile of tacos that he hadn't wanted to leave her. He was really glad, though, that she'd be there in the hotel waiting for him tonight, after this fundraiser was over. Even though he enjoyed events like this, they took a lot out of him. That wasn't something he'd expected when he first started a life in politics. He'd always been an extrovert, he'd always been good at parties, but political events were on a whole different plane than anything else he'd experienced. He had to be on all the time; he had to give every single person who wanted to talk to him his full attention; he had to show them all the Max Powell they'd come for. And it wasn't that he resented any of that—he wanted to do that, he liked meeting people, he wanted to hear their stories and give of himself to them. But he hadn't realized how exhausting it would be, every time. He was glad he wasn't going to have to go back to a lonely hotel room tonight.

He walked into the greenroom and snapped his mind away from Olivia and onto this fundraiser tonight. After the parade of likely boring speeches, it would be a zoo of picture taking with donors, and glad-handing and chatting with all of the other politicians in the room. These things were part of the job in any election year, even one where he wasn't up for reelection. Thank goodness Wes would be at this one—not that they'd even get to really talk to each other, but at least he'd have someone to make eye contact with when one of the speeches got boring, or annoying, or laughable, which happened every single time.

After the usual rigmarole with the organizers, they ushered him onstage, where the governor introduced him to lots of cheering. Max went on and gave an abbreviated version of the same speech he'd been giving at these things all year—he always tried to keep his speeches short, punchy, and just a little funny. He ended on a laugh line, waved at the crowd, and went backstage with a smile on his face, while their laughter echoed behind him. He walked past a group of press, and . . . yep, that reporter from the taco truck was there. He grinned as he made his way into the reception area.

"Max Powell, as I live and breathe." A woman with a very large hairdo and a lot of makeup pulled him into a hug, and he laughed and hugged her back.

"Congresswoman Strong! I didn't know you were going to be here!" This was a benefit of events like this; he got to see some friends he didn't get to see much of anymore.

"Well, you know, I'm retired now, so I get to pick and choose which of these things I go to, but I couldn't miss tonight."

Twenty minutes later, as Max chatted with the mayor of San Francisco, an older white man and a cheerful-looking Black woman joined their group.

"Senator, have you met the mayor of Berkeley?" The mayor of San Francisco gestured toward the older white man. "Mayor Emmitt, Senator Powell."

He and the mayor shook hands, and then the Black woman behind the mayor held out her hand to him.

"Senator, a pleasure to meet you. I'm Alexa Monroe, the mayor's chief of staff."

"Nice to meet you, Alexa," he said automatically. He turned back to the mayor, and then his head snapped back to Alexa.

Alexa . . . Monroe?

If he had any doubts, the knowing smile in her eyes removed them. He'd been so focused over the last hour, he'd completely forgotten Olivia's sister would be here.

"Great speech tonight," she said.

He grinned at her.

"Thanks, I appreciate it." They smiled at each other for a second, though she had a slight measuring-him-up look on her face. He suddenly felt nervous. Did he pass muster?

He made himself turn back to her boss.

"I've heard you're doing excellent things in the Berkeley school system with restorative justice," he said. "It's a good example for others who think it may not work."

The mayor smiled as Zachary snapped a picture of the four of them.

"I hope that's the case," the mayor said. "Though there's often such a bias against programs like that. I have high hopes for your criminal justice reform bill, you know."

Olivia's sister smiled and nodded behind him. Why did he feel so much pressure on how he answered her boss?

"I have high hopes for it, too," he said. "I'm not sure if the rest of Congress is where we are yet, but it's our job to convince them, isn't it? But I'm not sure if anyone in my office has talked to you about my town hall plan for the summer—I want to hear from youths themselves about what they need to recover and thrive. I want this to be about them, not the politicians, but I'll make sure we consult you about plans." He glanced at Alexa. "My office will be in touch soon."

She handed him her card.

"Just in case you don't know how to find me," she said to Max with a straight face.

Georgia tapped him on the shoulder.

"I'm sorry, I have to pull the senator away for a moment; he's needed in the photo line."

There was another round of handshakes as he said good-bye.

"I hope I get to talk to all of you again, and soon." He let his eyes twinkle at Alexa as they shook hands, and her smile widened.

He walked away with Georgia toward the photo area.

Had Alexa liked him? He hoped she liked him. He knew Olivia and her sister were close, and it would matter to Olivia if Alexa thought he was some pompous douchebag.

He walked by Wes on the way to the photos, but Wes was in the middle of a conversation, so all they had time for in passing was a quick fist bump. Even that, though, felt like a respite. To see someone who actually knew him, whom he could be real with, in the midst of this need to constantly be on, was like for one brief second someone had opened a window in a hot, stuffy room. The relief he felt even walking by Wes made him realize how great it would be to have Olivia here with him tonight. If she were here by his side, he could nudge her when he wanted to—but couldn't—roll his eyes, he could exchange "we'll talk about this later" looks with her when someone said something wild, or he could laugh with her when something ridiculous happened. It was incredible to even think about that.

He didn't see Alexa again for the rest of the night, until he ran into her and the mayor just as he was leaving.

"Mayor Emmitt, and . . . Alexa, right? I hope you had a good night."

They all shook hands again.

"It was a great night," Alexa said. "The speeches weren't too long, some of them gave me a lot of hope for the future, and I got to meet some really interesting people, so I'd call that a winner."

He smiled at her as he turned to walk out the door.

"I got to meet some people I've wanted to meet for a while, so it was a great night for me, too. Have a safe drive back to Berkeley."

Max walked back into the hotel room twenty minutes later to find Olivia sitting on the bed, fully dressed, with her laptop on her lap.

"So." He kicked off his shoes and flopped down onto the bed next to her. "What did your sister think of me?"

Olivia's eyes widened. They widened just a little too much, as a matter of fact.

"Oh, you got to meet her? I wasn't sure if that would happen, I thought the fundraiser might be too big for . . ."

He waved his finger at her.

"I'm not buying a single second of this, you know. I am one hundred percent certain your sister texted you before she even left the ballroom. I had to meet a member of your family, and I had to do it without you by my side, so I deserve to know what she said." He leaned over and kissed her on the lips. "Come on, I'm dying here."

She shook her head and laughed.

"Damn it, you're giving me those puppy dog eyes again. Fine, she liked you."

He waited, but she didn't say anything else.

" 'She liked you'? That's all I get? No, absolutely not, I know there was more to it." Olivia glanced toward her phone, and he reached for it.

"Come on, there was a lot more. Just for that 'she liked you,' you have to show me the texts!"

Olivia laughed and unlocked her phone.

"There was just one text, right after she met you, and fine, you can see it."

Just met you know who! You probably figured out that I was a little skeptical of him, but I was impressed; good speech, not an asshole behind the scenes like most people like him would be, was polite to me even before he realized I was your sister (and then gave me a big smile once he did realize). As hot as he is on TV, too.

Oh, but I know what you meant about his shoes.

Saw him again on the way out! Can't wait to meet him again, this time with you there too!

"What about my shoes?"

Olivia snatched the phone back from him.

"Shit, there was only one text the last time I looked! I was working and I didn't see the other two come in!"

He frowned at her.

"I believe you, but what does she mean, she knows what you meant about my shoes? What's wrong with my shoes?"

Olivia sighed and pointed at his shoes.

"Those brown suede shoes of yours. They're terrible, Max. I'm sorry you had to find out this way, but I keep wanting to sneak into your closet and throw them away. How is it that you have such great suits and such terrible shoes?"

He turned to look at the shoes in question and then back to Olivia.

"My, um . . . mom helped me buy my suits. She didn't *pay* for them," he said over Olivia's giggles, "but once I became DA she told me I had to start dressing the part, so she found me a guy at a store she knows and I went in and he measured me and had me try on a bunch of stuff and then I gave him my credit card number and then he sent four suits, ten ties, and twenty shirts to my house, with firm instructions on what went with what. Once a year I go back for him to measure me again and he sends over more clothes. But whenever I go there, I go in sneakers and use his shoes to try on the clothes; no one ever told me what to do about shoes, so I just kept wearing what I'd been wearing."

Olivia stared at him, an expression he couldn't decipher on her face.

"What is it?" he asked. "I can get new shoes, just tell me what to buy."

She took his hand.

"I love you." She looked down at their hands, then back up at him. "And it still feels early, but I can't ignore it anymore. I love you."

He hadn't felt this explosion of joy since the night he'd won his Senate race, a year and a half before. He wanted to jump off the bed and throw his arms in the air; he wanted to run around the hotel shouting. But instead, he took her face in his hands.

"I love you, too."

She leaned forward and kissed him softly.

"And you don't have to buy new shoes, I'll love you anyway. But . . . please do."

He tackled her onto the bed, and she laughed and laughed.

Chapter Thirteen

When Olivia got home from work the next Friday, Max was already there. She'd had a late afternoon meeting on the Westside, and by the time she'd battled traffic to get back home, Max had landed at LAX, so she'd told him to just let himself into her place. She'd given him her extra key a few weeks back so he could easily meet her at her house after an event. But he hadn't given her back her key, and she hadn't asked for it.

She couldn't believe she'd told him she loved him. And she'd meant it then and meant it more with every day that went by. Yes, it hadn't even been five months since they'd met, but by this time in her life, she was a pretty good judge of character. And she knew she loved Max, even though she never would have expected it. It made her so happy to let herself into her house and know he was there.

When she walked in, she heard banging coming from the direction of the kitchen.

"Max?" It must be him; that was his car she'd driven by on the way here. He tended to park a block or two away, and in a slightly different place every time so no one would notice his car in front of her house.

"I'm in the kitchen!"

Was he . . . cooking? Max had many strengths, but she'd never seen him do anything in the kitchen other than move takeout from boxes to plates.

She walked down the hallway and saw him leaning over the counter, a lump of dough in front of him and a rolling pin in his hands.

"What in God's name are you doing?"

He looked up at her and made a face.

"Well, I was trying to make you a pie. Strawberry rhubarb, your favorite. But . . . I've run into some difficulties."

She moved closer to the counter.

"I can see that."

He stuck out his tongue at her.

"I didn't do a . . . great job of reading the recipe before I started—I thought I'd be able to surprise you with a pie when you got home, but I didn't realize the dough had to rest in the fridge for an hour after I made it. And now I'm trying to roll it out, and it's rock hard!" He banged the rolling pin in the middle of the dough again and tried to move it from side to side. It didn't budge.

Olivia held in her laughter.

"Where'd you get the rolling pin?" she asked. "I don't have one."

He gestured to the bag on the other end of the counter.

"Yes, I realize that now. I bought it, along with a pie pan." He smiled sheepishly at her. "Also, um. I'm sorry about the mess. I promise I'll clean all of . . . that up once I'm done with this part. And I swear, I absolutely did not kill anyone in your house this afternoon!"

Olivia walked around him and saw the bowl of cut-up strawberries and rhubarb next to the sink . . . and the bright red spatter everywhere around it.

Now she laughed so hard tears streamed from her eyes. After a few seconds, Max joined her.

"It does indeed look like you committed a murder in this kitchen," she said as she gasped for air.

Max smashed the dough again with the rolling pin. Olivia thought she saw tentative movement.

"I knew conceptually that strawberries had lots of red juice, but I didn't quite understand what that meant in practice until today." He rolled again. "Oh, look, it's moving! Thank God."

Olivia opened the fridge and poured herself a glass of wine. This felt like the kind of thing where she should stand back and watch instead of offering to help out.

Plus, no one had ever made her a pie before. She didn't even care how it turned out; she wanted to enjoy this.

"There!" Max said, forty minutes and two glasses of wine later, when he slid the pie into her oven. "It should bake for . . . an hour? It takes that long for pies to bake? Damn, okay, good thing I'm not going anywhere for a while."

She grinned at him.

"And good thing I ordered dinner while you were occupied with the pie. Food should be here any minute."

He went over to the sink to wash his hands. That apron looked far too sexy on him, even though it looked like he'd stabbed someone in it.

"Oh thank God you're the smart one in this relationship," he said. He grabbed a sponge to clean up the counters. "I'm starving. Pie making is hard work, you know."

Olivia sipped her wine and smiled at him. She couldn't believe he'd done this, just to make her happy.

"It looked like it," she said.

After the food came, they went into the living room to eat, and he looked around and smiled.

"You got new bookshelves! No more stacks of books on the floor."

She put the food down on the coffee table.

"Yeah, I'd had them for a while, and I finally put them together last night. I knew I couldn't prep for the pitch today any more than I had, and I needed to do something to get out all of that nervous energy."

Max put the napkins and plates down on the table.

"How did the pitch go?"

Olivia put spring rolls onto both of their plates and sighed.

"I don't know. I mean, it felt like it went well; I know we did a fantastic job. But that doesn't seem to really matter—the one client that we got so far from a pitch was the one I thought hated us, and all of the other pitches have felt great and we haven't gotten them. They say they like us, but they want people with more experience, or a bigger firm, and even though our rates are on the low end, that doesn't matter."

"Is that code for 'they want to hire white men instead'?" Max asked.

She glanced up at him, surprised and pleased she didn't have to spell that out.

"Sometimes, definitely. Probably most of the time, even. Which I should be used to by now in my career, but still feels crappy."

"That's because it's fucked up," Max said. He put his hand on her knee. "How much . . . Are you . . . I mean, do you need . . ." He stopped, and she laughed.

"If you're trying to ask if I'm okay financially, I am, really. Ellie thinks I'm irrational for stressing this much—she says we both knew it would be slow going in the beginning, but we started with a few anchor clients and we have money coming in and we both saved up a lot before we started this." But she'd feel like such a failure if she had to dig even deeper into her savings. "And she's right, but I guess I didn't quite realize how uncertain it would all feel. Like all of it could disappear in an instant. I thought I'd feel more comfortable once we got our first new client, but it was for such a small case it didn't make me feel much better. If only we could get a case from a bigger company—all we need is to get our foot in the door. I know we'd do a great job; we're both excellent lawyers. We'll see what happens with the pitch from today, but . . ." She shrugged. "I'm not feeling that optimistic."

Max dished noodles on her plate and handed it to her.

"Here. Your favorite spicy noodles will help— the spice high will make you feel like a super-hero."

One of the things she liked so much about Max was that he didn't try to give her a pep talk unless she asked for one, and he didn't try to reassure her that everything would be fine. He just handed her spicy noodles. Which was exactly what she needed.

"Thanks," she said. Which felt inadequate, for the noodles and the pie and the sympathy, but she knew he understood.

He picked up a spring roll and turned to her.

"So. I wanted to talk to you about something."

That never meant good news.

"Okay. What is it?" She braced herself.

"I know we talked about this some a while ago—not specifics, but just in general—but that was when things were different and I feel like things have changed, so I wanted to ask about it again—"

Okay, now she needed him to cut to the chase. He was usually way more articulate than this. Was he breaking up with her?

"Max. What are you getting at?"

He rubbed his face and put his plate down onto the coffee table.

"I guess I'd better just say it: have you given any more thought—or any at all, actually—to us going public about this?"

Oh. Not a breakup.

The opposite of a breakup, really.

"Oh. I didn't expect . . . that's not what I thought you were . . ." She laughed out loud. "Max Powell, please do me a favor and never say 'I have to talk to you about something' again to me like that. Because I thought you were about to break up with me."

Max sat back, his mouth wide open, then leaned forward and grabbed her hands.

"First, I'll never say that again. Second, breaking up with you is the last thing I want to do."

She kissed him on the cheek.

"Same here. But . . . you want to go public?"

He squeezed her hands.

"I understand if you're not ready for that yet, just say the word, and it's fine. But the thing is, I was thinking all week about last weekend. How we ran into that reporter, and part of me—a lot of me—wondered if it really would be the end of the world if she recognized me with you. And then I killed it in my speech—not to be arrogant, but. . ." He grinned at her, and she grinned back. "And when I finished, and I knew it had been great, I looked around the room, and I realized I was looking for you out there. Even though I knew you weren't there, I wanted to be able to introduce you to people I've known for years, and meet your sister with you by my side instead of with knowing glances on both of our parts. And . . . it was more than that. Those things are a lot sometimes, and I wished so much that you were there. That I'd have you with me for a boost, or a smirk, or some sympathy."

She hadn't realized until right now how much she'd hated staying back in his hotel room while he was at the fundraiser. How much she'd wanted to be there with him, see him make his speech, introduce him to Alexa herself.

"And the thing is . . ." Max looked straight into her eyes. "That thing Wes said, when I first told him about you, and he was skeptical, and he said to make sure it was something real before anyone found out about us, for your sake as well as mine—this feels real to me. Does it feel real to you?"

She looked down at their joined hands.

"Yes," she said in a low voice. Sometimes it felt like she'd made this whole thing up, especially when she randomly turned on the TV or the radio and there was Max. But whenever she was with him, the connection between the two of them felt so real, so solid, it overwhelmed her.

"Good," he said. "Do you . . . What do you think?"

Beeeep.

They broke apart, startled. Then Max laughed and pulled his phone out of his pocket.

"It's the pie! I set my alarm for it. I'll be right back."

Olivia stayed where she was as Max raced into the kitchen. She was grateful for the extra time to figure out how to answer his question. A few minutes later, he came out with a big grin on his face.

"Well, the good news is that it *looks* like a pie, anyway. The bad news is we're supposed to let it cool for a while, which I didn't quite realize."

He sat back down on the couch and looked expectantly at her. She took a deep breath.

"This does feel real to me," she said. "And in a perfect world, we wouldn't have worried about that reporter, and I'd be there with you at that fundraiser, and to meet my family, and all of that. But . . . how big a deal do you think this is going to be? I don't really have any concept of how this will all work, or how many people will care."

He gripped her hand.

"I really don't think people will care all that much—maybe enough for a few news stories, if it's slow, but I think that'll be all."

She trusted him, but . . .

"Some people might really care that you're dating a Black woman," she said.

He pulled her close.

"Some, definitely, but then, I couldn't give a fuck what those people think anyway. But I completely understand if that makes you hesitant, especially in the current climate."

She thought about that for a moment.

"It does make me hesitant, but I don't want to give assholes like that power over my life." She pulled back so she could see him. "You're sure about doing this? Really sure? It feels like . . . a big step."

He looked her straight in the eye.

"As sure as I was when I heard your laugh at the bar, and knew I couldn't leave without talking to you. As sure as I was when I saw you across that luncheon and knew I couldn't let you leave my life again. I've been sure about you since the moment I met you."

She could feel tears come to her eyes, and fought them back.

"Damn it, Max! Whenever I try to get serious and cautious, you say things that go right to my heart and it always makes me want to throw caution to the wind. Please never ask me to jump out of an airplane; you'll hypnotize me with that damn cupid's arrow of yours, and before I know it I'll be falling to my death."

He kissed her softly on the lips.

"I promise I'll never ask you to jump out of an airplane."

She smiled at him.

"But . . . can you give me some time to think about this?"

He nodded.

"No rush. I'm just greedy—I want more time with you, and this feels like the best way to get it." He kissed her on the lips again. "Now, I know it's not cool enough to cut into it yet, but . . ." He beamed at her. "Want to come see my pie?"

She jumped to her feet.

"Absolutely."

Max checked his phone when he walked back into his office after a very frustrating judiciary subcommittee meeting Thursday morning. His heart jumped when he saw a text from Olivia, and then fell again when it was just a picture of the empty pie dish, with something about how she wished she had more pie. Yes, he was thrilled she'd liked his pie—even though they both agreed his crust needed a lot of work. But did she want to go public or not? It was already Thursday—he'd brought that up to her a whole six days ago! Sure, he'd told her that there was no rush, and technically that was true, but "no rush" clearly meant something very different to Olivia than it did to him.

The thing was, he'd completely understand if she said no, she wasn't ready, she didn't want the attention yet. But he hated being in limbo; he just wanted a yes or no. And it didn't look like she was going to give him one anytime soon.

Would she not bring it up again for a month and then finally say no? If they were going to have a future, they'd have to do it eventually; couldn't eventually just be now?

He wished he'd said that to her last Friday night, but it felt too late to open that conversation back up again.

He didn't even respond to her text about the pie; he was too frustrated. Instead he threw himself into meetings with his staff to plan the town halls, meetings with other senators and their staffs to talk through strategy for the environmental bill they still had hope of passing before the end of the session, and then his prep for another hearing the next day. All that helped occupy him enough so that by the time he went back to his office at seven, he'd almost forgotten why he'd been in a bad mood that day.

He pulled out the briefing book Lisa had made for his committee hearing the next day. The witnesses were all going to be heavy on the science, and he needed to be prepared with questions that didn't make him look brainless.

He only got halfway in before he glanced at his phone again. And was rewarded.

> In the car for the next hour or so, depending on LA traffic—give me a call if you're not too busy.

Now he felt bad for not answering her text from earlier that day. He knew Olivia took time to make decisions; he didn't need to be petulant and not respond to her.

He picked up the phone.

"Hey, I just saw your text," he said when she answered the phone. "Perfect timing, I needed a break. How's your day? Where are you off to?"

"Hey," she said. "I'm actually almost there, so I can't talk for long, but . . . I've been thinking. About what you said last weekend about going public."

He was suddenly completely alert.

"Yeah? Are you . . . What have you been thinking about it?"

Why did it suddenly feel like his whole world depended on her answer?

"I've been really on the fence," she said. "I just didn't know how it would all work, or if it would make everything too difficult, and . . . I don't know, I've just been scared about it."

"Okay," he said. He felt like she was leading somewhere, and he had no idea if it was somewhere good or bad.

"But then, last night, I went to grab food with Jamila, and she asked me how things were going with that guy I'd told her about, and I hated that I had to talk around everything when I answered her. I wanted to tell her all about you, and I couldn't, and it made me feel like I was lying to her."

Max felt hope start to rise inside of him.

"Uh-huh?"

Olivia went on.

"And then she said I should bring him to the food pantry some night. And I realized I really wanted to; I'd love to bring you there and introduce you to some of the other volunteers to see the great work they do, and the incredible community they've built, and everything we're working on for the future. But there's no way we could do that the way everything is right now—we might be able to go on a hike together without people figuring out who you are, but not something like that."

Max let himself smile.

"Uh-huh," he said again.

"So," she said. "Okay. We should do this."

Max stood up and danced around his office. Thank God Olivia couldn't see him; she might break up with him then and there.

"Fantastic," he said. "Here's a thought: I have season tickets to the Hollywood Bowl, and Dolly Parton is playing on Saturday night. That seems like a perfect time to do something low-key, but still public. What do you think?"

Olivia was quiet for a second.

"This Saturday? That soon? I figured it would take some time to . . . I don't know, for me to talk to your staff, or do a background check and get everything ready."

Max laughed.

"You don't need a background check, and you don't need to talk to my staff, I can handle that. I don't think either of us wants this to be a big, complicated rollout, do you?"

He respected his staff a lot, but the less they had to do with this, the better, as far as he was concerned.

"Definitely not," she said. There was silence on the line for a few moments. "Okay. Saturday night, Dolly Parton. That sounds good."

He couldn't wait.

"Fantastic. And see you tomorrow night. Want to meet me at my place? I shouldn't be home too late. I love you."

"I love you, too," she said. "See you tomorrow."

He hung up the phone and immediately picked up his office line to buzz Kara.

"Can you come into my office for a minute?"

She was there within seconds.

"What's up, sir?" she asked.

He couldn't help the smile that spread across his face.

"I've been wanting to tell you this for a while, but I had to wait until it was okay with her. I've been dating someone. She's a lawyer in L.A.; you'd love her. We've been trying to keep it quiet, but we're ready to be less quiet about it."

Kara grinned back at him.

"I've been waiting for you to tell me this, sir. Congratulations. You seem very happy."

He sat back and stared at her.

"You knew? How did you know?"

She laughed.

"I already suspected, but if you thought you didn't make everything clear when you told me about your 'friend' who had the great idea for the town halls . . . well, we need to work on your poker face. It also helped explain why you've been in such a great mood lately. So after we had that conversation, I came up with a plan. I drafted a press release, you can look at it shortly, but first, we can—"

He held his hand up to stop her.

"I appreciate that so much, but I think we both want this to be pretty low-key. No plans, no briefing, no press releases—we're just going to go to the Hollywood Bowl together this weekend without me in any baseball cap or glasses or anything like that. We'll just take it from there."

Kara sat down across from him.

"That's lovely, sir, it really is, but this weekend? Can you at least hold off another week? Maybe I could just have a call with her, to talk about . . ."

He shook his head.

"Thank you, Kara, I really am grateful you think about all of these things for me, but I don't want to make a whole thing about this. I don't think people will care all that much about my personal life. Plus, she's nervous about this, understandably, so I don't want to make this more stressful for her."

He wanted to ease into this—do something fun with Olivia this weekend, and then maybe by the end of the summer she'd be able to come with him to all sorts of events and it wouldn't be a big deal.

"I understand that, sir, but I'm pretty sure people will definitely care about this. You were on those most-eligible-bachelor lists in both DC and L.A., remember?"

He brushed that off.

"Those were both last August in very slow news weeks, but the news has been more of an onslaught these days; I don't think we have to worry about all of that."

Kara folded her hands together.

"Can I convince you to let me make sure there's a friendly photographer around? There will be a ton of people there—someone is likely to take a picture of you, and it'll get out, I promise. Think about this from her point of view—you may not care if the pictures are unflattering, but she likely will."

This was yet another reason why he was glad he had Kara.

"Good idea, please do that."

Kara stopped, right before she opened his office door.

"And, may I ask—what's her name?"

He smiled.

"Olivia Monroe."

Kara smiled back at him.

"Congratulations again, sir. And good luck this weekend."

Chapter Fourteen

Olivia took longer to get ready for her date with Max that Saturday night than she had for any other date in her life. She'd been a little taken aback when Max told her his chief of staff had arranged for a friendly photographer to take photos of them on their way into the Hollywood Bowl. That seemed so . . . intentional. But she agreed that she'd rather have good photos out there of her than bad ones, so "friendly" photographer it was. Friendly photographer or not, though, she had to look perfect. She'd searched Instagram for pictures of people at the Hollywood Bowl to see what they wore to concerts there; she'd washed, moisturized, and twisted her hair the night before so it would be perfect and bouncy today; and she'd spent an entire hour doing her makeup, when she usually spent no more than five minutes.

She was a little surprised she hadn't had to talk to Max's staff before this, but she was relieved, too. That probably would have stressed her out even more. She still didn't quite know why she was doing this, but that was the story of her entire relationship with Max. Why had she talked to him at the bar? Why had she gone out with him in the first place? Why had she started dating him? Why had she told him she loved him, no matter how true it was? There was just something about Max—the way he smiled at her, the way he looked at her, the way he loved her— that made her feel as if he saw her, all of her, and loved every single thing about her. And against all odds, she felt the same about him.

Finally, she was ready, thirty minutes before Max was due to pick her up. She took a picture of herself and her outfit in her full-length mirror (long, flowy blue sundress, jean jacket, gold wedge sandals) and a close-up selfie to get her jewelry and makeup (dangly gold earrings, tortoiseshell sunglasses, pink lip gloss, and just a hint of highlighter) and texted both pictures to Alexa and Ellie.

> Okay, we're really doing this. How do I look? I'm going for woke up like this

Ellie immediately responded.

> You look fantastic!

That was all well and good, but this was a time she actually wanted some constructive criticism on her outfit. She would have trusted Ellie better if she'd told her to change her lipstick or to wear the yellow dress or the gold hoops instead. It was like how she always trusted a proofreader better as soon as they found a typo.

> I'm with Maddie and she says you look excellent but that you need a bracelet— don't you have a gold one? Oh, and roll up the sleeves

Thank God for little sisters and their best friends for giving her the notes she'd been looking for. She grabbed her gold bangles out of her top drawer and slid them on her left wrist, and rolled up the sleeves of the jean jacket. She snapped a new picture and sent it to Alexa.

> How's this?

The text came back in seconds.

> PERFECT

"You ready to go?" Max appeared in the doorway of her bedroom. "Oh wow, you look amazing."

She tucked her phone into her pocket and picked up her bag. Shit, she hadn't consulted with her fashion advisers about the bag, but she thought it worked—a big caramel leather tote she'd bought a few weeks ago. Well, if it didn't work, it was too late now.

"Thanks." She smiled at him. He looked great, too, in jeans, sneakers, and a blue-striped button-down. But tonight, he had no fake glasses, no wig, and no baseball cap. And instead of the tousled hair he usually had when he was off duty, his Ken doll hair was in all of its shellacked glory. That told her more than anything that tonight was going to be different.

"Are you sure you're ready for this?" he asked.

She definitely was not.

"Thank you for giving me room to back out, but let's do this."

He smiled and kissed her lightly on the lips.

"Okay. Let's go."

He touched her knee on the car drive over.

"Nervous?" he asked.

She shook her head.

"It's just a concert, right? I'm fine."

That wasn't exactly true, but maybe if she said it enough, she'd feel fine.

"You talked to your staff about me, right? Did you tell them—"

Max slid his hand in hers.

"Don't worry. They're very happy for us, and my chief of staff completely embarrassed me by saying she already knew I was dating someone because I seemed so happy."

She shot her head in his direction.

"Really?"

He laughed.

"Really. Also, Kara says there might be a flurry of stories about us for a day or so and then people will get bored and move onto something else in the news cycle." He squeezed her hand. "I'm really glad we're doing this."

She nodded again, and tried to ignore that *What have you gotten yourself into?* rattling around in her head.

They pulled into the parking lot. Max turned off the car, and they looked at each other.

Olivia smiled at him.

"I'm glad we're doing this, too," she said. Despite all her fears, she was.

Max took her hand as they got out of the car. Olivia tried to look straight ahead as they walked into the Hollywood Bowl, when all she wanted to do was to look around for the photographer in the crowd. But no, she was trying to look as natural as possible, so she just kept a smile on her face and her hand in Max's and kept walking. The whole crowd was amped up tonight—it was mostly lots of women of all ages who seemed just as excited to see Dolly Parton as Olivia would have been if she weren't vibrating with anxiety about everything else going on tonight.

They walked through the first level, up the stairs, and to the box seats, where Max waved her in front of him into their seats. As soon as she sat down, she let herself relax. No one would probably take a picture of them up there, right?

"So is this what it's going to be like, then, going out in public with you?" Max asked under his breath. "Complete silence except for periodic sighs of relief?"

She realized she hadn't said a word to him since they got out of the car, which was at least ten minutes ago.

"Give it some time, okay? I'm just trying to figure out how to do this."

He touched her elbow with his.

"I know, I know, I'm sorry. I was just teasing you." He stood up. "I think we both need a drink. Wine?"

She looked around for the first time—really looked, instead of surveying the crowd.

"Oh wow, we're in the fancy seats, aren't we?" She let herself grin. She found it sort of hilarious that her first time at the Hollywood Bowl was with a damn millionaire senator. "God yes, a glass of wine is exactly what I need. Rosé if they have it, whatever white they have if not. Normally I'd be a lot more picky than that, but tonight isn't a night to be picky about the wine selection."

While Max was gone, Olivia forced herself to relax. She just had to pretend that this was simply a fun outdoor concert on a beautiful night with her boyfriend, which, technically, it was. None of the rest of that stuff mattered.

"Glass of rosé for the lady, beer for me, and I couldn't resist a cone of french fries. One for each of us."

See, this is why she'd fallen in love with him. He not only got her french fries without her asking for them but had gotten one for each of them.

Damn it. Even french fries made her all gooey.

She took the fries in one hand and the rosé in the other as he sat down.

"Thanks. I needed this." She smelled the hot, salty, greasy goodness of the fries and smiled.

He sat down next to her and took a sip of his beer. She took a sip of her wine. They each slowly ate their fries. She looked around the amphitheater, careful not to look right at Max.

He leaned in close to her.

"I'm so happy to be here with you right now, I hope you know that." He looked straight at her. "I really hope you know that."

Warmth spread through her body. She couldn't quite trust herself to talk, so she just nodded.

"Good," he said.

The lights onstage went up, and it seemed like every single one of the thousands of people there cheered wildly. Including both her and Max. And thank God for that—she was delighted Max was the kind of guy who would yell at a Dolly Parton concert before Dolly even came out onstage.

As soon as the opening act started, Olivia felt her whole body relax. She didn't know if it was the music itself, or the way the whole crowd swayed back and forth as they listened, or the energy in the crowd, or Max's hand in hers, but she felt calm and happy, and like she could—and would—conquer the world. And when Dolly finally came out onstage, there was an explosion of noise like Olivia wasn't sure she'd ever experienced. Pure, loud, joyful screams and yells and cheers rang out and kept on ringing until Dolly started singing, and then they all shut up so they could hear her.

In the middle of "9 to 5," Max took her hand. She turned to him and smiled so hard her face hurt.

"I love you," he said in a low voice, but she could hear him as clear as if he'd shouted it from the stage.

"I love you, too," she said.

Max was relieved as they walked back to the car. Olivia walked with the bounce back in her step, and didn't seem as skittish or closed off as she had on their way in. Maybe they'd be able to have fun like this all summer—especially in August when Congress was in recess and he'd be back in California for five fantastic weeks.

"Olivia! Hey, Olivia!"

Max shook himself out of his daydreams when Olivia stopped. They both turned toward the direction of the shouts.

"Jamila! Hi!" Olivia greeted the woman walking toward them, but her whole body was tense again.

"Hey, I thought that was you!" the other woman said. "You look great, I love this dress."

"Were you just at the concert?" Olivia asked. She shook her head in answer to her own question. "Of course you were just at the concert—did you have fun? Wasn't it great?"

He'd never seen Olivia babble like this before. Was this how she got when she was nervous? She'd said she was fine, but he knew she wasn't—at first she'd been stiff and silent, and now she couldn't stop talking.

"Yeah, it was so fun, right? We got tickets last minute, otherwise I would have texted you to see if you wanted to come with us." Jamila looked back and forth from Olivia to him and back again, and smirked slightly at Olivia. "Glad you made it anyway."

Olivia glanced at him, and he could tell she was gearing herself up to introduce him. After a few too many seconds of silence, she turned back to Jamila.

"Oh, I'm sorry—Jamila, this is Max, Max, Jamila."

First names only; that was a nice compromise.

He reached out to shake Jamila's hand.

"Nice to meet you, Jamila," he said.

She shook his hand.

"Nice to meet you, too . . ." She looked up at him, and recognition dawned over her face. He winked at her as her mouth gaped open.

"Um. Max. Nice to meet you, Max," she said.

Jamila turned back to Olivia, her eyes still wide. He couldn't see the look on Olivia's face, but after a few seconds, Jamila smiled at her.

"We should probably get out of here; it'll take forever to get home," Jamila said. "And I have to find my friend, she was supposed to meet me out here, but . . ." She looked down at the phone gripped in her hand. "Oh, she says she's already at the car, what the hell? Okay, I should run. See you on Wednesday, Olivia?"

Olivia nodded.

"I'll be there," Olivia said. "Maybe we can get dinner after?"

Jamila glanced back and forth from her to Max. Max tried to pretend he didn't know exactly what was going on.

"Mmmm, definitely," Jamila said.

Jamila dashed off into the crowd, and Olivia and Max walked off toward the car.

They didn't say anything to each other until they were in the car and a block away from the stadium.

"So," Max started.

Olivia burst out laughing, and then he did, and they laughed so hard he almost pulled over.

"No offense," she said through gasps, "but that was one of the weirdest dates I've ever been on. The middle part was good, the part with Dolly Parton and holding hands and all of that. But the beginning and the end were very stressful! I thought dating a famous person was supposed to be glamorous!"

He poked her in the arm.

"Oh, you think you were stressed? You didn't have to stand there and take it while your friend Jamila looked me over like I was a piece of meat and she was measuring me up to see if I was good enough for you. *Or* try not to react when she was looking straight at me and made that face when she suddenly realized who I was!"

Thank God there was so much traffic that he didn't really have to pay attention to the road, because when he thought about Jamila's face at that moment, it set him off again.

Olivia reached for her phone, connected it to his car Bluetooth, and cranked up a Dolly Parton playlist.

"Thank God for Dolly," she said. "See, she was the best part of the night."

They spent the rest of the drive back to her house singing along with Dolly, and they could tell a bunch of the cars around them were doing the same thing.

They didn't talk about any of the other events of the night until they got back to her house. He parked around the corner, and as they walked down the sidewalk, he reached for her hand. She hesitated, and looked around her quiet street before sliding her fingers through his.

"Sorry," she said as they walked up to her door. "I guess I'm just not used to this yet. And still a little—or maybe a lot—paranoid."

He shrugged.

"You have reason to be paranoid, don't apologize. You notice that I'm still not parking in your driveway."

She unlocked her front door and he followed her inside.

"I noticed." She kicked her shoes off and walked into the kitchen. Max grinned and followed her. "I was terrified when Jamila saw us together. I felt like a teenager again, like I'd been caught. Then I remembered I wasn't doing anything wrong, and also that Jamila is my friend, not my mom."

Olivia turned to look at him and finally saw the box in his hands.

"What's that?"

He looked down and pretended to be surprised.

"This? Oh God, I don't know. What *is* this? I just saw it on the counter, what could it be?"

He flipped open the top and turned the box toward her.

"CAKE!" She stared at the cake then back up at him. "Is that for me?"

He grinned at her and opened the sides of the box so he could slide the cake out onto the counter.

"Who do you think it's for? I got it this afternoon. I had a feeling tonight might be stressful—Dolly notwithstanding. I thought we both might need a pick-me-up afterward." He picked up the cake cutter from where he'd left it on the counter, cut a fat slice, and slid it onto a plate.

"Yellow cake with chocolate frosting!" Olivia took a fork out of the drawer and took a big bite of the cake.

"Oh God. Oh God, this is just what I needed."

She dropped the fork on the counter and wrapped her arms around him.

"I love you," she said.

He tasted the sugar and butter and chocolate as he kissed her.

"I love you, too," he said.

She stepped back and picked up the fork.

"And I really, really love yellow cake with chocolate frosting."

He cut another slice and grabbed his own fork.

"So do I."

Olivia woke up absurdly early the next morning to find Max standing over her.

"What's wrong?" she said as she squinted up at him.

He bent down to kiss her.

"Nothing, I just have an early flight this morning back to DC, remember? I'm sorry I woke you up, but I have to go and I didn't want to leave before saying good-bye."

She sat up and kissed him again.

"I'm glad you woke me up." She touched a finger to his cheek and brushed down his hair. "Have a good week. I'll miss you."

He kissed her hard on the lips, then stood up all the way.

"I'll miss you so much. I'll be in touch. About everything."

He kissed her again and left. When she heard her front door open and close a few seconds later, she flopped back down on her bed with a long sigh.

She tried to drift back into sleep again, but even though it was just after six a.m. and she almost never woke up before seven thirty, she was wide awake. She missed Max's warm, comfortable, soothing body next to her, and now all she could think about was the "everything" he'd meant. Maybe all hell had already broken loose and he hadn't told her? No, Max would have told her, that wasn't his style.

The problem was, this was a hell of a bigger deal to her than it was to Max. Max was *already* famous—this wasn't going to change his life that much, maybe even at all. But it was going to change hers, at least somewhat. She just had no idea how much. Or what was going to happen next.

She threw back the covers with a sigh—there was no point in staying in bed and pretending she'd go back to sleep. She might as well drink some coffee and eat some leftover cake for breakfast.

Ten minutes later, she was back in her bedroom with a cup of very strong coffee and a big slice of cake. She took a sip of coffee and a bite of cake and smiled—the super chocolatey frosting cut through the bitterness of her coffee perfectly. She should definitely have cake for breakfast more often.

She reached for her phone and laughed out loud when she saw Jamila's text, sent approximately one minute after they'd said good-bye last night:

THE MYSTERY MAN YOU ARE DATING IS MAX POWELL. THE MAX POWELL. WAS I JUST IMAGINING THINGS. HOLY SHIT OLIVIA I NEED TO KNOW EVERYTHING.

Olivia laughed out loud again and took another big bite of cake. THE Max Powell indeed.

She shrugged. She had no choice here but to go all in, did she?

You free tonight? Come over for dinner.
This is a story that has to be told over a
bottle of wine—for me, not you—and
also not in public

Jamila texted back a lot faster than Olivia
thought she would this early in the morning.

Just tell me what time and I'm there

At 6:03 that night, Olivia finished making a
cheese and charcuterie plate that even her sister
would be proud of her for, and opened one of
the bottles of wine she'd picked up along with
the cheese. Thank God Jamila was one of those
people who was always five to ten minutes late,
which Olivia considered to be perfect timing. The
worst people were the five-to-ten-minutes-early
people—half the time she wasn't even dressed
ten minutes before someone was supposed to
arrive at her house.

At exactly 6:10, the doorbell rang. Olivia swung
open the door and handed Jamila a wineglass full
of sparkling water.

"Come on in. I hope you're hungry, I got us a
ton of food."

Jamila was smiling from ear to ear when she
followed Olivia inside.

"Starving—I haven't eaten since brunch, and
that was at eleven. Brunch always throws me

off for the rest of the day—it makes me want to eat again at like three, and then again at nine. But I refrained from doing so because I knew I was coming over here and why the hell am I still talking about brunch when all I care about is what the HELL IS GOING ON BETWEEN YOU AND SENATOR MAX POWELL?"

Olivia laughed as she poured herself a glass of wine.

"I was waiting for you to get there. Come into the living room so we can get comfortable; this story will take a while."

They sat down on the couch, and Jamila looked at Olivia expectantly. Olivia took a sip of wine and started with that first night at the bar, giving her an edited version of the past few months.

"And that's why I went up to the Bay Area a few weeks ago—yes, to see my sister, but also because Max was there instead of in L.A. that weekend, and we . . ."

Jamila put her hand to her heart.

"You didn't want to go two weeks without seeing each other!" Olivia hadn't planned to put it exactly that way, but it was the truth. She nodded. "Oh my God, that's adorable!"

Olivia reached for more cheese as she absorbed that. She wasn't used to being one half of an adorable couple. It didn't feel like her—the Olivia who had worked her ass off for years and had kept relationships at bay, the Olivia who never took a plus-one to a wedding, the Olivia who rolled her eyes at a guy clearly trying to hit on her at a bar, the Olivia who men found intimidating, or too closed off, or too self-assured, the Olivia who had hardened herself against the world because of all that and refused to let herself hope. Was she still that Olivia?

She poured Jamila more sparkling water.

"Anyway, we decided we were tired of being a secret, so last night was our first semipublic night out." She bit her lip. "It'll be actually public soon—his chief of staff leaked it to a photographer that we'd be there, so pictures should pop up online of us any minute."

Jamila opened her eyes wide.

"Wow, that's a big deal. How are you feeling? About all of this, I mean. You looked kind of . . . shell-shocked last night."

Yeah, that was a good description of how she'd felt.

"Last night was kind of overwhelming, to be honest. I did—I do—want to be public with him, I'm getting tired of sneaking around. But when we got to the Hollywood Bowl, and he wasn't in any kind of disguise, and there were so many people there, and they all had their phones out . . ." She let out a deep breath. "I didn't know what I'd gotten myself into. I'd relaxed a lot during the concert; Dolly Parton can make anyone feel better, I think, but then I saw you, and it all hit me again. Sorry if I looked like I was mad at you or something, that wasn't it."

Jamila shook her head.

"No, I get it. I'm sure this is all a lot."

It sure was. It had all happened so fast, and Max had become such a fixture in her life so quickly that she hadn't stopped to think about just how wild this whole thing was.

"It feels totally normal most of the time, when we're together. But sometimes I'll be flipping channels and hear my boyfriend's voice, and it feels really fucking weird." They both laughed. "I'm sorry I didn't tell you before. I really wanted to, but . . ."

Jamila brushed that aside.

"Of course you couldn't tell me. And don't worry, I won't tell anyone until you give me specific clearance to do so."

Olivia let out a deep breath.

"Thanks. I really appreciate you saying that. I have no idea what's going to happen here—which is not a phrase I enjoy saying, trust me—but I just hope whatever happens, I can handle it."

Jamila clinked her glass of sparkling water against Olivia's glass of wine.

"I'll toast to that, but then I've only known you for a few months, and I have full confidence that you can handle anything."

If only that were the case.

"I'm glad I give off that impression, anyway," Olivia said. "Truthfully, I can handle a lot, but I sort of feel like I'm in uncharted waters right now. Max is very chill about the whole thing, but then Max is always either very chill about things or very fired up; there's no in between with him."

Olivia poured herself some more wine and piled more cheese on her plate. She'd been talking so much she'd barely eaten any.

"So. That's the story. Stay tuned for updates."

Jamila turned and looked in the direction of the kitchen.

"Not to be greedy, and I know you said there are more snacks, but . . . is there more of that cake you mentioned?"

Olivia waved her toward the kitchen.

"On the counter, in the pink box. Cut me a slice, too, now that you brought it up." Dessert in the middle of a meal was exactly what she needed tonight.

While Jamila was in the kitchen getting the cake, Olivia reached into the pocket of her yoga pants for her phone. She'd been so intent on talking to Jamila that she hadn't thought about checking her phone for at least an hour.

Nor, apparently, had she felt it vibrate.

The photographer was as advertised; you look fantastic

And then there was a link to some website she'd never heard of:

MAX POWELL STEPS OUT WITH A MYSTERY WOMAN!

Here we go.

"I'm a mystery woman!" She waved her phone in the air as Jamila walked back into the room, plates of cake in her hand.

"Oh shit, the pictures are out?" Jamila put the cake down on the coffee table. "How are they?"

Olivia tried not to let her hands shake as she scrolled down the page.

"Okay, I guess? I tried to smile the whole time we were walking around, so I look kind of weird, but mostly fine?" She handed her phone to Jamila. "What do you think?"

Jamila scanned the pictures and nodded.

"I think you look great. I mean, I see what you're saying about the smile, but it's fine, don't worry about it. And your outfit is great." She held up the phone to Olivia. "And that one? It's perfect. The way Max is looking at you? Every woman in America will be jealous of you."

Olivia took the phone back to see what Jamila was talking about. She'd concentrated on how she looked in all of the photos; she hadn't stopped to look at Max. But Jamila was right— in the third picture, she was smiling that weird smile and looking straight ahead, while Max was looking straight at her and just . . . beaming.

That look on his face made her fall in love with him all over again.

"Wow," she said. "This might have all been worth it, just for that picture."

Jamila handed her the cake.

"I wonder how long it'll take the press to find out who you are."

Olivia clicked on the picture to save it to her phone.

"Hopefully weeks. Maybe months."

Chapter Fifteen

It took until 10:25 Monday morning. Olivia was at her desk at work, her gossip with Ellie over, her third coffee in her hand, when she got the first call.

"Is this Olivia Monroe?" the caller asked.

"Speaking," she said. "How can I help you?"

Olivia hoped it was about that potential pitch to Clementine, a huge local biotech company. Bruce had introduced her to someone in their legal department, and she'd had coffee with him the week before in the hopes that she and Ellie could get some of their vast amount of legal work. If Monroe & Spencer could get some Clementine business, maybe she could finally take a deep breath.

"Can you answer some questions for me about your relationship with senator Max Powell?"

She froze. She'd expected some warning before this happened. From Max, or his office, or something. She didn't even know what she was supposed to say.

"Um, no comment," she said finally, and hung up the phone. Then she texted Max.

I just got a call from a reporter—is there something I'm supposed to do?

"Ellie!" Ellie came running into her office.

"Was that a good call?"

Olivia made a face.

"The opposite. It was from a reporter. I texted Max, but during the day he's usually so busy I don't hear back from him for hours. I don't . . ." She picked up her coffee, then put it down. "What am I supposed to do? They didn't prepare me for this."

Ellie sat down.

"What did you say?"

Olivia stared at her phone, willing Max to respond.

" 'No comment,' which made me feel like I was on TV or something. Is that what people actually say?"

Ellie got up.

"Yes, that's what people actually say. Just keep saying that until you hear back." She came around Olivia's desk and leaned in for a hug. "You knew this was going to happen, right? This will be fine."

Olivia nodded slowly.

"I mean, I guess I knew it would happen eventually, but this was all so fast. I guess I just wasn't ready."

The phone rang again, and she and Ellie looked

at each other. Olivia took a deep breath and picked it up.

"Olivia Monroe." She paused for a second, and locked eyes with Ellie. "No comment."

"I guess that's what today is going to be like," she said when she put the phone down.

"Olivia Monroe," she said yet again, thirty minutes and ten phone calls later. She'd started answering the phone like that, instead of "Monroe and Spencer" like she had before, just to make these interactions move along faster.

"Ms. Monroe, this is Kara Ruiz from Senator Powell's office." Oh thank God. "I owe you an apology—I started getting calls from reporters about you about an hour ago, but I was outside of the office at a meeting where I couldn't have my phone. I assume you've gotten some calls to this number?"

Olivia had assumed she'd like Kara, just from the way Max talked about her. But the competent, brisk, warm tone to her voice immediately made her feel better.

"Kara, it's good to talk to you, I've heard a lot about you. And yes, there have been many calls to this number over the past hour or so. I've just said 'no comment' to all of them—was that right?"

This was definitely one of those rare times where she couldn't wait for someone else to tell her what to do.

"Yes, that was right, just keep saying that. I'll ask them not to call you again, and many of them will respond to that, but not all, I'm sorry to say. It'll probably be best if you have your secretary answer this line, at least for the next few days. You're pretty easy to find; this is the number on your website."

Easy to find: great for business, bad for when you were trying to dodge the press.

"Unfortunately, I don't have a secretary; it's just me and my business partner. If it gets bad, she might step in, though."

Ellie had offered to take over and blow off all the reporters for her, but she'd felt like at least one of them should be able to get work done today.

"That might be a good idea, at least for a little while. It's a rare slow news day, which must be why everyone's running with this. And again, I'm so sorry we haven't spoken before. I should have insisted on speaking to you last week, but this all moved so fast. That's no excuse, though."

Olivia brushed that off.

"Please don't apologize. I should have expected this to happen this morning; I was naive not to. Can you tell me . . ." She didn't even know how to phrase this. "How bad will it get?"

She didn't know why she was asking this of Kara, a woman she'd never met, or even talked to before, and not Max, her boyfriend. But then, maybe it was because she already got the sense that Kara might know the truth more than Max would.

Kara's voice softened.

"I don't think it'll be that bad—probably a flurry of phone calls over the next day or so, and then there will be another big story of the day, and people will lose interest. There might be some racial elements to some of the stories, though—I just want to prepare you for that."

Yeah, she'd expected that.

"I figured there would be. I just didn't know if the calls and stuff would go on for, like, days, or weeks or months."

If it went on for months . . .

"Don't worry, it shouldn't last that long. Though . . ." Kara paused. "There might be a rush to get more pictures of the two of you together. You can do it whatever way you want; it could be easier to just get that over with early on, but I understand if you may not want to do that."

Olivia tried to imagine that. Her and Max, out to dinner, and then walking out of the restaurant to an army of paparazzi. That sounded like a nightmare.

"I'll . . . I'll think about that." The phone rang again, and she heard Ellie pick it up in her office. "I should go; I think that was another reporter calling for me. Not that I want to talk to them, but . . ."

Kara laughed.

"I understand. And hopefully the calls will quiet down soon. I'll make a number of calls as soon as I hang up. Also, Ms. Monroe—"

Olivia broke in.

"Olivia, please."

Kara laughed.

"As the senator will tell you, I tend to stick with formality. But I'm going to make sure the senator gives you my contact information; I'm often more reachable than he is, so please feel free to contact me at any time if there's an issue, okay?"

Did that mean Kara expected there to be an issue? *No, don't think that way, Olivia.* She was probably just planning for all contingencies; she seemed like that kind of person.

"Okay, will do. And thank you. Thanks very much."

Seconds after she hung up the phone, Ellie ran into her office, a broad grin on her face.

"Oh no," Olivia said. "What did you say to those reporters?"

Ellie laughed.

"Nothing, nothing, I just told them all you were unavailable in my most Southern accent. They almost purred at me. Men are so easy that way. No, it's something else: that was Clementine calling—they want us to pitch them for some of their IP work!"

Olivia jumped up from her desk, and she and Ellie threw their arms around each other.

"When?" Olivia asked, when they finished jumping up and down.

"Not for a few weeks, their general counsel is going on vacation, so we have some time. They're emailing us the details now."

Olivia sat down at her desk and rubbed her hands together. This was the big chance they'd been waiting for. Who cared about a handful of phone calls from reporters now?

But . . .

"Ellie, I know we talked about this when I was deciding whether to go public with Max, but . . . what if this whole thing affects our firm? What if people think I'm not serious about my job, or that my focus is on my relationship, not my career, and don't want to hire us?" She put her head in her hands. "I made that decision too fast; I shouldn't have done it."

Ellie dropped into the chair across from her.

"Liv, honey. Part of the reason we started this firm in the first place was that we were tired of caring what a bunch of assholes think about us, remember? The assholes will think what they think, but we don't want to work for assholes anyway—better to have something like this to show us who they are. And plus . . ." Ellie winked at her. "Did you ever think this might be excellent publicity for us?"

She hadn't thought of that, as a matter of fact.

"But, El—it feels gross, somehow, for us to get publicity and business because of who my boyfriend is."

She'd always done everything, gotten everything, because of her own hard work and on her own merits. It had never occurred to her to try to use her relationship with Max for her own gain.

"Do you think two guys who started their own law firm wouldn't use their rich daddy's name and connections to get ahead?" Ellie asked. "No, of course not. We all have to use anything that's to our advantage in this life. Of course you didn't go public with Max to get us business, you and I both know that. But if some news stories about your new boyfriend give us the opportunity to make sure people know that we're damn good lawyers, it's just our way of making lemonade out of the lemons that are the dozens of phone calls we've already gotten this morning." She grinned. "At least one of the stories already out about you calls you an accomplished Harvard-educated lawyer—just the kind of branding we like to see."

Ellie, as usual, had an excellent point.

"Make sure you answer the phone 'Monroe and Spencer!' " Olivia said.

Ellie grinned.

"Oh, I have been."

• • •

Wes looked up from his phone as Max walked into their apartment.

"If it isn't 'now-taken Max Powell' as I live and breathe!"

Max dropped his briefcase on the floor.

"Shut the fuck up, will you?" He really wasn't in the mood to joke about this.

Wes laughed at him.

"These headlines are cracking me up. 'Max Powell, off the market!' 'Has the bachelor senator given out a rose?' 'Just who is the woman who won Max Powell's heart?' " Wes laughed again. "Wait, here's another one—"

Max stopped him before he could go on.

"I don't want to hear it, okay? I've heard enough of them already today."

Even though Kara had told him she thought people would be interested, he didn't expect this level of interest in his dating life at all. He'd expected maybe one or two articles about it, but nothing like the volume that there'd been only that day. All of it had been mostly positive, which his staff was happy about, but that didn't really matter to him—what mattered was that Olivia didn't seem happy about it at all.

Wes turned to look at him as he went into the kitchen.

"What's wrong? You knew this was going to happen, right?"

Max got a beer out of the fridge and shook his head.

"I knew something would happen, I just didn't realize people would care this much." He dropped down on the couch next to Wes. "I don't care about the headlines about me, whatever. But when they talk about Olivia like that, it makes me so angry. Especially since I told her it wouldn't really be a big deal, and . . . now I feel like a jackass."

Wes's eyes widened.

"You told her it wouldn't . . . Okay, well, in the grand scheme of things, you're right. This should all blow over in a few days. Maybe even tomorrow, depending on what else happens in politics tonight. Did you tell her that?"

Max shook his head.

"I haven't even talked to her—she talked to Kara earlier, but we've been playing phone tag all day—I called her as soon as I could, but it went to voice mail, then when she called back, I was in the middle of a TV hit. I just tried her again, and nothing."

He'd texted her an apology as soon as Kara had told him what was going on, and Olivia had said it was okay, she was dealing with it. But he hated that he'd given her something to deal with.

Wes picked up the remote.

"Don't stress. You'll make it up to her this weekend."

Max shrugged.

"I hope so."

He could tell Wes felt bad for him, though, because he turned the TV from MSNBC to baseball. He even clicked past soccer to land on it.

After thirty minutes of watching soccer with his phone in his hand, Olivia finally called. He jumped up and went into his bedroom before answering.

"Hey. I hate this, I'm so sorry," he said when he picked up.

"Well, saying 'no comment' that many times isn't how I thought I'd spend my Monday, but I'll survive," she said. He could tell she was trying to joke about this, but she sounded off. She had a tense, wary tone to her voice. Like she was steeling herself up for what was to come.

"I really thought no one would actually care about this, but I was wrong," he said. "But Kara thinks it should all blow over soon—Wes thinks so, too. So it's not just me this time."

She sort of laughed at that.

"Thanks, Kara told me that, too. And I hope she's right. By the end of the day, Ellie and I both became experts at figuring out who was press within a second or so on the phone, so at least that's something. Oh!" Her voice changed. The life came back to it. "Here's some actual good news—we're going to get to pitch Clementine in a few weeks! I've been dying to get an in there. I ran into Bruce Erickson last week at the community center, and when he asked me how the firm was going, I mentioned that our expertise would be a perfect fit for Clementine, and he connected me with a friend of his there. Keep your fingers crossed for us—this could be the big break Monroe and Spencer has been looking for."

He hoped that excited tone in her voice was there to stay.

"Fingers and toes crossed," he said. "It's fantastic that Bruce hooked you up like that."

She laughed.

"Well, let's hope it bears fruit. Speaking of, I have to run—I told Jamila I'd help her out with a bulk produce pickup tonight."

He was glad she was going to be with Jamila tonight, but God did he wish he could be with her.

"Okay, talk to you later. I love you."

"Love you, too," she said.

As soon as he hung up, he picked up the phone again. Carrot cake this time, maybe? Or coconut?

Chapter Sixteen

＊

On Thursday of the following week, Max called Olivia a few seconds after Kara left his office.

"Hey, what's going on?" Olivia said when she answered the phone.

He smiled just at the sound of her voice. Thank God it didn't have that tight, anxious pitch it had last week. He'd hated that sound in her voice, and he'd hated even more that he'd done that to her. And it had killed him to be so far away from her in those first few days when it was all so stressful. Just remembering that made him hesitate. Maybe his great idea wasn't so great after all.

"Max, what is it?" she said.

"I had an idea," he said. "But . . . if it doesn't work, just tell me, okay?" He probably should have waited to run it by Olivia first, before he'd told Kara.

"Okay," she said. "What is it?"

He grabbed a pen so he could doodle on his notepad.

"Well, next week is the Fourth of July."

He'd have a whole week of recess, though a lot

of that was going to be full of travel to fundraisers and party events. He'd still get to see Olivia a lot more than he would in a normal week, though.

"I know it's the Fourth of July," she said, amusement in her voice. "Was that it?"

He laughed.

"No, that wasn't it! It's this: for the past few years, I've done a volunteer thing on the Fourth, where I would bring some people from my staff, do some good, get some easy publicity for whatever nonprofit I was helping, and yes, some easy publicity for me, too. This year, it was going to be to help build furniture and toys for a foster-care center."

" 'Was'?" Olivia asked.

Max took a gulp of water.

"Yeah, 'was'—they just called Kara and said they had a fire; everyone is okay, but the building flooded. We're going to reschedule for when they're all moved back in, because they'll need our help more than ever, but of course, next week is too soon. So here's my idea. What if I came to your food pantry to help cook? With you, I mean. This seems like the perfect way for the two of us to be in public together again without it being a zoo. But if you don't want that, I understand. I'll be at the community center later this summer for one of the town halls, so we could always wait until then."

Kara had told him the week before that he

and Olivia should go out somewhere in public again in L.A. when he was home, just to get the inevitable second set of photos over with. But last weekend Olivia had seemed so exhausted he hadn't even wanted to bring it up. Instead, they'd spent almost the entire weekend in his house; relaxing, working, watching movies, and just being together. It had been wonderful.

But he didn't want them to feel stuck inside his house every weekend—the whole reason he'd wanted to go public was so they could go *more* places together.

"That is a good idea," she said slowly.

There was silence on the other end of the phone for a while. Max just waited.

"This will be really good publicity for them," she said. "Especially since people tend to volunteer and give money to food banks more during the holidays than the summer. And summer is such a difficult time for food insecurity, with kids home from school and not getting free lunch. No matter what, you should definitely do this. I'll text Jamila and find out the right contact info for your office to use. But can I . . . think about whether to come with you?"

He'd probably get used to Olivia's reluctance to make decisions without some sort of waiting period and matrix at some point. He tamped his irritation down; it made sense that she'd need more time.

"Of course," he said. "I love you."

"I love you, too," she said.

A week later, they were in the back seat of his car together, on their way to the community center. His aide Andy was driving, and another member of his L.A. staff, Brittany, was in the passenger seat.

"You ready for this?" he asked.

Olivia looked around the car and held tight to his hand.

"I think so," she said in a low voice. "I'm glad you're going to get to see the food pantry. I did always want to bring you there." She glanced into the front seat. "But maybe not like this."

She straightened her dress; it was a blue-striped sundress—very patriotic. Her hair was in a big knot on the top of her head. She looked professional, well put together, and also beautiful. He squeezed her hand.

"It'll be great. And the fundraiser tonight will be . . . well, we won't have to stay long, at least."

She laughed. They were going to a Fourth of July fundraiser that night at the home of one of the big party donors. He'd been to dozens, maybe hundreds of events like this by now, but he was really looking forward to going to this one with Olivia by his side.

"Good thing I have a different dress for that one," she said. "Just in case I spill barbecue sauce on this one." She pressed her hand to her forehead. "Oh God, that'll be the picture every tabloid runs with. 'Max Powell's new girlfriend, the slob!' "

They both laughed. He was glad she could make jokes about all this. From what Kara said, after these pictures came out, there would be another small flurry of local news stories, and then everything would calm down. He hoped so, for Olivia's sake. And he was pretty sure she was right; July would be such a busy news month that no one would have much time for gossip about the relationship of a senator who wasn't even up for reelection this year.

Andy pulled into a parking spot outside the community center, and Andy and Brittany both jumped out of the car. Max and Olivia stayed put.

"Remember, I'll come around the car to you, and . . ."

Olivia took off her seat belt and nodded to him.

"I know, then we'll walk in together, I remember!"

Their doors opened simultaneously, and he smiled over his shoulder to her.

"Just wanted to make sure you knew I'd be right there by your side."

He squeezed her hand one more time before they got out of the car.

Olivia smoothed her dress down again, then swung both of her legs together out of the car.

She'd been practicing how to do that all week. She was barely on her feet when Max came around the car and took her hand. Oh, okay—she hadn't realized they were going to do the hand-holding thing again. At least this would give her something to do with her hands as they walked into the building, with what felt like a hundred cameras around them. Fine, there were only four cameras. It was just that they all kept making that clicking sound, making it feel like more.

She'd never exactly been a person who sought a spotlight, nor had she been afraid of one. But she'd never experienced anything like this before. This kind of spotlight felt more like when little kids would hold magnifying glasses to catch the sunlight, and it would get so concentrated on one tiny pinpoint that it started a fire.

She forced herself to look up and smile at Jamila, who was standing with the head of the community center at the entrance to the building. Jamila looked more excited than Olivia had ever seen her. She'd been over the moon when Olivia had called her about Max's idea.

"Oh my God, I cannot wait to call my boss!" she'd said. "No, wait, sorry—I'm going to email my boss."

Olivia grinned. It was great to be able to help Jamila this way.

"Email him and cc the board president!" Olivia had said.

"I will," Jamila had said. "You're coming, too, right?"

"Oh, well . . . I'm still deciding that," she'd said. But that tone in Jamila's voice had decided for her. Plus, she couldn't let Max go to her place without her.

There was a flurry of handshakes when they got to the front door. When Olivia shook hands with Jamila, both of them could barely keep a straight face. Finally, they all walked together into the building and to the kitchen, where a group of volunteers—some regulars, some Max's staff—were waiting for them.

"Thank you all for having me and my staff here today!" Max said in his booming senator voice. "We're all so impressed with the important and necessary work you do here, and we've been really looking forward to helping out."

Jamila handed Max an apron.

"We're thrilled you're here," she said. "And we're ready to put you to work!"

The whole room laughed, and Max rolled up his sleeves. Olivia saw two of the college-age women in the room look at each other and whisper. She didn't blame them—if Jamila had been standing next to her, Olivia would have turned to her to whisper, "Holy shit, my boyfriend is hot, isn't he?" Okay, she wouldn't have actually done it, but she would have really wanted to.

They divided into groups to work on the day's

menu: barbecue chicken, potato salad, and baked beans. Olivia slid her own apron on and looked around the room. She was more grateful than she would have thought possible that she'd come to the food pantry that first night. What a difference it had made to her life to be in a job where she could come here every week—she never would have been able to do something like this at her old firm. And now that she had room in her life, she'd found a community here. And—she smiled when Jamila winked at her—a friend.

She'd wanted to bring Max here for a while, but as soon as she told Max she'd come along with him, she'd become increasingly anxious about this event. She'd worried it would feel weird to have Max in her space, with her people, and that it would feel like he was invading the one place—other than work or home—she'd made her own since she moved to L.A.

But she'd been wrong. It felt natural to have him here. And it made her heart so full to introduce him to this place, and these people, that had come to mean so much to her over the past few months. She wasn't just happy he was here, she was happy he was here with *her.*

Jamila came by to check on them, and Olivia moved over so Jamila could tell Max more about the pantry and kitchen and the work they did. Soon she was making fun of him for not knowing how to use a vegetable peeler for the potatoes, and Max in turn made fun of her for a typo in the recipe. Damn, it was good to see her friend and her boyfriend getting along so well.

"It's so easy to see the difference between your real smile and your camera smile," Jamila said in her ear.

Olivia laughed.

"I have resting bitch face, okay? I have to fake the camera smile; it does *not* come naturally to me. But the press dug up all of these old pictures of me, and people said I looked angry—I'm not angry! My face just looks like that!"

Jamila laughed.

"I think that's why we got such a good deal on your car—the guy kept thinking you were mad."

Olivia laughed as Jamila moved on to another table. Soon, a few more volunteers came over to their group to meet Max.

It was interesting to see him being Senator Powell, something she'd really only seen glimpses of since she'd known him. Sure, she'd seen him on TV lots of times, but that was different. It had always felt like he was two people: her boyfriend, Max, who brought her cake and made her laugh and gave her great orgasms, and Senator Powell, who argued with other people on TV about politics, pontificated a little too much, and occasionally cracked very dorky jokes. But now she was here with her boyfriend Max, but she was also with Senator Powell, who chatted warmly with everyone there. He smiled and shook hands and took selfies and asked intelligent questions and had a pleasant smile on his face, and did it over and over and over again.

Would she have to learn how to do that if she and Max kept going like this? Is that what he had meant when he suggested they do an event together, that she see how events like this worked for politicians . . . and politicians' wives? If she married Max, would this be what her life was like? Would she have to learn how to put a fake smile on her face all day whenever she was in public so she could look pleasant and harmless? Would she have to remember talking points and details about charities in different cities in California and the name of someone who had volunteered for a campaign two years before, like Max just had? Would she be some sort of Max appendage, where people wouldn't see her as an individual but only as "the senator's wife"? Would the world expect her to nod and smile next to him no matter what he said or did? Would she have to go everywhere in some sort of politician's-wife suit?

"How's the potato salad coming?" Max came around the counter to her. "Can you put me to work?"

Yes, right, she was supposed to be concentrating on potato salad, not a whole pile of what-ifs. Why was she even thinking about marriage?

Ridiculous. She handed Max the washed herbs.

"Here, dry off the parsley. And I thought you were working, what happened to the potato peeling?"

He took the parsley out of the bowl and carefully rolled it in the towel.

"Well, I had a few pictures to take and hands to shake, so Jamila took over." He lowered his voice. "That always happens when I do this stuff, and for a while I felt guilty about it, like I wasn't pulling my weight with volunteering, but then—"

"But then you realized your presence here is pulling the bulk of the weight, so you should give yourself a break? I'm sure those photos you just took—which will be posted everywhere—will bring in tons of volunteers and money, and will do an incredible job to spread the news of the good work we do here."

He shrugged.

"Well, I hope so. That's the goal, anyway."

She smiled at him.

"It's a great goal."

After they were done at the food pantry, Max and his staffers dropped her back off at his house, before they took off for a parade on the other side of L.A. He would meet her back at his house before they headed out to the fundraiser. She had no idea how Max managed to go to three events in a day and stay sane.

She sat down on Max's couch with her laptop

in her lap to work on their pitch to Clementine. It wasn't for two weeks, but their PowerPoint and script were mostly already done—at this point both she and Ellie were just tinkering with it, but neither of them could help it; they both wanted to get it perfect.

The next thing she knew, she woke up to the sound of the front door closing. She opened her eyes to see Max walk into the living room and smile at her.

"Hey." He moved her laptop off the couch and onto the coffee table. "Get some good work done on the pitch?"

She nodded as he pulled her into his arms.

"I did. And I got in a very good nap. How was the parade?"

He kissed her on the shoulder.

"Very exuberant. Did I tell you this morning that you look incredible in that dress? Because I kept thinking it, but we were with my staff the whole time, so I can't remember if I said it out loud."

She pulled off his tie.

"You did say it, as a matter of fact, right after I got dressed. But I'm happy for you to say it again."

He smiled as she unbuttoned his white shirt, which he'd somehow managed to keep crisp through all of that cooking and a parade outside in the July heat of Los Angeles.

"Do you know the only thing you look better in than that dress?" He pushed her back on the couch. "Nothing at all."

She smiled as she ran her hands up and down his warm, firm chest, and then down to his waistband.

"I think that could be arranged."

She couldn't stop touching him. She'd seen him last night and this morning, but that didn't make a difference. It was like he was a magnet, drawing her to him, and she was powerless to resist.

"How much time do we have until we have to be at this fundraiser?" she asked as he tossed her dress onto the floor.

"Plenty of time."

She closed her eyes as his hands roamed over her body.

"Oh thank God."

Forty minutes later, they got out of Max's big shower, and she pulled her shower cap off.

"Okay, but really—what's tonight going to be like?" she asked.

He rubbed a towel over his hair.

"Did your old law firm used to have holiday parties?"

She opened the drawer where she kept all of her toiletries.

"Yeah—lots of standing around, holding a drink in one hand and a plate in the other, and trying somehow to shake hands with people. Occasionally someone would get too drunk and make a fool out of themselves, a few boring speeches, frequent low-level sexual harassment, the usual."

Max nodded.

"It'll be a lot like that, hopefully without that last thing. Though—incredibly—the egos will all be bigger." He combed a dollop of gel through his hair with his fingers. "The good thing, though, is that I always get to arrive late and leave after exactly an hour. It's amazing what you can get away with as a senator, I'm telling you."

He gave her that cocky grin, and she couldn't help but grin back at him. Damn, she loved this man.

As soon as they walked into the party, though, all of her fears and what-ifs from earlier in the day came back to her with the first words out of their host's mouth.

"Senator Powell! This must be Olivia! Shouldn't your woman be in blue, not red?"

No *So nice to meet you,* no *Hi, Olivia, my name is Asshole,* not even a *Would you like something to drink?* before he was calling her Max's woman and assuming Max had decision-making power over her wardrobe.

Max ignored the last sentence, and put his hand on her back.

"Olivia, this is a very old friend of mine, Cary

312

Thompson. Cary, this is my girlfriend, Olivia Monroe."

Olivia forced her face into a smile and reached out to shake Cary's hand.

"Hi, Cary, thanks for having me." Was it petty that she refused to say *Nice to meet you?* Maybe, but did she care? No.

She kept the fake smile on her face as she and Max and Cary walked outside to Cary's enormous multilevel deck.

"Jerry! Hey, great to see you, happy Fourth!" Max said to someone who came up to them. "I'd like to introduce you to my girlfriend, Olivia Monroe."

Then it hit her. Max was introducing her to everyone tonight as his girlfriend. He'd never done that before.

She liked it.

Jerry nodded to her and shook her hand.

"Olivia, it's lovely to meet you. You're a lawyer, I hear? Tell me about the kind of work you do."

What a relief that not everyone here would just see her as a Max appendage.

Cary brought her a glass of wine—at least he was good for something—and Max a beer, and they each stood there nursing their drinks for thirty minutes while they chatted with an endless number of people. Most of them were perfectly nice and friendly to her, though obviously *very* curious. Max stayed glued to her side the whole time, which she found both unnecessary and completely charming—she'd been to lots of cocktail parties, she knew how to play this game, but it was lovely of him to want to protect her.

After a while, Max's staffer Andy came up and nodded to him. Olivia hadn't even realized Andy was at the party. Max turned to wink at her, then walked over to Cary's side.

"If you'll all indulge me for a moment," he said into a microphone that seemed to magically appear in his hand, "I'd like to thank you all for being here, and wish you all a happy Fourth of July!"

The whole party cheered, Olivia among them. Max kept talking—just your standard politician patriotic speech, but somehow, it sounded great coming from him. Olivia felt a swell of pride for Max and what a good man and politician and public servant he was, and that she was here with him. To be here, by his side, with his eyes on her, and that special smile just for her—that felt incredible. Suddenly the publicity and the reporters and the photographers and the constant smiling and the people who looked at her strangely and talked down to her didn't matter anymore. What mattered was Max, who was both a senator and a man she loved very much. And he mattered more than anything else.

As soon as his speech was over, Andy was at her elbow.

"Ms. Monroe, the senator would like you to meet him at the front door as soon as you're able to do so."

She glanced at her watch. It had been exactly an hour since they'd arrived. Max hadn't been kidding.

"Will do. Thanks, Andy."

Granted, it took Max fifteen more minutes to actually get out of the event, but at least he'd made the effort.

"I'm impressed by that exit," she said as they got in his car. "It's getting dark—I assumed we'd stay for the fireworks."

He turned to grin at her as he turned on the car.

"I have another plan for the fireworks."

He drove them up into the hills, where they joined a bunch of other cars at a lookout point. Before they got out of the car, he pulled a hoodie over his button-down and put his old UCLA hat on. She took the sweatshirt he tossed her, and pulled it on over her dress. They sat on the trunk of his car, and he wrapped his arm around her.

"We made it just in time," he said.

There were crackles in the sky, and they both looked up to see the first explosion of white stars over their heads. She laughed and clapped.

"I love fireworks so much," she said.

He kissed her cheek.

"So do I."

They watched the bursts and shooting stars

light up the sky, her head on his shoulder, their fingers intertwined. After a while she looked up at him and saw the red and white lights of the fireworks dance across his face.

"I'm really happy," she said.

He looked at her for a long moment.

"I am, too. It was really good to have you with me tonight, you know." He brushed an invisible hair off her face. "We make a good team."

She looked into his eyes and smiled.

"We sure do," she said. "And speaking of that: I thought we were going to eat at that party, but all I had was two glasses of wine, and I'm starving. Can we get burgers on the way home?"

He laughed.

"Absolutely."

Chapter Seventeen

✳

Two weeks later, Max was in his office in DC, reading briefing materials for his afternoon committee meeting, when Kara walked into his office with barely a knock and shut the door.

"Excuse me, Senator? We have a situation."

He dropped his papers on his desk. Whenever Kara used those words and that tone, it wasn't good.

"What's up?"

Her mouth was in a tight line.

"I just got a call from someone at Politico, wanting to know if we had a comment about the story they're going to run about Olivia Monroe's arrest as a teenager."

He made a fist and then forced himself to flex his hand. Shit. This was bad. He had to call Olivia.

"What did you tell them?"

Kara narrowed her eyes at him.

"I told him I would get back to him in ten minutes. Before I can do that, I have two questions for you. The first is, did you know about this before I walked into your office just now?"

He put his hand flat on his desk.

"I can't see how that's any of your business."

She walked closer to his desk.

"Oh, really? You can't? Because *you* are my business, everything about you is. I can only be as good at my job as you allow me to be. Did you know about this?"

Oh shit, this was what Kara looked like when she was mad. He'd forgotten that. She was usually so calm and collected.

"Yeah, I knew. She told me early on."

Kara nodded, opened her mouth, closed it, and nodded again.

"Okay. Good, that was smart of her, I'm glad to know she was watching out for you. Now I know which one of you to be mad at. Because, if you knew that, why the FUCK didn't you tell me?" She closed her eyes and took a deep breath. "My apologies, sir. I didn't mean to say that."

He just looked at her.

"Yeah you did, don't give me that 'I'm sorry, sir' bullshit. It happened when she was a teen-ager, and those records are sealed, so I thought it wasn't relevant."

Plus, he hadn't wanted to make this whole thing even worse for her.

Kara sat down in the chair across from him.

"Sealing records means nothing if you have people who know and who will talk, which is I'm sure how this reporter got hold of this story. If only we'd known this, we could have prepared for it; I could have talked to Olivia in advance, we could have maybe even controlled the release, depending on what she'd said, but now . . . Do you know what people will say about your criminal justice bill now? Not to mention what will happen to her." She let out a breath and stood up. "I'm sorry, I know you didn't want to hear that, but I had to prepare you. At least the news cycle the rest of the summer will be so bananas that I think this might be a few days of stories and that's all. But Ms. Monroe should know this is coming."

He closed his eyes and nodded. Dread filled the pit of his stomach at the thought of telling Olivia this.

"I know. I'll call her."

Kara walked across the room and opened his door, but before she walked out, he raised a hand to stop her.

"Kara."

She closed the door again and looked at him.

"I'm sorry," he said.

She nodded.

"I'm sorry, too. I shouldn't have said . . . most of what I just said. But . . ." She shook her head. "I'm just going to tell that reporter my standard 'no comment,' just FYI."

He had to call Olivia right away. Before a reporter did. Or . . . oh shit, had a reporter already called her?

He picked up the phone.

She answered right away.

"Hey, I was just about to call you—I got a weird message from some reporter, and it's been a few weeks since that happened, do you know what this is about?"

Shit, she sounded so relaxed and cheerful. How was he going to tell her this?

"Yeah, I know. Olivia . . ."

He should have told Kara. It didn't have to be a big thing, he knew he could trust Kara not to tell anyone. He should have done everything in his power to protect Olivia.

"What is it? What happened?" He could hear the change in her voice.

He just had to let it out.

"There's going to be a story coming out soon—Kara just got a call about it—about your arrest as a teenager. We're saying 'No comment', and you should do that, too, or just don't say anything at all, but Olivia, I'm so sorry."

"Sorry" seemed like such an inadequate word.

"I see. Okay. That's . . ." She was quiet for a moment. "Okay. I thought the worst was over, that's all. And this timing couldn't be worse, our big pitch to Clementine is tomorrow." She sighed. "Damn it. I wish you were here."

She sounded so stunned. He'd never heard her like this before.

"I wish I was there, too. This is all my fault. I

hate that you're going to have to deal with this because of me."

He really should have thought of this. Why did he have to do it all so fast? This was what he had staff for, damn it.

"It's not your fault," she said. "I should have assumed someone would be nosy and dig this up. I guess I just wasn't thinking."

Fuck, he had to tell her this part, too.

"I have to apologize: I never told my staff about this, and I should have. They would have prepped you—us—for all of this."

There was a long silence on the phone. So long he wasn't sure if she was still there.

"Olivia?"

"Yeah, I'm here," she said. "I'm just . . . kind of stunned. You didn't tell them? I thought you talked to your staff before the Hollywood Bowl? Didn't you think they should know this? My God, I would have told Kara if I knew you hadn't!"

He had nothing to say. Well, nothing good to say, anyway.

"I hoped no one would have to know. I didn't want you to have to deal with all of this. I did talk to my staff—well, Kara—but . . . obviously not enough."

She laughed, but there was no amusement there.

"Yeah, obviously. Okay, well, I guess I'll just see what this story is, and figure out how to deal with it."

He hated that it was only Tuesday. He wouldn't get to see her until Friday night. She was so mad at him, and there was nothing he could do, and he felt like if he was there and they could talk about it and maybe she could yell at him some, they could resolve this a lot faster.

"Can Kara call you? She's as mad at me as you are, but she'll be able to give you good advice on how to deal with everything."

Olivia sighed.

"Yeah, that's a good idea. Have her call me."

He noticed she didn't deny she was mad at him. She was right to be mad at him. He knew that. He just wished she wasn't.

"Okay, I should probably call my family now," she said. "Just so they know this is out there. And so my dad doesn't yell at a reporter if they call him."

Oh God, her family. He hadn't even met her parents yet, and they were going to hate him.

"I love you. Talk to you tonight?"

There was silence for a moment.

"I love you, too, but maybe not tonight. I'm going to try to relax and get to bed early so I'm in good shape for the pitch."

He wished there was something he could do about that defeated tone in her voice.

"Okay, tomorrow, then. And I hope you kick ass on the pitch."

"Thanks," she said.

"I love you," he said again. But she'd already hung up.

Wednesday morning, Ellie picked Olivia up on the way to their pitch at Clementine.

"It's not too late to cancel, you know," Ellie said when Olivia got in the car.

"You know as well as I do that if we postpone this pitch, it would be the same thing as canceling it," Olivia said to Ellie.

If only the pitch had been scheduled for next week. By then, hopefully everything would have died down some—that's what Kara had told her, anyway, and she trusted Kara not to bullshit her. But apparently the universe had conspired against her.

She'd seen only a few of the stories about her arrest, and they all seemed predictably titillated by a teenager who broke into her high school twenty years ago. She'd anticipated that—people had always reacted that way, and she'd seen what the media did to other Black women, after all—but she hadn't realized just how much it would all hurt her. And she hadn't prepared herself—enough, anyway—for the stories referring to her high school "in the ghetto," or the one suggesting she'd manipulated Max into a relationship with her. And all of this just because she happened to be a Black woman who fell in love with a famous, attractive white man.

She was mad at Max for not telling Kara about her arrest, but she was just as angry at herself. She should have done her best to control this whole situation, instead of trusting other people to do it well. What had that ever gotten her? How had she let Max convince her to go public in such a rush? That was so unlike her. She should have taken a lot more time about that decision. And she should have insisted that she talk to Kara first. If they hadn't rushed to go public, if they'd talked to Kara and made sure she knew about the arrest, maybe they wouldn't have gone public at all. And then she wouldn't be dealing with any of this. Especially not on one of the biggest days in Monroe & Spencer's short life.

"We could postpone the pitch, cancel it, what-ever—either one would be fine," Ellie said. "I'm worried about you."

Olivia shrugged that off.

"I'm fine. And I'm not going to let our firm suffer because of me." She sighed. "Though it has, already. I got a fucking message from fucking Jeremy Wright this morning—that ass-hole I hated at my old firm. He said he'd seen the news, and he hoped everything was going well with me. That was his way of telling me that everyone at my old firm knows about this, and they're laughing at me." She never wanted those people to know a damn thing about her, and now they knew far too much.

Ellie shook her head, then abruptly pulled into a grocery store parking lot. Once they were parked, she turned to Olivia.

"Who cares about any of those assholes? Who cares about this fucking pitch? I sure as hell don't right now. What I care about is my friend! Liv, one of the reasons we both left Big Law in the first place was because we wanted to be treated like human beings, and not just cogs in a wheel, remember? Did you blink when I barely worked for a week in the spring when Sophia was so sick? No, of course you didn't."

Olivia shook her head.

"That was different, you had to be with her."

Ellie grabbed her hand.

"It wasn't different, though, that's what I mean. We both have to be able to take breaks, and take care of what matters in our lives, before we fall apart."

Olivia squeezed Ellie's hand.

"Thank you." She closed her eyes for a second. "I love you a lot, you know that?" she asked.

Ellie smiled.

"I love you a lot, too."

Olivia let go of her hand.

"And I promise I can handle this pitch today. It'll be good to get the first time I have to deal with strangers about all of this over with, if that makes sense."

"That does make sense," Ellie said. "But

remember, whatever these people say doesn't matter."

Olivia wasn't sure if she believed that, but damn if it wasn't helpful to think it.

She grinned at her friend.

"Let's do this."

Ellie grinned back and started the car.

They walked into Clementine shoulder to shoulder.

"Gentlemen, I'm sure you're busy, so we should get right to it," Ellie said once everyone sat down. She started up their PowerPoint, and Olivia smiled at the men at the other side of the conference table.

"Thank you for meeting with us today. We've learned a lot about Clementine and what your needs are for this case, so now it's time to tell you about Monroe and Spencer, and why we are the best choice for your business."

Once they launched into their well-practiced routine, Olivia felt good, even great. This, she could do. Maybe she couldn't deal with the press who kept calling her office, or the photographers outside her office building—who, luckily, couldn't get into the garage, so hadn't gotten a picture of her yet—but she knew how to do this. All three of the men at the other side of the table seemed like they were listening to what Olivia and Ellie were saying. When they occasionally jumped in to ask questions, they were thoughtful ones, and the men made eye contact with both of them, instead of just with one another.

Olivia flipped to a blank sheet of paper and nodded to them when Ellie finished up.

"Do you have any more questions for us?"

They got questions about how new their firm was, how small it was, and their knowledge of the technology of the case, all of which they'd prepared for. The line of questioning worried her some, though—they seemed to want a bigger, more experienced firm, which made Olivia wonder why they'd even had Monroe & Spencer pitch in the first place. At least Olivia knew if they didn't get this client, it had nothing to do with how hard they'd worked.

Despite her frustrations, Olivia gave them her best politician-style smile. She knew it was her best; she'd been practicing it for weeks now.

"Any other questions or concerns? As we said earlier, we'd be happy to pass on the contact information of some of our other clients if you want to consult them."

The three of them looked at one another, and then the one in the middle—Brad, the one in charge—shook his head.

"No need for that." Her heart fell. Damn it. This one had been a long shot, but they'd worked so hard on it, and she'd been so sure it had gone well. "Bruce Erickson is a friend of mine and he speaks very highly of you, so I don't need to talk to anyone else. And I was impressed by how you've handled all of that nonsense in the press in the past few days—I thought you might cancel our meeting today, but on the contrary, you didn't let any of that distract you. Says a lot for what you'd be like as our lawyer. Anyway, we like you. You're hired."

The three guys across the table all grinned at her and Ellie. Olivia was too stunned to grin back. Had that really just happened? She took a sip of water to help compose herself.

"Thank you, all," Ellie said. Thank God for Ellie. "We look forward to working together."

Olivia turned to look at Ellie, and their eyes danced at each other. They'd done it. They'd motherfucking done it.

"Plus, I have a little more faith in any lawyer who has had some personal dealings with the law. Who among us didn't get into a little trouble in high school anyway? For some of us, it didn't end in high school, right, guys?" He and the other two chuckled and elbowed one another, as Olivia tried not to let the astonishment show on her face.

Had he really just. . . . You know what, nope, she was just going to ignore that.

She joined in the smiles and handshakes and jokes as the five of them stood up and she and Ellie got ready to leave.

"Oh, and another thing," Brad said to her by the conference room door. "Tell that boyfriend of yours I like him a lot, but that he should lighten up on all of the talk about taxes, will you? We have high enough taxes, living in California, I'm sure you agree!" He would have patted her on the shoulder, but Olivia stepped backward, so his hand just swatted through the air.

"You should give his office a call and let him know your thoughts. The number is on his website," Olivia said. Her face was devoid of the politician smile or, indeed, any smile at all.

Had this man really just given her a message to pass along to her boyfriend, the senator? And then tried to pat her on the shoulder? Was that why he'd hired her? Not for her experience, or her accomplishments, or her preparation, but because he thought he would have a direct line to a senator with her as his lawyer?

"Gentlemen, we should be clear," Ellie said. "If you're hiring Monroe and Spencer, you're hiring the two of us. And that's all. I hope no one has a problem with that?"

All three men shook their heads.

"I was at that Dolly Parton concert at the Hollywood Bowl, too, wasn't it great?" one of the men behind Brad blurted out.

Olivia tried to remember how to smile.

"Indeed. It was my first time at the Hollywood Bowl, actually."

All of the men exclaimed at this, and spent a few minutes relating their favorite trips to the

Hollywood Bowl as they ushered Olivia and Ellie out of the conference room and waved good-bye.

Ellie smiled brightly at Olivia as they walked out of the building and toward her car.

"We'll talk about it when we get into the car," Ellie said between her gleaming white teeth. "You never know who is listening around these tech companies."

They got in the car, and Ellie gunned the motor.

"We're getting the hell out of this parking lot before we talk about anything," she said. They drove a mile down the road without speaking, a Beyoncé song from Olivia's power playlist the only thing breaking the silence in the car. Ellie pulled into a fast-food parking lot and threw the car into park. Olivia started talking before the car was off.

"Ellie, what the HELL just happened back there?" She stopped herself. "I'm sorry, I'm not yelling at you, I'm yelling with you, you know that, right? I just have to yell right now."

Ellie slipped out of her blazer and folded it on her lap.

"Yell as much as you want. Yell for the rest of the day, at minimum, as far as I'm concerned. I can't believe he did that."

Olivia shook her fists in the air.

"I can't believe he did that! 'Tell your boy-friend'—what the fuck? In what world is that ever appropriate? But it's especially inappropriate when my boyfriend is a fucking senator! I let that comment about getting in trouble with the law go, even though it annoyed me; I'm sure his experiences getting into trouble as a privileged white dude were a lot different than mine. But 'Tell your boyfriend' was my limit, Ellie!"

Ellie pulled out her phone.

"Say the word and I'll email that asshole and tell him we don't want his business."

Olivia pulled her blazer off and tossed it into the back seat.

"Let me think about that. I can't decide which one would be better: a cold refusal to do business with them or charging them a great deal of money for our work."

Ellie grinned.

"Either one would be satisfying, but you're the one to make this call."

Olivia put her hand on Ellie's arm.

"Thanks. I really appreciate that. And I'm sorry, again, that all of this drama has had an impact on our firm. That's the last thing I ever wanted."

Ellie patted her on the cheek.

"You don't have to apologize for that, either. We're in this together, remember?"

Olivia smiled at her.

"I remember." Ellie started the car and rounded the parking lot to pull into the drive-through.

"Two large fries, one regular Coke, one diet," she said into the speaker.

Ellie took the cash Olivia handed her and pulled forward.

"And, Olivia Grace, you hear me, you're not going back to the office, you're going straight home. I can tell you didn't get a wink of sleep last night, and I need you to rest. I'd take your phone away from you for the night if I didn't think you'd kill me for it."

Olivia took the bag of food from Ellie and pulled out a fry.

"I know when I get Olivia Grace'd I'd better do what you say."

Olivia fell asleep about five minutes after she walked into her house. She woke up in a panic to the sound of a door opening and closing. Had someone just broken into her house?

Before she could react, Max appeared at the door of her bedroom, suit on, briefcase over his shoulder, hair in full Senator Shellac.

"Max?" She sat bolt upright. What was he doing here? It was still Wednesday, wasn't it? She hadn't somehow slept for two days straight?

He smiled and dropped his briefcase on the floor.

"There you are. I didn't expect you to be home this early, but then I saw your car outside."

She rubbed her eyes.

"I . . . what are you doing here? Aren't

you in DC? I mean . . . you know what I mean."

He sat at the foot of her bed.

"I fly back tonight on a red-eye. I had to see you. These past few days, those stories . . . I'm so sorry, Olivia. I didn't realize how bad this would be. I couldn't wait until Friday. I hope you meant it when you said you wished I was here."

She stared at him. Was this a dream? Had he really flown across the country just to see her for a few hours, because of an idle wish on her part? Her lingering anger at Max faded away.

"I'm so glad you came." She blinked away the tears that had sprung to her eyes. "It's really good to see you."

He pulled her into his arms.

"I don't think I've ever been happier to see someone," he said in her ear. "I'm so sorry. I should have done something to prevent this."

They sat like that for what felt like hours, just holding each other.

Finally, she kissed his cheek and pulled back, but kept her hand in his.

"Thank you," she said. "I needed that."

He kissed her softly.

"I did, too. Badly. How did the pitch go?"

She laughed.

"At first really well. I was worried they'd say something shitty to me, especially after those stories over the past few days, but . . . well, they sort of did, but they also offered us the job. In part, it seems, because of you." She held up her hand at the look on Max's face. "I know, I know, I was pissed, too, and so was Ellie. We're still figuring out whether we're going to take it."

"I'm not sure whether to congratulate you or commiserate with you," Max said.

Olivia leaned her head against his chest.

"Both sound great right now."

Max kissed her again, then pulled his phone out of his pocket.

"Speaking of those stories. Kara didn't want me to read them, but I did, and on the plane I drafted this press release telling them all to stop being so racist and also to fuck off." He shrugged. "Not quite in those terms, but close. I sent it to Kara on my way here so it could go out first thing in the morning, but she suggested I show it to you first."

Olivia's eyes widened as she scanned the draft on his phone. She quietly sent up a thank-you for the existence of Kara.

"Max, this is one of the most romantic things anyone has ever done for me, so thank you, and also, I'll murder you if you send this." She paused, and then raised her voice. "Wait, I won't actually murder you, sorry about that; this is not a threat to a member of Congress, if you're listening, FBI, that was a figure of speech. What I meant by that was, I'm thrilled by your vigorous defense of me, your ability to recognize racism, loud and subtle, and especially your recognition of your own privilege, but no, absolutely don't send out this press release. We want these headlines about us to die down, not flame back up, remember? This is like pouring oil on the embers; it'll start another round of articles and summaries and phone calls to my parents and sister, and I want all of that to stop."

He sat back.

"You didn't tell me they'd called your parents and your sister."

Damn it. She hadn't told him that on purpose; she knew he'd lose it.

"Of course they have; come on, you knew they would. But what I'm saying is, they'll stop after a while, once we get boring to them. Please let us get boring to them, okay?"

He slid his phone back into his pocket.

"Okay. Even though I really want to tell those assholes off, okay."

She stood up, and pulled him with her.

"Good, now that's settled. Hopefully, in a few months, this will be nothing more than a lovely story someone tells a kid in trouble about rising from adversity. 'If Olivia Monroe could get arrested as a teenager and later be the founding partner at one of the top law firms in Los Angeles, you can, too!' they'll say."

Max followed her into the kitchen.

"One of the top law firms in Los Angeles, huh?" he said.

She took leftover pizza out of the refrigerator.

"People always told me to dream big, you know."

Chapter Eighteen

※

Max was home for the weekend a week later—
the last weekend before August recess—and
he had to admit Olivia had been right. Maybe
because they'd been boring, or maybe because
much bigger news had knocked them out of the
headlines, but the stories about them had almost
completely died down. Random pictures of
Olivia still popped up from time to time—once
heading into the community center, another time
walking into the gym—but even the paparazzi
didn't care about them anymore after those first
few awful days.

They still took precautions—Olivia had
swapped cars with different friends to make
it harder to follow her; she and Ellie had hired
a temp for a few weeks to answer their phones;
and Max had stopped going to her house, for fear
the press would discover where she lived. But
other than all of that, life had mostly returned to
normal.

Max looked over at her, in her spot in the corner
of his couch, and smiled. That line of tension that
had been there on her forehead for the past month

had faded. But . . . her shoulders still looked too tense as she hunched over her phone.

What she needed was a vacation.

Wait. Yes. What they *both* needed was a vacation! Max pulled up his calendar on his phone and smiled.

"What are you doing next weekend?" he asked.

Olivia sat up and narrowed her eyes at him.

"I sort of assumed I'd be here—why, are you gone then? I thought your town halls didn't start until the second week of August."

His staff had built in a few days of break for him, which he hadn't had time to think about until just this moment.

"This last month has been so hard, and I think we deserve an actual vacation," he said.

A smile spread across Olivia's face.

"What do you have in mind?"

Max grinned at her.

"Hawaii."

Olivia's mouth dropped open.

"Hawaii? For just the weekend?"

Max shook his head.

"For, let's say . . . five days, if you can manage it? I get back here from DC on Thursday night, God willing—we can leave Friday morning, and come back, like . . . Tuesday night. I know the office has been pretty busy lately—can you take a few days off?"

He'd fallen in love with this idea in the last two

minutes. Now he just had to convince Olivia.

"Ellie was lecturing me the other day to take a few days off," she said. "But Hawaii? You know, I've actually never been. It was always too expensive for us to go there on vacations when I was growing up, and then I've been on the East Coast for so long and Hawaii is so far from there I didn't even really think about it. Isn't that kind of far for a five-day trip, though? And isn't this kind of last-minute?"

Max ignored that last question.

"It's a shorter flight from L.A. to Hawaii than it is from L.A. to DC—okay, barely, but it is shorter—and the amazing thing about flying to Hawaii is that, because of the time difference, you can take a nine a.m. flight from LAX and be on the beach by noon."

Well, that was a slight exaggeration, but it was worth it. He could already see the glimmer in her eye.

"I like the sound of that. Go on."

Shit, that had been his main selling point; he hadn't had to sell anyone on Hawaii in a while. What to say?

"Second, I know a great hotel there—we won't have to deal with press or anyone who gives a shit about either one of us. We'll just lie by the beach or snorkel around and look at sea turtles, or lie by the pool drinking mai tais and eating poke, and it'll be perfect."

She pressed her lips together, in that way he knew she did when she was fighting back a smile.

"Beach, turtles, mai tais, poke . . . I love all of those things. But . . ." She stopped and looked at him. He tried to make his eyes extra pleading, and she laughed out loud.

"If you think those puppy dog eyes are going to win me over . . . well, you're correct, but to be fair, I was mostly already won over by all of that other stuff. Are you sure we can get a room in your dream of a hotel at this late date, though? It's summer vacation, isn't everyone in Hawaii?"

He pulled his phone out of his pocket.

"Let me make a call."

Five minutes later he hung up the phone with a grin on his face.

"We have a room at the hotel from Friday until Tuesday. Are you in?"

With a smile on her face, Olivia looked up from her phone.

"I just double-checked with Ellie to make sure there's nothing crucial, and she told me she'd fire me if I don't take this trip, so . . . I guess I'm in."

Which is how they ended up in two first-class seats from LAX to Oahu that Friday morning. She fell asleep on his shoulder as soon as they took off, but he nudged her awake about an hour before they landed.

"I don't want you to miss your first descent into Hawaii," he said.

She smiled sleepily at him and turned to look out the window. For a while, nothing disturbed the endless blue of the ocean. And then, suddenly . . .

"Is that it?" she asked.

He peered over her shoulder and nodded.

"That's it. I can't wait for you to see it."

They landed during a soft, warm rain. At first Max was disappointed that Olivia's first views of Hawaii would be in the rain, until she pointed.

"A rainbow!"

She had a look of pure awe on her face. Max could have watched Olivia look at that rainbow for hours.

The rainbow wavered in front of them as they drove away from the airport, but finally the sun came all the way out, and the rainbow disappeared, just as they made the turn toward their hotel.

"Now," Max said. "Let's see just how fast we can plant our asses in lounge chairs by the pool."

They checked into their hotel in a flash, and raced, giggling, into their room to change. Olivia threw off her clothes almost before Max had his suitcase open, and before he could pounce on her, she'd pulled a bright red bikini on and slipped on flip-flops. He reassured himself that he'd have plenty of opportunities to pounce on her this weekend.

"What's taking you so long? I thought this was

a race." Olivia grinned at him, her hat in one hand and a bottle of sunscreen in the other. "Get my back, will you?"

She handed him the sunscreen and turned her back to him. And then she gasped and walked toward the window.

"What is it?" He dropped the sunscreen on the bed and followed her.

"This view. Holy shit." She stared outside at the golden beach, bright blue water, and choppy white waves, then turned back around to him. "Why do you still have pants on? Let's go!"

But Olivia didn't let him stop at the lounge chairs by the pool. Instead, they went straight to the beach. She dropped her beach bag in the sand, and they ran into the water holding hands. They both recoiled at the impact of the freezing cold Pacific Ocean, then grinned at each other and went in deeper.

"You're right," Olivia said to him, once they'd both treaded water in silence for a few minutes. "Hawaii is perfect."

He leaned forward and kissed her. She tasted like salt water and lip balm and happiness.

"Now Hawaii is perfect," he said.

Later that afternoon, Olivia pushed back her wide-brimmed straw hat and smiled up at the sky, and at Max, in the lounge chair next to hers. She'd been more stressed about this last-minute vacation than she'd let on to Max. She'd had to get a ton of work done, bring Ellie up to speed on her clients in case she had to cover something while Olivia was gone, *and* find a swimsuit that not only fit her boobs and ass, but one that actually looked good on her, and all in less than a week. But it had all been worth it. The sun felt so good on her skin. She'd spent so much time this year inside her office building or her house—or Max's house—she'd barely taken advantage of the L.A. weather. She hadn't even been to the beach since she'd moved back! Sure, the beach was all the way on the Westside, but that was still closer than Hawaii. She made a pledge to herself to get to the beach more often.

She kept her sunglasses on as she looked around the pool; after the past few weeks in L.A., she constantly felt like she was being watched, which was only partly paranoia, after that one really bad week. She still felt smug about one of the paparazzi pictures, though—someone had taken it as she'd walked toward her gym, brand-new athleisure on and yoga mat in hand. She'd looked sporty and friendly, and like she had no idea anyone was taking her picture. As soon as she walked into the gym, the employees had smuggled her out the back door. When that picture had popped up online, she cheered.

Luckily, everyone—including photographers—had seemed to lose interest in her and Max, so she'd begun to let her guard down. Plus, already this morning she'd seen two people far more famous than Max here at the resort. If they trusted this place, she would, too. Oh wow, and there was a third, over there stepping out of a cabana. Now she could definitely relax. And speaking of relaxation . . .

She turned to Max.

"Do you see those people over there? They have a drink inside a pineapple—how do we get one of those? No, two of those."

Max grinned at her.

"You're getting into the Hawaii spirit, I see. Next time one of the waiters walks by, we'll ask him to bring us one. No, two."

Ten minutes later, they grinned at each other over their boozy pineapples.

"Cheers to one of the best ideas I've ever had," Max said as he touched his pineapple to hers.

Olivia wanted to roll her eyes at him, but she was too relaxed.

"Cheers," she said, and took a sip of . . . oh wow, that was a strong pineapple drink.

"I'm going to be drunk within the hour," Max said as he put down his pineapple.

"I think I'm already drunk," she said. And then she took another sip.

Max glanced down at his phone. Even though it was a Friday during recess, he still seemed to get an email about every minute. They'd both spent some of this time by the pool working on their phones, but it still felt like vacation.

He turned to her with his eyebrows raised. Oh no, she knew this look.

"You know," he said, in his most convincing voice. "The last town hall meeting is going to be in L.A., at your community center."

Olivia picked up her pineapple again.

"Excellent," she said. "I hope Jamila takes credit for that."

She took another sip from her pineapple. She probably didn't want to know how much rum was in this thing, did she? Well, whatever was in it, it was delicious.

"I know how you feel about that center, after all the time you've spent there," Max said. "What would you say to coming with me to the town hall there? Especially since this whole thing was your idea, after all."

Olivia couldn't help but smile back at Max.

"With an offer like that, how can I say no?"

Olivia took another sip of her pineapple and smiled at the world. If only every workday could be spent in the sunshine with pineapples full of rum. She'd get very little work done, but she'd be in an *excellent* mood.

After they finished their pineapples, Max reached for her hand.

"Let's go take a walk along the beach," he said. "I'm getting hot."

"You've always been hot," Olivia said, and giggled.

Max grinned at her.

"I think I like Hawaii Olivia a whole lot. Can we bring her back to California?" He stood up and pulled her up out of the chair.

Olivia pulled on her cover-up.

"Look, I'm still trying to get rid of New York Olivia, okay? But if you can manage to bring me one of these drinks every day, I feel like Hawaii Olivia will just naturally take over." She slung her beach bag on her shoulder. "She won't have a job anymore, but she'll be real cheerful about it."

They walked down to the beach, hand in hand, and strolled along the water's edge.

"This was a very good idea on your part," Olivia said.

Max turned to her, that cocky grin she loved on his face.

"I know," he said. Then the grin faded and his eyes opened wide. He turned her in the direction he was looking and dropped his voice to a whisper.

"Look!"

A man was on one knee, and the woman in front of him had her hands in front of her face. Slowly, she lowered them, and took his hand. Olivia and Max couldn't hear what the couple was saying, but everyone on the beach knew exactly what was happening. After a few minutes, the man slid a ring on the woman's finger and stood up. Everyone around them—including Max— applauded. Olivia joined in.

"Wasn't that romantic?" Max said, after the couple waved at everyone and walked back up to the hotel.

"It was," Olivia said.

Max turned to her and smiled. Olivia saw something in his eyes change. He opened his mouth, almost in slow motion. A sudden apprehension hit Olivia.

"You're not going to propose, are you?" she blurted out.

His face dropped. That crestfallen look made her want to take back what she'd said, but it was too late. Damn that pineapple drink and all this sunlight; she would have done that much better if she hadn't been this tipsy.

"Would it be so bad if I was?" he asked.

No, it wouldn't be so bad, but also yes, of course it would be.

Shit, shit, shit, how could she say this to him?

"It wouldn't be, if now was say . . . a year from now. And if in that year, we'd had even one conversation about getting married—though I'd prefer more like four or five conversations."

Max threw his hands in the air.

"Four or five? Who needs to talk four or five times about getting married? I love you, you love me, isn't that enough?"

347

Olivia took a deep breath. Every time he said he loved her like that, it made her heart want to burst.

"I do love you, so much, but that's not the only thing. Even normal people in normal relationships need to talk through this, and our relationship has at least two or three major abnormalities."

Max dropped down on the sand and pulled Olivia down next to him.

"Okay, fine, what do normal people in normal relationships have to talk about?"

Olivia looked sideways at him.

"You don't . . . I mean . . ." Why was her mind suddenly blank here? "Um, things like . . . money, children, family, work—you know, the hard stuff. You used to be a normal person; I know you've had other serious relationships. Didn't you guys have conversations about this kind of stuff?"

He shrugged.

"I mean, I guess so, just as they came up, but not specifically. Let's talk about it all now. Money: what's mine is yours. Children: love them, but having them might be hard with two busy jobs, so we can explore. Family: your sister seemed to like me, except for the shoes; I'll work on everyone else. My mom and sister will adore you; my dad will, too, he just won't seem like it at first. Work: I feel like we've talked about this a lot, haven't we? We've handled it okay for now, right? What else?"

Olivia stared at him. He just smiled back at her.

"Max, I . . . I wasn't prepared for this right now! I need to think of questions to ask, and things that are important to me, and I want to find out what's important to you, and you didn't even touch on race or your specific job and all of the stuff I'd have to do because of that and the press and everything and I can't do all of this when I just drank that whole pineapple!"

Max laughed, and put his arm around her.

"I know you think I rush into things, and maybe I do. And I know my job makes things complicated. But you know, I only rush into the big things when I know to my core that they're right. I know to my core you're right for me, Olivia Monroe." He kissed her cheek. "But no, I won't propose right now."

Olivia leaned her head against his chest. His words made her want to wrap her arms around him and not let go, and they filled her with panic at the same time. How did they get from pineapples full of rum to talking about marriage this quickly?

Granted, she had thought about what it would be like to be married to Max. But she'd worried about how to be in the public eye, and how to keep that damn smile on her face, and if she'd have to lose some of herself in order to do everything involved with being a politician's wife, and if it was all worth it. Was it all worth it?

He tightened his grip around her waist, and she sighed. It all felt worth it when she was with him like this. She'd never had anyone love her this completely, this unconditionally, with this much certainty. And she'd never loved anyone like she loved Max. He threw himself into everything he did, and he did it all with such enthusiasm and joy. But he rushed into things, he so often didn't think things through, and he was terrifyingly impulsive, which had already made life so much more stressful for her. Could she deal with that forever?

Max got up and pulled her to her feet.

"Come on—I think we've both recovered somewhat from those pineapples, and we're supposed to go on that snorkeling trip in an hour, remember? Let's go see some turtles."

Olivia forced herself to shake off the fears that had all descended on her. What was wrong with her? Hawaii was no place for that.

"Oooh yes, I forgot about that." She looked up at the cloudless sky and smiled. "Also, I have a bone to pick with you—I heard that there are some sort of special doughnuts in Hawaii, but we've been here hours now and I haven't had one yet—what's going on?"

Max slapped his forehead.

"Malasadas! Oh God, I've failed you. We're

going to stop to get some right after snorkeling, I promise."

Olivia smiled at the world. Sun, sea turtles, and sugar—could she ask for more? What had she even been so worked up about?

Chapter Nineteen

✳

"Thank you all for coming today, and for sharing so much with me. You've given me a lot to think about. I appreciate it more than I can say." Max put his microphone down and waved to the Bakersfield crowd. He turned from side to side with his hand in the air and a smile on his face for the benefit of the sea of camera phones that looked back at him, and then stepped off the stage to take selfies with anyone who wanted one.

It was the fourth, and second to last, of his statewide town hall meetings. Some of them had been difficult—he'd heard a lot of painful stories from teens and educators about the impact the school-to-prison pipeline had in their communities, and he'd been yelled at by more than one parent—but he'd also connected personally with advocates around the state, and had gotten excellent ideas for the future. Not only did he think he might be able to get some of those ideas through Congress, he'd also heard from some excellent sources that the governor of California was now planning to throw his support behind one of the state juvenile justice reform laws.

He couldn't believe he'd been so single-minded about his bill that he hadn't broadened his scope to see how else he could accomplish his goals. He was so grateful to Olivia for this idea, and he couldn't wait to get back to L.A. to tell her that in person.

Plus, he couldn't wait to see her. After their fantastic trip to Hawaii, they'd been able to spend only a few more days together in L.A. before he flew up to Sacramento to start this tour around the state, and that had been ten days ago. They hadn't gone that long without seeing each other since their first date.

He wished they were at the point where she could come with him on trips like this, even for part of the time. He couldn't stop thinking about how nice it was to have her with him for those two events on the Fourth of July. When he'd looked out into the crowd and seen her smile, he felt like he could do anything and everything. He wanted that again. But even more than that, he wanted to be able to relax with her after events like this, when he got back to a lonely hotel room, both wired and exhausted. That vision of his future—of their future—felt so good to him, so real to him.

Ever since that conversation on the beach, he'd become more and more certain he wanted to marry her. At least three or four times a day, he winced when he thought back to that moment he'd almost proposed to her, and how she'd reacted. His feelings were still hurt—of course he wanted her to celebrate and jump in feetfirst and not worry about anything but how much they loved each other. But he should have known she would hate a beach proposal like that, with people taking pictures of them like they had that other couple. And he also knew Olivia well enough by now to know she liked all of her i's dotted and t's crossed before she made any sort of decision, especially such a big one. Well, after the town hall in L.A., there would be a few days before he had to go back to DC—maybe they could have some of those Conversations about Big Issues she wanted to have.

He wished he could drive straight back to L.A. tonight, but that would have been too much to ask of his local staff, who had been working all day to pull off this event. But tomorrow he'd be back in L.A., and tomorrow night he'd get to see Olivia again—before, during, and after the town hall. He couldn't wait.

When Olivia drove to the community center that Friday night, she felt like a kid on Christmas Eve. It had almost been two weeks since she'd seen Max, and that was far too long. In the time they'd been apart, all of her old doubts and worries had sprung up again. Was this all happening too fast? Was this too good to be true? It would be so good to see Max again; she always felt better when she was with him.

She was nervous about this event, though. She'd said yes immediately when he brought it up in Hawaii, but that had been because of way too much of whatever was in that pineapple. When he'd brought it up in passing again, she felt like she couldn't say no after having said yes. But the press had *just* relaxed on them, she hadn't gotten a weird phone call all week, and part of her hoped she could stay out of sight and they'd forget about her. The problem was, if she and Max were in this for the long haul—and after that conversation on the beach in Hawaii, it seemed like they were—she couldn't stay out of sight forever. So here she was.

Had he been about to propose? She thought so at the time, but had she been imagining things? Had she forced an awkward conversation with him for no real reason? He hadn't brought it up again, and neither had she, but she'd thought about it every day since it happened. Maybe now that he was home for a few days, they could talk about all of that. But first, she'd need to make it through tonight.

At least Jamila was going to be there, and probably a few other people she knew from the food pantry. It would help to have friendly faces around, and hopefully even someone to sit with during the town hall, since she wasn't sure if she wanted to be surrounded by Max's staff.

When she pulled up to the community center, her status as The Girlfriend was clear. One person waved her into the reserved parking area, and then another person escorted her to the "greenroom" to wait for Max.

He and his whole entourage—it was a big one this time—walked in ten minutes before the event was scheduled to start. And for the life of her, Olivia couldn't stop the smile that spread across her face. Max immediately crossed the room to her.

"Hi," he said under his breath. "I missed you."

There were people all around them, and she knew they were all looking at them, even if they pretended not to. She and Max couldn't touch or even stand that close to each other. But the way he looked at her felt like a caress.

"I missed you so much," she said. His Hawaii sunburn on his nose had faded, and he was wearing that pale blue shirt and striped tie combination she particularly liked. And . . .

"I like the shoes," she said.

He glanced down at his new shoes and blushed.

"I hoped you might." They grinned at each other. It was so good to be with him again.

"Okay, everyone!" Someone with a very cheerful voice and perfectly straight hair stood by the door. "The community members are mostly here;

we'll just wait a few more minutes for stragglers and then get going."

Max's staff always seemed deeply competent. Olivia liked that so much.

"This'll be fun," Olivia said to Max as they walked down the hall toward the auditorium. "I haven't really seen you do your thing since that first luncheon—Fourth of July was all softballs. I'm sure I'll have some notes for you."

He looked at her sideways, and she giggled. The doors to the auditorium swung open, and Olivia started to step to the side so she could drop behind Max and out of the spotlight. But before she could do so, he took her hand.

The hundreds of people inside scrambled to their feet, flashbulbs went off, and Max and Olivia walked inside, hand in hand. Knowing Max, he hadn't planned for this in advance, he'd just grabbed her hand at the last second. She tried not to let her irritation show on her face. Instead, she forced a smile as Max gave high fives to the people in the crowd closest to him.

As soon as they were toward the front of the room, Olivia let go of Max's hand and looked around for somewhere to go. Jamila gestured to her from her seat at the side of the stage, where she sat with some of the staff from the center. Olivia made a beeline for her and then tried her best to fade into the background. But she knew that no matter how much she tried to disappear, it was impossible; everyone in this room knew who she was, and many of them were probably taking pictures of her right now. She had to look alert and interested and friendly and intelligent, and she had to keep a smile on her face the whole time. She felt the tension settle into her shoulders as she tried to do all of that. Shit, her shoulders—she had to think about her posture, too, didn't she?

The executive director of the center made a too-long speech that tested Olivia's ability to keep that damn smile on her face. At one point she made eye contact with Max, who of course had a perpetually interested, intelligent smile on his face—how the hell did he do this? He had to deal with this every day, all day, didn't he? He winked at her, almost imperceptibly, and she winked back.

Finally, the executive director introduced Max, and Olivia smiled for real. She'd teased him about giving him notes about his speech, but he was good at this—really good at it. She'd heard parts of the speech before, of course, had seen bits of it on TV, but it was smart and substantial and also made it clear that he really wanted to hear from the audience, and cared what they had to say. And he was funny, too—he got everyone clapping and laughing again after the director had almost put them to sleep.

Then the town hall part of the program started,

and a bunch of Max's staff dispersed through the crowd with microphones. Both adults and teens asked questions and raised ideas: about schools and how overcrowded they were, about health care, about after-school care, about jobs and job-training programs, about access to mental health services, about the police. He got some tough questions, but she was proud of him for how he handled them—he listened, he didn't get defensive, and he gave honest answers whenever he could.

And then a tall, lanky kid toward the back took a microphone.

"My name is Jerome Thomas. I . . . um . . . last year I got in some trouble at school, and I served some time. It wasn't . . . Well, anyway, I don't want to ever have to do that again. But I don't want that to brand me forever, you know? But I don't know how to get away from it: jobs ask you if you've been arrested, and I know people are going to look different at me at school. What can I do? Where can kids like me get help?"

Olivia looked at the stage without seeing it. She felt so bad for this kid, and she understood him so well. The world was stacked against him—she hoped he had people around him who would support him through this, and help him succeed and thrive, despite his mistakes, like she had. But no matter what, he had a hard road ahead. She slid a hand in her bag to see if she had her card case with her. She'd ask if someone on Max's staff could run back over to the kid and hand him her card so she could try to help him.

"Thank you so much for asking that question, Jerome," Max said. "I'm doing my best to get a bill through the Senate to help people like you—one thing I especially want to do is to ban that box you have to check if you've been arrested; some states have banned it already, but I want to do this nationwide." Max paused for the applause to die away. "But as for what you can do, I know there's someone in the audience today who has some expertise on that . . ." Max looked straight at her, that smile still on his face.

At first, Olivia didn't understand what was going on. And then she realized, and fury swept over her. Had Max really called on her, spontaneously, in front of this huge crowd, and the press, to talk about one of the most difficult experiences of her life? For what, to give him street cred, or something?

She shook her head at him. But instead of looking away, he put on that smiling, pleading look, like he did when he wanted the last dumpling at dim sum, or when he wanted to watch one of his comic book movies. And the worst part was, it had usually worked on her before. Did this man really fucking think his stupid puppy dog eyes would convince her to rip open a wound in front of a huge audience? She shook her head again and glared at him, and he seemed to finally get the picture.

"My office can definitely help you," Max said to Jerome. "Someone will give you contact information before you leave, and we can get you connected with services that can help, like getting you hooked up with mentors who can help guide and advise you, and job-training programs. But one of the reasons we're all here is that we need to do a lot more. Does anyone have any other great ideas for me about ways we should be helping Jerome and people like him?"

Olivia would be impressed with Max's recovery right there if she hadn't been so angry that it felt like actual smoke was coming out of her ears.

Was everyone in this whole room staring at her? She certainly felt like they were. They were staring at her like Max had. All these vultures from Max's office and from the press who just wanted their own curiosity satisfied, who wanted her to talk and cry and talk some more so they could judge her afterward even more than they'd judged her before. All of these people who wanted her to humiliate herself even more than Max had just humiliated her. Angry tears sprang to her eyes, and she fought them back.

Someone nudged her, and she flinched.

"It's just me," Jamila said in a low voice. "Are you okay?"

She shook her head. She was many things right now, but "okay" was not one of them.

"Do you want to go?" Jamila asked.

God yes.

"I've never wanted anything more in my life," Olivia said. "But I can't get up and leave right now. The last thing I want are pictures in the newspaper of my ass as I walk out the door."

She could feel the rumble of Jamila's laughter, even if she couldn't hear it.

"Okay, as soon as the town hall is over, we're out of here." She pulled out her phone. "I know they locked some of the back doors for security, but I'll get Sam to let us out."

The next fifteen minutes felt interminable. Olivia kept a fake smile on her face the whole time, and her face turned in the direction of the stage, but she couldn't and didn't look at Max. Finally, Max thanked everyone for coming, and got a round of applause. As everyone in the whole room staggered to their feet, talking and laughing and banging chairs around, Jamila grabbed Olivia's arm.

"Follow me."

Olivia didn't let herself glance in the direction of the stage as they fled. They went away from the main doors to a little door in the corner of the room, almost hidden behind the AV equipment. Jamila opened the door, and they slipped through.

"This takes us to the back; we have to walk

around the block to the parking lot," Jamila said. Olivia just nodded.

They didn't speak as they rushed to Olivia's car, thank God. She just wanted to get out of there, away from Max's staff and the press and everyone else who had been in that room. But most of all, away from Max, who knew she never wanted to be in the spotlight, who knew how hard it had been for her to be thrown into public because of him, who knew that she'd only done that for him because she loved him, and who had tried to drag her and her story and her pain and her struggles in front of the world, like she was some kind of trophy for him. She had to get away as fast as she could before she broke down.

They stopped right by Olivia's car.

"Do you need me to drive you home?" Jamila asked.

Olivia shook her head.

"I really appreciate that, but no. I just need to . . . I just need to go."

Jamila touched her arm and looked into her eyes.

"Text or call later if you need to talk. Okay?"

Olivia looked away so she wouldn't cry.

"Thanks," she said. "And thanks for getting me out of there."

Olivia gave Jamila a quick hug and then got in her car and sped out of the parking lot as quickly as she could. Part of her wondered if there were photographers around waiting for her or maybe even following her home, but at this point, she was past caring about that.

She felt so relieved when she pulled up to her house. All she wanted was to be inside, in her own space, alone. In a place where she didn't have to worry that anyone was watching her or judging her or taking pictures of her. A place she wouldn't have to hold on tight to herself and everything she was feeling.

She opened her front door, walked inside, and slid to the floor with her back against the door.

How could he have done this to her?

She'd given so much of herself to Max. She'd thought he understood her. She'd thought he knew just how hard it was to deal with the public part of his life, how much of a compromise it was for her to even come to events like this for him, to be in public with him, to let him tell the world they were together. But he obviously didn't understand at all, or else he never would have done what he did tonight. He never would have looked to her in that room, full of the press and his staff and so many people, and tried to get her to talk about one of the hardest moments of her life, one she'd spent years trying to get over, one she'd long ago forgiven herself for, but she knew the rest of the world wouldn't. How could he have done that?

She curled her knees up to her chest and let the

tears that had pricked her eyelids for the last hour finally flow.

Where the fuck did she go? Max fumed in the back seat of his car as Andy drove him home.

After the town hall ended, Max had been busy shaking hands and taking selfies and talking to community members and staff from the center, but he'd looked around for Olivia over and over again. He hadn't seen her anywhere, but he'd just assumed she was hidden behind the crowd, or talking to someone else, or waiting for him in the greenroom. But when he'd made it back there, no one on his staff seemed to know where she was.

He wouldn't be quite so worried about this if it hadn't been for the look on her face the last time they'd made eye contact. That kid had asked the perfect question to allow Olivia to finally easily address everything in an optimal, press-friendly way—it couldn't have been better if the question were planted! Max had looked to her gratefully so she could stand up and briefly talk about her background, how she'd succeeded, and give the kid advice for his future. She'd seemed to want to be an example for kids who had gone through what she had. But instead she'd just stared back at him with that look of stone on her face. He hadn't understood at first, so he kept looking back at her, but she'd just looked angrier and angrier.

And then she'd disappeared. And she hadn't texted to say where she was, and she hadn't replied to any of his texts asking her where she was, and he couldn't call her because he was in the car with his staff right now, and he still had no idea where the fuck she was or what that look on her face had been about and why she wasn't answering his texts.

Maybe she was at his house right now. Maybe she'd needed to drive her friend home and had forgotten to text to tell him so. She had a key; maybe she was already there waiting for him. Maybe she was in his bed right now, waiting for him. Oh God, he hoped so—it felt like forever since he'd had her in his bed. He couldn't wait to slide into bed with her tonight, and kiss her, and make love to her, and then wrap his arms around her and never let go.

Andy pulled up in front of his house, and Max thanked him for the great event before he raced into the house.

"Olivia? Olivia, are you here?" he shouted as soon as he walked in the door.

No answer.

Maybe she couldn't hear from his bedroom. Or maybe she'd fallen asleep there, waiting for him.

He ran up the stairs and burst into his bedroom. "Olivia."

But his bedroom was silent, his bed empty. And he realized what should have hit him as soon as they'd pulled up to his house: her car wasn't there.

Okay, seriously, where the fuck was she?

He called her, once, twice, but she didn't answer.

He thought back to that frozen look on her face. Now that he thought about it, had she avoided his eyes for the rest of the town hall? He'd looked at her a few other times, but she'd always been looking at a random corner of the stage, definitely not at him.

He grabbed his car keys off the hook by the garage. Thirty minutes later, he banged on her front door.

"Olivia? Are you there?"

Her car was there, at least, so that was a good sign.

He rang her doorbell, then reached for his keys to let himself in. But before he could, her door swung open.

"So is your goal to let the whole world know exactly where I live, on top of everything else?"

She was still in the black pants and silk blouse she'd worn to the community center, but everything else about her looked different. Her hair was gathered in a tight knot at the top of her head, instead of the soft curls that had skimmed her shoulders. She had smudges around her face that he knew hadn't been there earlier. And now, instead of either the laughter in her eyes he'd seen in the greenroom or that stony look on her face he'd seen in the auditorium, the look on her face was pure fury.

"Olivia, what happened? Where did you go?" He stepped inside. "What do you mean, 'on top of everything else'?"

She slammed the door behind him.

"What do I mean? Have you forgotten what happened back there at the community center? What you did to me up there on that stage, in front of your staff and the press and hundreds of other people?"

He stared at her as realization dawned.

"This is all about that kid? Is that what all of this is about? I don't understand why you wouldn't give him advice in the first place—you told me you wanted to be able to be an example for kids like him!"

She took a step away from him, and that stony look was on her face again.

"I'm making a big deal out of nothing, is that what you think?" she said. "You ambushed me! In front of hundreds of people and dozens of reporters! I'd be happy to give that kid advice; I was planning on it—privately, afterward. I've helped out many kids like him, as a matter of fact—I've volunteered and mentored and given them advice and made connections. But I do that as my decision, not yours! When I said I wanted to be an example to kids like him, I didn't mean like this!" She shook her head. "How could you even think I would want to stand up in front of the whole world and talk about all of that? After these past few months, when my past was thrown in my face—all for you, I might add—and you wanted it to start all over again?"

Fuck. He'd gotten this all wrong.

"No, Olivia, that's not what I wanted. I just thought you might—"

But she wasn't listening to him.

"Does it give you some sort of street cred, or something? Having a girlfriend who got arrested? Is that why you paraded me around today, in front of that group? So they might trust you more? So they might vote for you next time?"

Now she was making him mad.

"That's really fucking unfair and you know it. I didn't want you there today for any of those reasons—I wanted you there today because I like having you there with me, because I love you, because this was an event that was important to me and I wanted to share it with you. I thought you wanted to be there! I'm sorry I put you on the spot, but the timing and setting seemed perfect." He remembered something, one of the reasons he'd thought it was okay to bring it up today in the first place. "Plus, you talked about it at that city council meeting a few years ago, I don't know why it's so different."

Olivia clenched her jaw so hard he could see it from across the hallway.

"It was my choice to talk at that city council meeting, and I had the freedom to talk about it in my own way. And that was before my name was already in the fucking tabloids! No one cared one iota about me two years ago at the Berkeley City Council meeting! But now, today, if I said one single thing in public about my arrest, too many fucking people would care! They would ask me questions, they would write articles about it for weeks, they would call my office over and over again, and I don't want any of that. I've never wanted any of that."

He couldn't ignore the implications of that. He really hoped she wasn't saying what it felt like she was saying.

"I thought . . . from what we talked about in Hawaii, anyway . . . that you saw a future for us. Did you think that you and I would stay together and you would stay in the public eye—as much as you don't want that, that's what would happen—and you would never talk about it?"

"Yes!" she yelled. She stopped and took a deep breath. "I don't know. I guess I didn't get that far in thinking about it. But what I do know is that if I ever did address it, I wouldn't do it your way, where you just leap into something without thinking about the implications, say the first thing that comes to your mind, and smile and charm your way out of every hole you dig yourself in."

That wasn't fair. He started to break in, but she held up a hand to stop him. "I can't do things like that; I'm a Black woman, I don't ever get the benefit of the doubt in the way someone like you does. I can't afford to make split-second decisions and assume they'll work out. I have to plan, and think, and plan again, and strategize. I prepare like hell for everything I do, so if I did ever decide to say anything publicly about the time I was arrested as a teenager, and the aftermath, and the way I recovered and flourished after that, I would prepare like hell for that, too. What I wouldn't do is stand up at a few seconds' notice at a community center and say whatever came into my head, because that's not how I live my life."

She looked at him with tears in her eyes. "That's how you live your life, though, isn't it? You just make impulsive, snap decisions all the time, and maybe they work for you, but you can't make them for other people like you keep doing for me."

He'd made her cry. He'd really fucked this one up, hadn't he?

"Olivia, I'm sorry. I'm so, so sorry. I just thought it was the perfect opening, and you were right there, and I know how much you care about teens like that, and I wanted everyone to see how warm and caring and smart and accomplished you are, and I thought this would be the perfect opportunity to show the world who you really are."

He walked toward her with his arms open, but she shook her head.

"What if . . . what if I don't want to show the world who I really am? What if I don't want the world to know anything about me? What if I'm so tired of smiling all the time and wearing perfect outfits whenever I leave the house and thinking about what the world thinks of me?"

The tears were still in her eyes, but she also looked . . . determined. Like she'd come to some sort of decision.

He didn't like that look on her face. He didn't like it at all.

"Olivia. What are you saying?"

She shook her head.

"Max, I'm sorry. I just don't think I can do this anymore."

He stepped toward her again, but she took a step backward, and he froze.

"No. No, please don't say that. You're mad at me, I understand, but we can work through this. I love you. So much."

She dropped her face into her hand and wiped away tears before she looked back up at him.

"I love you, too. And I'm not mad at you, not anymore. I was mad, don't get me wrong, I was furious. But I can never stay mad at you. The thing is, I don't think we *can* work through this. You're impulsive, you're an idealist, you want to help everyone, and that's part of the reason I fell in love with you. But . . ." She stopped, closed her eyes, and took a breath. "But I don't think I can live like that. This is all so hard for me, and I keep trying, but it's too much." She sighed. "I wish we could go back to how it was before. When we were just Olivia and Max, two people falling in love. I didn't . . . I never expected to fall in love with you, you know. I thought we would have a fun little fling and it would all be over. But I kept getting in deeper and deeper. And your job makes everything so much more complicated."

He felt like his whole world was crashing around him.

"No, please, don't do this. Fuck my job, this is about us. I don't have to . . . I would do anything for you."

Another tear fell from her eye, and she brushed it away.

"You love your job so much, and you're so good at it, and we need you there, now more than ever. But I just can't take this anymore. The calls from reporters, the nasty articles, the photographers, the weird comments from clients . . . I can't keep doing this, Max. Every week it's something else. And you need the kind of partner who I can't be—you need someone who looks perfect all the time by default, someone who doesn't have any baggage, someone who isn't obsessed with her job, someone who can be a perfect political wife in all of the ways I can't. I don't want to mess this all up for you."

He couldn't let this happen. He couldn't lose her.

"Olivia. No. Please. I need you. All I need is you. Please don't do this. You say you don't like impulsive decisions, don't make this one! Take some time, think this through, don't give up on us."

She shook her head.

"Max, I . . . We're just too different. I can't change you, and you can't change me, either. I have been thinking this through—I should have listened to that voice in my head every time I agreed to go out with you, or to date you, or to go public with you, or to go to Hawaii with you. Or to . . ." Her voice caught. "Fall in love with you, though that one isn't your fault. I kept slowly giving in to you, because I loved you, but if I keep doing that I'm going to lose parts of myself. We can't do this anymore. I'm sorry."

She walked around him, and opened the front door.

"You should go."

He tried to think of something else he could say. Some way to change her mind, some way to convince her he belonged to her, and she belonged to him, forever. This had always been his strength, one of the reasons why he'd always been such a good politician. He'd always been able to change minds; he'd always been able to think of the right thing to say, even to people who hated him. And Olivia loved him; she'd said so. He knew her; he should be able to do this.

But somehow the words wouldn't come.

So he walked out the door.

Chapter Twenty

Olivia fell into an exhausted sleep shortly after Max left. Miraculously, she slept well, but when she woke up the next morning, all she could think about was that frozen, devastated, empty look on his face before he'd walked out the door. And then she hated herself for breaking up with Max. No, she hated herself for falling in love with Max in the first place. She should have headed this off at the pass months ago—she knew this would never work! Why did she even let herself, and him, think it might?

Had she done the right thing? Had Max been right, that she should have thought this through more, that she shouldn't have given up on them? But no, she'd thought about it for that hour between when she got home and Max showed up. She'd thought about how different they were, and how she'd have to keep conforming to him if she stayed with him. She thought about how determined she'd been at the beginning to not get in too deep, to not get too attached, because if she did, she knew bad things would happen. She should have trusted her instincts.

She loved him so damn much. She never should have let herself get to this place. What a nightmare love was.

She stumbled into the kitchen to make coffee, and as she did, her doorbell rang. Hope rose in her heart—it was Max, he'd come back, he had a solution for everything, he'd figured out a way for them to work after all.

She raced to the door, without bothering to put on a bra or do anything to her hair. But when she stopped to look through the peephole, her heart dropped. It wasn't Max at all, just some sort of deliveryman. Probably with those shoes, or purse, or dress she'd ordered the week before in her fit of missing Max. She watched through the peephole until the deliveryman put down whatever he was holding and drove away. But when she cracked open the door to grab her package, it wasn't the box she'd expected. It was a bakery bag.

She sighed and brought the bag into the kitchen.

"I love you" the cake read, in blue letters on top of the chocolate frosting.

Yeah, she knew. She didn't doubt his love for her, that wasn't what this was all about—hadn't he listened at all to what she'd said? She shut the box and took her coffee back to bed.

Three more cakes arrived over the next two days. She stacked them all on her kitchen counter, untouched. She should drop them off at the food pantry, but that would mean she'd have to answer some difficult questions from Jamila, and she'd spent all weekend ignoring her texts. Instead she'd watched marathons of the *Real Housewives* of New York City, Atlanta, *and* Orange County. Strangely, these women and their awful relationships all made her feel better about her own choices. That was, until she was in bed in the middle of the night, without Max next to her, without his love and affection and desire for her. He'd loved her, wholly, completely, in a way no one had ever loved her before. And never would again, she was sure of that. How could she have let that go?

She probably should have told him long ago how hard all this was on her. But for so many years, she'd learned how to suck it up, pretend to the world everything was fine, even when she was miserable inside. A lot of times, she even pretended that to herself. She didn't blame Max for not knowing what a hard time she'd had with everything. But she knew she couldn't go back to the way it had been.

Sunday night she couldn't sleep. None of her regular tricks—hot bath, soothing book, warm boozy drink—worked. Finally, she turned on a documentary, and the soothing voices talking about an old sports scandal lulled her to sleep, at least for a few hours. But she woke up at four with that look on Max's face in her head, and she knew she'd never get back to sleep.

At five a.m. Monday, she went to the gym for a spin class. She thought it would make her feel better, but instead she cried the entire time. Thank God she also sweat so much no one had seemed to notice.

She showered at the gym and threw her work clothes on there. At least she didn't have any meetings that day and could hunker down in the office and get work done and not talk to a soul.

She shut off her feelings and worked steadily for almost two hours—she finished a brief, she replied to dozens of emails, she went through a pile of documents for discovery prep, and was deep into the PowerPoint for their next pitch when Ellie knocked on her door.

"I was wondering why the light was on in your office. What in the Lord's name are you doing here?" Ellie asked. "It's barely eight a.m. I'm trying to remember if I've ever seen you at this hour in my life."

Olivia shrugged. She really wasn't in the mood to get into everything with Ellie right now. Hopefully, she could play this all off— the makeup she'd thrown on when she got to the office after the gym should mask any of the lingering signs of her tears, and she'd learned from her many years working for terrible bosses how to pretend she was okay at work.

"I couldn't sleep. I was worrying about all of this stuff, so I decided to just come in and dive into it." She made herself laugh. "It's made me realize you've been right all of these years about getting into the office early—it's great to be able to dive into work without any of the distractions that are there in the late afternoon, operating on adrenaline and a huge cup of coffee instead of a sugar high and then low from my three p.m. snack."

Ellie narrowed her eyes and came farther into her office.

"This feels like one of those things where in six months I'll look back on it and say, 'I should have known my best friend had been kidnapped and a robot had replaced her that time she showed up at the office before eight a.m. and told me how great it was to get up early.'" She came around the desk and touched Olivia's forehead. "You seem like a real person, but I'm not convinced. What was the name of that shot that made you so sick that one night in law school? And don't ask me which night!"

Olivia forced herself to grin. She would joke around with Ellie about this, and Ellie would go back to her office, and she wouldn't have to talk about anything hard.

"The Three Wise Men: Jack, Jim, and Jose. The most disgusting thing I've ever put in my body; my body clearly agreed, because it revolted against it very quickly afterward. That was the fault of our damn friends, but I mostly blame Nathan. Satisfied that I'm who I say I am?"

Ellie pursed her lips.

"I'm still not convinced. A robot could probably come up with that one; that's probably the shot that's made a lot of people that sick." She looked around the room, and her eye landed on Olivia's gym bag in the corner.

Oh shit. It was all over now.

"Olivia. What's that?"

No, no, she wasn't going to concede defeat just yet.

"Just my gym bag. I went to the gym this morning but I didn't want to put my makeup on in the crowded mirror there, so I waited until I got here. Though, the lighting situation in the bathroom here leaves a lot to be—"

Ellie closed the door. Then she sat down in the chair across from Olivia.

"Okay. Spill it. What did he do?"

Olivia looked in her eyes for a few seconds, and it all fell apart.

"He didn't . . . he did something, but it wasn't . . . but it made me realize we . . ." She swallowed. "I broke up with him. Friday night. I'm a wreck, El."

It felt real, to say it out loud to Ellie. She hadn't wanted it to feel real.

"Oh, honey." Ellie jumped out of her chair and

pulled Olivia into a hug. "Do you not want to talk about it? Is that why you didn't tell me before? I'm sorry for quizzing you—I was mostly just joking until you said you went to the gym in the *morning*. Then I knew something was up. But if you want to just keep your head down and get work done today, I understand; I've been there."

Olivia shook her head. Now that she'd said part of it, she had to get it all out.

"It all started because of that community center event I went to with him on Friday night. Thanks for your text about that; I'm glad I looked good in the pictures, at least." She took the tissue Ellie handed her, and then let the whole story spill out. "I never thought this could work between us—I guess I was right."

She took a deep breath.

"But worst of all, I let it affect our firm. I'm so sorry about that. All of those news stories brought our firm up, too; I hate that all of these people know things about me I never wanted them to know, and I've probably destroyed my career because of a man, but I'll never forgive myself if I've destroyed yours, too. I was so afraid our firm would fail because I didn't work hard enough or people didn't have enough faith in us, but I never thought it might happen because I got myself in an ill-advised relationship."

Ellie dropped the tissue box back on the desk.

"Olivia. What in God's name are you talking

about? *If* anything happens and our firm doesn't survive, we'll manage. I'll get another job, and so will you. We are both fantastic lawyers, with successful careers, and one stint at a law firm that didn't make it won't do a damn thing to either of us. Neither, by the way, will a few news stories about you getting arrested over twenty years ago—do you know how many lawyers we both know who have multiple DUIs and are still partners at law firms? But none of this is an issue, because our law firm is not going to fail! And it's certainly not going to fail because of anything that happened in your relationship!"

Olivia looked down at her lap so she wouldn't have to meet Ellie's eyes.

"Okay, but what if it does? I will have let you down, and myself down."

Ellie banged her fist on the desk, and Olivia looked up in surprise.

"Pardon my language, but that's bullshit. You haven't let anyone down. You've worked your ass off for us. As a matter of fact, you're the one who decided to take the Clementine case when I know we both wanted to tell those jerks we didn't need their business. And we didn't! We have plenty of work! Our firm is doing great! We've already surpassed some of our end-of-the-year goals, and it's only August."

Olivia wiped her eyes again.

"I know. But—"

Ellie shook her head.

"No buts! Our business is thriving, but even if it wasn't, the most important thing is us. Our firm is not the important thing here, our firm is not a person. You and I are what matter. Olivia and Ellie are more important than Monroe and Spencer any day. Never forget that, okay?"

Olivia closed her eyes for a second, and took a deep breath.

"You're right. I did forget that, for a . . . while. I'm just not used to prioritizing Olivia over Olivia's work product."

Ellie pulled her out of the chair and into another hug.

"I know. But you've got to do it. Because I want to be working with you for a long damn time, and that's not going to happen if you turn your own damn self into a robot."

Olivia held on tight to her friend.

"I'll try," she said in a small voice. "Ellie, I love him so much."

Ellie squeezed her hard.

"I know you do. Damn that man." She pulled back and dabbed at Olivia's face with one tissue, and her own with another.

Olivia took the tissue from her.

"I'm sorry about all of the crying."

She hadn't cried at work—at least where anyone could see her—since her third year as an associate, when a terrible partner had yelled at her. Other terrible partners had yelled at her after that, of course, but she'd never let them see her cry again.

"Like I say to Sophia, it's okay to feel your feelings," Ellie said.

Olivia made herself laugh.

"I felt enough feelings this weekend to do me for the rest of the year, thanks. Actually, no, for the rest of the decade. I'd like to stop feeling any feelings for a while."

Ellie gave her one more hug.

"Oh, honey. I've been there." She stood up. "Now, this is what I'm going to do—I'm going to go to that bakery on the corner and get two of the most delicious-looking pastries they have, and make you choose which one you want, even though I know you're going to hem and haw and in the end I'm going to cut them in half so we can each have both. And I'm going to get you another coffee, because I bet that one sitting in front of you is cold by now. And then I'm going to book us a spa day this Saturday, and neither work nor my husband nor my child will keep us away from it. And then I'm going to check on you every few hours and see if you need me until you yell at me and tell me to stop. Does that sound good?"

Ellie opened Olivia's door and disappeared without waiting for an answer. Olivia hoped Ellie didn't come back with the pastries in one of those bakery boxes like all of those cakes had come in.

She took a deep breath and pulled out her phone.

Max. Please stop sending the cakes.

There. That was done.
She put her head down on her desk and sobbed.

The last week of recess, home in L.A. by himself, without Olivia, was one of the most difficult weeks of Max's life. He'd pretended to his staff that he was fine, great, thrilled with the town halls, in love with the great state of California, so happy he'd gotten to meet so many of his constituents, having fun at all of the fundraisers! But he felt like he was carrying a heavy, ice-cold weight on his shoulders the whole week.

Every room in his house made him think of her. The kitchen, where they'd eaten pie straight out of the dish and laughed the whole time. The living room, where they'd spent hours working at opposite ends of the couch with comic book movies (his choice) or Bravo (her choice) on the TV in the background. The backyard, where she'd dragged him outside to look at the full moon on clear nights. And good God, the bedroom. He couldn't sleep there anymore; after that first awful night, he crashed in the guest bedroom—the only room in the house that didn't have memories of her. Especially over the past month, when they'd spent so much time at his house together because he hadn't wanted to lead the press to her place—something he'd stupidly forgotten that night he went over to her house. That night she'd broken his heart.

All of a sudden he had so much sympathy for every one of his friends who had ever gone through this kind of heartbreak, and felt like an asshole for whatever he'd said to them at the time. Like "cheer up" or "get back out there" or "she didn't deserve you!" He definitely remembered saying at least that last one. If anyone said that to him right now, he'd want to punch them in the jaw. Olivia deserved far more than him. He didn't deserve her. God, he loved her so much. Why wasn't that enough?

He wasn't supposed to be back in DC until Sunday night, but he changed his ticket to go back on Saturday instead. He couldn't take one more night in that house, in that city, with Olivia right there and not there with him, especially after that text she'd sent him. He'd thought the cakes would be a sweet callback to how she'd first agreed to go out with him, and would make her realize all the good times they shared, and that she couldn't throw it all away. Apparently not.

He let himself into the DC apartment and sighed in relief. He was so happy to be in this generic, boring apartment, a place Olivia had never been.

He dropped his suitcase on the floor of his bed-room and went back out into the kitchen to see if either he or Wes had left beer in the fridge before they left for recess. At least luck was with him today—there was an entire six-pack. It was alone in the fridge with a bottle of sparkling water, a jar of pickles, and three different kinds of mustard.

Just as he opened the bottle, the apartment door opened and Wes walked in.

"Max! What are you doing here?"

Shit. He'd been really looking forward to this night alone, before he had to pull himself together and talk to people in this damn city again.

"I could ask you the same question," Max said. "I assumed you wouldn't be back until tomorrow night."

Wes shook his head and came into the kitchen.

"Give me one of those, will you?" Max pulled the cap off a second beer bottle and handed it to his friend. "No, I got back late last night—they booked me on one of the Sunday morning shows, so I came back early to prep. And so I wouldn't be so fucking exhausted first thing tomorrow morning."

"Congratulations," Max said. Getting booked on a Sunday morning news show was a big coup, especially for a freshman House member. But God, did he wish he had the apartment to himself tonight.

"What are you doing back so early? I thought

388

you'd spend every moment you could in California with your girl. Or did she come back with you?" Wes looked in the direction of Max's bedroom with a smirk on his face. Max probably would have thought that was funny before.

"She broke up with me."

God, did it suck to say it out loud.

"What?" Wes dropped his beer on the counter, and it tipped on its side and spilled everywhere. "Shit, wait." He grabbed a dish towel out of the drawer and mopped up the mess as he stared up at Max. "Are you serious? Are you okay?" Wes looked at Max and answered his own question. "No, you're definitely not okay."

Max took a swig of his beer and sat down on the couch.

"No. I'm definitely not okay." He held up his hand. "I haven't . . . I haven't told anyone else, so if you could keep this between us for the time being?"

Wes took what was left of his beer into the living room to join Max.

"You mean, I shouldn't let it slip while I'm on CNN tomorrow?" He glanced over at Max with a grin on his face, and Max just glared at him. Wes held up a hand.

"Right, sorry, I'm being an asshole, aren't I? You're not at the 'let's joke about this' stage yet. Tell me what happened."

He didn't want to tell him. He didn't want to

even think about that day. Even though he'd done nothing but think about it for the past week. But before he realized it, he was telling Wes the whole story.

"And please don't tell me I shouldn't have called on her in front of the world, I know that, trust me, I know that. If I could only go back to that moment, if I could just take that back, everything would be different. Because that's the thing that made her break up with me, that was her last straw." He told Wes about rushing to her house, and then their fight, and then the moment when he'd—just for a second—thought she'd forgiven him. "She said she loves me, but we're too different, I'm too impulsive and public, and she's too measured and thoughtful and private—she didn't use those words, but that's what she meant—and we'll never be happy together."

He sank back into the couch cushions and drank his beer. There. At least that was over. Maybe now that he told someone about it, he'd feel better.

He doubted that, but it was worth a try.

"And then what did you say?" Wes asked him.

Max just stared at his friend.

"I didn't say anything," he said after a long moment. "She told me I'd better go, so I left."

He didn't want to think about that moment he'd left Olivia's house ever again. Or that nightmare of a drive home.

"Have you reached out to her since then?"

Max shrugged.

"I sent her cakes. That first weekend after. With messages on top. I thought . . . But I was wrong. She texted me and told me to stop."

Wes started to laugh, then looked at Max and stopped.

"How . . . how many cakes did you send her?"

Max pushed his fingers through his hair.

"Four or five, I don't remember now. Does it matter? It didn't work."

Wes folded his hands together.

"Well? What are you going to do next? Nothing? Are you just going to give up?"

Max slammed his empty beer bottle down on the coffee table.

"I don't know! I don't know what to do here! She doesn't want anything to do with me, what the fuck am I supposed to do?"

Wes was silent for a moment.

"Do you agree with her that the two of you could never be happy together?" he asked.

Max threw his hands in the air.

"No! I was happier with her than I'd been in years. I might have been happier with her than I've ever been! I wanted to spend the rest of my life with her! I know she had hesitations because of my job, and the media, and the storm she's been through, but I tried to support her through that, I thought I supported her through that. I wish she'd told me that she needed more from me; I would have given it. I know I fucked up, but good God, I'm miserable without her."

God, he sounded so pathetic. But to be fair, he felt as pathetic as he sounded.

Wes nodded.

"Okay, but I asked you if the two of you could be happy together. You just told me about you and your happiness. Can Olivia be happy? With you?"

Fuck.

"Did I really . . ." Max dropped his head in his hands. "Of course I did. I'm a selfish jerk, that's why she broke up with me in the first place, isn't it?"

Wes smacked his shoulder after a few moments and Max looked up.

"Okay, enough wallowing. How are you going to try to get her back?" Wes asked.

Max knocked his beer bottle onto the floor.

"If I knew that, don't you think I would have done it already?" he yelled. Then he looked at the bottle, aghast.

"I can't believe I'm throwing things. I'm an asshole, what's wrong with me?"

Wes picked up his phone.

"I'm ordering some food. Like my momma always says, you can't have important conversations on an empty stomach. This is why toddlers have so many tantrums; they get hungry and lose it. You probably haven't eaten all day, have you?" Wes looked him over. "Actually, from the looks of you, you probably haven't eaten all week."

Max tried to remember the last time he'd eaten.

"I think there were crackers on the airplane. And yesterday I had a few Girl Scout Cookies for dinner; there were some Thin Mints left in my freezer."

Wes clicked a few buttons on his phone, then went to the kitchen and tossed Max a bag of potato chips.

"First of all, pizza is on its way. Second, eat those. Third, drink this." He put a glass of water in front of Max. "After all of that, we can talk. Chips are the wrong thing, you need an apple, or some vegetables, but it's all we've got, so make the best of it."

Max didn't want the water, or the chips, but he knew that look on Wes's face all too well. He opened the bag and stuffed a handful of chips in his mouth. After that, and a few sips of water, he turned to his friend.

"Thanks. And . . . Wes, I don't know what to do. I'm usually good at countering any argument, you know I am. But I don't know how to deal with this one. You're right, I need to figure out how to make her happy; I want to make her happy, more than anything. I told her I loved her, I told her I was sorry, I told her I miss her, but that was the wrong thing, and I don't know what the right thing is. I feel like I'm letting my chance at the woman I love slip away, but I'm frozen."

Wes tipped the bag of chips toward him and took one, then pushed it back to Max.

"Eat more of those. Now, do you know why those were the wrong things to say?"

Max ate another handful of chips.

"I feel like I'm back in law school and got called on and didn't do the reading. No, of course I don't know why! If I knew why, don't you think I would have said something else?"

Wes took a sip of his beer and relaxed against the couch cushions.

"Yes, I do think that, asshole. The point is you gotta figure it out."

There was silence in the room for a while as Max finished the bag of chips and took two more sips of water. Then he took a long, deep breath.

"Because those things are about me. Not about her, or how she's feeling, or the problems she brought up, or how we can resolve them."

Wes gave him a smug smile that Max was sure his political opponents hated.

"See, I knew all you needed was a snack."

Max would get furious at Wes's treating him like a damn toddler, but he knew he deserved it. Plus . . . maybe he had needed a snack.

"That's exactly right," Wes continued. "In order to get her back, you need to tell her how you're going to fix this, how the two of you can fix this together." He looked at Max for a long moment. "Do you think you can? Fix this, I mean?"

Max closed his eyes.

"I don't know. Maybe she's decided there's nothing I can do, maybe she wants nothing to do with me or politics or anyone who has ever had their name in the paper, but I've got to try. I've got to see if there's a way around or through this for us." He winced. "Why didn't I realize that before? Am I that self-centered?" He looked at Wes. "Please don't answer that."

Wes patted him on the shoulder.

"It's not important how long you took to get to the party, what's important is that you got here at all. And if I can give you some advice . . ."

" 'If,' he says, like there's any way I could stop him from doing it," Max said to his water glass.

Wes kept talking like he'd heard nothing.

"Take your time with this. She doesn't like snap decisions; be thoughtful on this one, as much as it kills you."

Max grinned.

"Speaking of, I think I forgot to tell you I almost proposed to her on the spur of the moment when we went to Hawaii. Scratch that—I *would* have proposed to her, but she stopped me."

Wes turned to face Max, his mouth wide open.

"Yeah," Max said. "So. You're probably right about taking my time with this."

A few minutes later, the buzzer rang.

"And there's our food," Wes said. "I'm warning you, I got a salad and I'm going to make you eat at least ten bites of it before you have any pizza."

Max ignored that. He'd just remembered something Olivia said a long time ago. He might have an idea of how to do this.

But he still had to figure out what to say to make her realize how serious he was about her, about them. And the biggest question was, would she be willing to give this another try, despite everything?

God, he hoped so.

Chapter Twenty-One

※

In the two and a half weeks since she'd broken up with Max, Olivia had tried to be angry. It was always easier to get over something—or someone—when you were angry at them. Pure, righteous anger, that's what she needed. She thought of that moment when he'd looked at her across the auditorium with that patented charming smile, to try to get her to talk publicly about her arrest, and she hoped she'd feel that wave of fury she did at the time. But instead, all she could feel was sorrow.

How had she let herself fall in love with Max in the first place? He'd been determined to date her from the very beginning, but she'd known they wouldn't work—she should have listened to herself. And now she just missed him so damn much.

Just to get it over with, she'd sent Alexa and Jamila identical text messages on that Monday afterward: "Max and I broke up, I don't want to talk about it." Jamila had obeyed her command and hadn't asked her a single question about it, and so had Alexa . . . for the first few days. After that, she'd somehow gotten Olivia to spill the whole story to her. She was fiercely on Olivia's side, but also kept beating the whole "don't give up on love" drum, which Olivia ignored.

She decided to go back to the New York version of Olivia, without all these damn ups and downs. Yes, fine, the ups had been incredible, but the downs weren't worth it. Some combination of dating Max and moving back to California had made her emotions so heightened, and she was sick of it. She tried to put Max out of her mind, to go to the gym and work and home and the gym again and get up and do it all over again. And, for the love of God, to stop feeling her damn feelings.

She still thought about Max constantly, but keeping busy helped. Those first few nights she cried herself to sleep, but after a while she didn't even have the energy to do that.

And then one night at the gym, as she flipped channels to find something to watch while she ran on the treadmill, she accidentally turned it to MSNBC. And there was Max. A surge of happiness went through her as she heard his voice. It felt like an automatic, instinctual reaction; apparently her body hadn't caught up to her brain. She'd been so used to being happy when she saw him, it was hard to remember she was supposed to be sad now. She stared hungrily at the tiny screen. She stopped flipping, turned off the treadmill, and just stood there watching him. She'd missed him so much. When his segment ended and they cut to commercial, she realized tears were streaming down her face.

After that night, she watched the news every single night to see if she could get a glimpse of him. God bless cable TV bookers who were so susceptible to perfect hair and charming grins—he was on at least two weeknights out of five. He always had something smart to say, and seemed like he was always in a great mood . . . though was it just her imagination he'd lost weight? It probably was. Maybe he'd already found someone else. Someone who lived in DC and could be around all week with him and didn't have a job that got in the way and who liked impulsive romantic gestures and would beam and wave at the press like she'd been doing it her whole life.

The depression that hit when she thought of whom Max would date next didn't stop her from watching him whatever chance she got. Ellie had told her to feel her feelings, well, now she would feel them all! She'd probably never see him again in real life, so if she needed to watch him on TV for a few weeks or months to help herself get over him, that's just what she was going to do.

One night, he was on along with another senator to talk about climate change, and the topic got heated very quickly, as climate change conversations often did. Oh hell, who was she kidding, as every kind of political conversation did these days. Finally, the other guy shouted at Max, "Senator, if you care so much about the environment, what are YOU doing about it? If you think all of this helps so much, you should pledge right now that you and your entire staff will walk to work, and you'll all go vegan. If you're asking all of us to make changes, shouldn't you make all of these changes yourself?"

Max's eyes narrowed and his cheeks got pink, even under all the TV makeup. She was still charmed that he blushed when he got excited or heated about something, damn her. But she cringed as soon as he opened his mouth—she knew Max was mad enough to spit out an immediate agreement on behalf of himself and his entire staff; that's just how he was. She'd seen him do things like this on TV before.

"As a matter of fact, I . . ."

But then Max did something that surprised her. He stopped himself and took a breath. Then he started over again.

"I think you're trying to distract from the point, Senator. My point has always been that it's not individual personal choices that matter, it's about the need to regulate corporations and get them to commit to reducing their carbon impact. Corporations are responsible for the vast majority of global emissions—not individuals. This isn't to say I encourage irresponsible use of our natural resources; as a matter of fact, I do walk to work every day while I'm here in Washington, DC. But we have to attack this problem from the source; unfortunately there's no amount of plastic a family can give up, or straws we can stop using, that will make a significant difference to climate change—this is a structural problem, and we need to solve it with structural solutions."

Olivia paused the TV and sat back on the couch. Not only was that a fantastic answer, but Max had behaved in a very un-Max-like way. She'd seen it in his eyes; he'd almost made the rash, quick decision that would impact not only him but every member of his staff. But he'd pulled himself back from the ledge, and thought about it, and had done something a whole lot smarter.

Had he paid attention to what she'd said that night? And had he really listened and made a change? Or was she being irrational and taking this personally when it had nothing to do with her?

Just then, her doorbell rang. She stood up automatically to go get her delivery. It was only when her hand was on the doorknob she realized she hadn't ordered delivery.

Who the hell could be knocking at her door?

Her heart jumped. Could it be Max? Maybe he'd come back to say how much she mattered to him. How much he wanted her back. How he'd do anything.

She stood on her tiptoes and looked through the peephole. Jamila, not Max. Of course, not Max. He was in DC, remember? On TV? Granted, she'd recorded the show, it had been filmed hours before, but that wasn't enough time for him to get from DC to L.A.

She took a step back and opened the door.

"I was wondering if you were going to let me in," Jamila said. She strode past Olivia into the house.

"Oh, I didn't . . . did we have plans?" Jamila had a bag of food in her hand and walked straight toward the kitchen with a determined look. Maybe she'd texted Olivia about dinner and Olivia had texted back without remembering it? That was unlike her, but the past few weeks had been unlike her, too.

Jamila set the bag down on the counter and took a bunch of food cartons out of it.

"Sure, we had plans. If by 'plans' you mean you haven't shown up for the Wednesday volunteer night in three weeks, and that I haven't heard from you since I walked you to your car when you ran out of the community center except for that curt text that you and Max broke up, and you've ignored all of my texts, and I was worried about you. That's definitely what 'plans' mean to me—that's also what friends mean to me, by the way—but you might have a different definition."

Olivia felt guilty and touched, all at once. She hadn't wanted to show up to the food pantry, because everyone there had met Max, and they all knew the two of them were dating, and she didn't want to deal with their kindness right now. She knew it would take only one question and she'd throw herself into the arms of one of the sympathetic older ladies there and sob for hours. So she just hadn't shown up. But she should have texted Jamila to say she couldn't come. And it made her weirdly happy Jamila had worried about her like this.

"I'm sorry. I'm not doing . . . great about all of this, and I didn't want to have to answer questions about Max or listen to people talking about him or wonder if anyone was talking about me . . . I couldn't deal with any of that. So I just stayed away." She put her hand on Jamila's shoulder. "But I'm really sorry for ignoring you these past few weeks. Thanks for being a friend. I appreciate it. I really don't know what I would have done without you that night. Or for these past six months, really."

The stern look on Jamila's face softened. She took plates down from the cabinet and scooped food onto both of them. Olivia just stood back and let her do it.

"Okay. And me, too. No one was talking about you, and no one knew," she said, "but I understand how you felt. Do you want to talk about what happened? And how you're doing? Or do you want to watch *Housewives*?"

Ooh. Thai food and *Housewives* seemed like a much better idea for a Wednesday night than MSNBC and the crackers from the back of her cabinet.

"That second thing, please. I'll get the drinks."

A few minutes later, she followed Jamila into the living room, holding their glasses in each hand. It wasn't until she saw Jamila stop cold as soon as she walked into the room that Olivia remembered what was paused on the TV.

Jamila looked from Max's face, frozen on the screen, to Olivia, and back.

"Okay, change of plans. When you said you weren't doing great, I thought maybe you meant you were 'doing too much online shopping' not great. I didn't realize you were 'watching your ex-boyfriend on TV just so you could get a glimpse of him' not great! I assumed you were far too together for that!"

Olivia sat down on the couch.

"Yeah. I'm good at seeming together. But I . . . we . . ." She sighed. "I broke up with him, but I still love him so much, and I don't know how to handle it. So yes, I've been watching him on TV to get a glimpse of him. But he just now did something that really confused me, and I still don't know what to think about it."

Jamila sat down next to her and handed her a plate.

"Just now as in he called you, or as in TV Max did something?"

Olivia picked up a spring roll and dipped it in peanut sauce.

"TV Max, but—so one of the reasons we broke up was because he would always jump into things without thinking about what would happen, or about how other people would react. You saw that, a little bit, at the community center."

Jamila nodded.

"Right," Olivia said. "Well . . . okay, I'm going to show this to you."

Olivia rewound the clip and pressed play. Afterward, she pressed pause again.

"Well, he looks like hell, if that's what your point was," Jamila said. "Thin and miserable, and even his always perfect hair is all wrong. He's missing you. Bad."

"Really, you think so?" Olivia asked. She looked at the TV again. His hair really was all wrong; way too long, far too much gel. She shook her head. "No, that wasn't my point, and while that's nice of you to say, that's not what I was asking for."

Jamila shrugged.

"Whether you were asking for it or not, it's true. That's a depressed man trying to pretend

405

he's fine if I've ever seen one, and I've seen lots of them."

Olivia bit her lip. Was Jamila just saying that? She sounded serious, but she could just be trying to make Olivia feel better. And was it true?

"Okay, we can talk about that later. And maybe I'm making too much of this. But I was absolutely certain he'd yell back at that jerk that yes, he would walk to work, and he would become a vegan, and so would his whole staff. Because that's how Max is—he talks first, and thinks afterward, or not at all. And it's worked out for him for the most part, so he's never thought he needed to change things. But this time, he didn't do that."

Jamila waved a chicken satay skewer at her.

"You got to him. He's trying to win you back, by coded messages on MSNBC."

Olivia laughed out loud.

"Okay, when you put it like that, I sound ridiculous."

Jamila picked up her fork and pulled the chicken off the skewer.

"I'm not kidding! He was also wearing that same tie he wore when he came to the food pantry."

Olivia put her fork down.

"Are you sure?"

"Oh, he definitely was," Jamila said. "I'm sorry if it sounds creepy that I remember that, but I always remember clothes. It's a message to you, I tell you. That man loves the hell out of you, Olivia."

It felt great to hear that, and it hurt so much, all at the same time.

"Maybe he did. But he'll be better off with someone who can be a political wife in the way I can't be. Who is friendly to reporters and can wave and smile all the time and looks perfect at a moment's notice and doesn't have anything scandalous in her background, or any radical opinions people can get mad about."

Jamila tossed a pillow at her.

"Or maybe he'd be better off with you than with that imaginary boring-ass person. And maybe you'd be better off with him than with whatever dull, perfect guy you could conjure, one exactly like you in all ways and therefore will bore you to tears. I'm not saying the two of you didn't have real problems—what relationship doesn't? And I'm definitely not saying he didn't deserve everything you threw at him—he sure as hell did. But I am saying he is absolutely so in love with you that he'd try to show you and everyone who knows you he's trying to become a better man, just for you."

Olivia thought about that for a second, then flicked the TV off.

"That's what my sister says, too."

Alexa had been trying to get her to give Max

another chance, with some bullshit about how she couldn't give up on love at the first sign of adversity, and that she was clearly miserable without him, and that sometimes relation-ships took hard work, and no, their fight wasn't a sign that she never should have dated him in the first place. First of all, yes it was a sign, and secondly, how did her sister know her so well?

"And that's nice and all, but unless he says any of that to me, it doesn't really matter, now does it? I haven't heard from him since I told him to stop sending those cakes. Granted, I'm not sure if any of it would matter at all—I still think we're too different, no matter how much we both love each other. Maybe if we'd met when we were in our twenties, we'd be able to figure all of this out together, but as it is, we're just both too old, too set in our own ways to change for other people. And when you add his job to all of that . . . it seems impossible."

Jamila took a bite of Olivia's favorite spicy curry and her eyes widened. She jammed her fork into the pile of rice on her plate.

"I'm just saying, don't be too definite about that, okay? And please stop acting like you're some old crone, too old to change—you just moved across the country this year! You're not all that set in your ways!"

Olivia tossed the remote to Jamila.

"And I started watching a show I've scorned for years, and now I'm addicted to it. Find it for us, please."

Jamila apparently got the message that Olivia was done talking about Max, because she scrolled through the channels and found *Housewives* for them without another word.

When the episode was over, Jamila got up.

"I should go home, I have an early day tomorrow." She raised an eyebrow at Olivia. "That is, unless you need me? I can stay if you want to talk, but I wasn't sure if you wanted that."

Olivia shook her head.

"No, you go home. But . . . I might take a rain check on that? Thanks for dinner. And for coming over."

Jamila grinned at her.

"You're welcome. And you can have that rain check anytime."

After Jamila left and Olivia had put the leftovers away, she got back on the couch and pulled her phone out of her pocket to check her email.

Draft contract was the subject line of the email that popped up. Olivia went to click on it, but stopped, confused. What contract? Was this some sort of spam?

Then she looked closer, and froze. After a few seconds, she opened the email.

I thought about what you said. I thought about it a lot. First, I owe you a huge apology—you're right that I was using you and our relationship to try to make that crowd like me. That sucked. I didn't do it consciously, but I did it. I'm angry at myself for that, and so, so sorry I did that to you. I hope you believe I will never do anything like that again. Second, you're right that we're very different, and you're right that if we go on like this, it won't work. But I love you too much to give up on us. I think—I hope—that I can make you happy; I know you can make me happy. And the great thing is, we can make our own rules for our relationship, and we can figure this thing out together, if we want to. And I really want to. And I really, really hope you do, too. So I thought I'd start. Let me know what you think; you know how to reach me. I miss you.
Love,
Max

That all sounded good—sounded great, even—but she was scared to believe it. Scared to open herself back up again. Scared to get hurt again. She let her finger hover over the attachment.
Then she closed out of her email, dropped her

phone and hid it in the couch cushions, and went to bed. No. She couldn't do this again.

Max sat at his big, beautiful, shiny desk in his Washington office and stared at his computer. Emails kept coming in, hundreds every minute, it seemed like, but none of them was the one he was looking for.

He'd sent that email to Olivia Wednesday night, after working on it, and the silly, but—he hoped she knew—very earnest attachment, for over a week. He'd thought the best way to show her how serious he was about this wasn't just an apology—he'd already apologized, and anyone could say they were sorry and keep doing it over and over—but was something concrete. What could be more concrete to a lawyer than a contract?

But it was now Friday morning and he hadn't heard from her. Of course, he'd wanted an immediate response and a "come over this weekend so we can sign it together and then stay in bed all damn weekend," but a simple "I love you and miss you, too," would have been an excellent start. Honestly, at this point, he'd be happy for a "thanks, looking this over now," or something equally cold. But he reminded himself again, as he'd done once every ten minutes for the past two days, that Olivia needed more time than that.

Had he overstepped by sending her that email? Should he have tried to talk to her in person instead? But he didn't want to show up on her doorstep again, or at her office. Those both felt like shitty things to do to her, even if she did want to see him again, which was questionable now. Maybe always had been.

He was staying in Washington all weekend, for the first time all year. Sure, partly it was because he was booked on one of the Sunday morning shows, so it didn't make sense for him to fly to California on Friday and back here on Saturday. But if he'd still been with Olivia, that wouldn't have stopped him. He'd hoped, after he sent that email, he'd have a reason to fly back to California this weekend.

He sighed and spun around to look out the window. Apparently not.

At some point, he was probably going to have to tell his staff they'd broken up. He was pretty sure Kara suspected; partly because he'd never doubt her ability to see through him again after how quickly she'd realized he was dating someone, and partly because she'd asked about Olivia twice that first week back and not again. He hated that his staff had to know anything about his relationship failures, but that was his fucking life as a senator, wasn't it? He'd probably tell Kara at some point and have her spread the word, but that didn't feel any less humiliating.

There was a knock on his door, and Kara poked her head in.

"Sir, your ten thirty appointment is here."

He glanced down at his calendar.

"It's blocked off in my calendar, but I thought this was an appointment with you—do I have any briefing papers for this?"

Kara grinned at him.

"I don't think you need them, sir."

She threw open the door, and in walked Olivia. She had on a dark gray suit, a blue blouse, and black high heels. She looked incredible. And, most of all, she was here.

Max stood up and gaped at her.

"Senator," she said, with a nod to him. "Kara, thank you."

Kara winked at Max and closed the door.

Max couldn't stop looking at Olivia. He just wanted to drink her in. Just being in her presence made him happy. He'd missed her so much.

"You're here," he said. And then he wanted to kick himself—why didn't he say something more articulate, more romantic? Something that made it clear to her how much he loved her, and how serious he was about working through this with her?

She walked toward him, but before he could move around his desk to pull her into his arms, she sat down in the chair across from his desk.

She reached into her briefcase and pulled out some papers.

"I got your initial contract, and I had some edits to it. I thought it made the most sense for us to talk in person." She looked down, and then up at him. "First, I have a question. Do you mean this? All of this?"

Hope rose in his chest. He wanted to jump up and come around the desk to embrace her, say he'd do anything to get her back. But he knew that was the wrong thing to say—he knew if he said that, she'd think he wasn't serious. So instead, he looked right into her eyes.

"Yes," he said. "I do."

She closed her eyes for a second and nodded.

"Okay," she said, and pushed a few sheets of paper across the table to him. It was his side of the draft agreement he'd sent to her, with her edits and additions.

I, Maxwell Stewart Powell III, agree to the following:

1. I will never put you on the spot in public.
2. I won't push you to go to events with me, I won't even suggest it, except for the very important ones; for those I'll give you as much warning as possible. And I will always make it clear you can say no.

You can suggest that I, Olivia Grace Monroe, come with you to any event you want to, but you should make it in the form of a question. And don't push me to say yes if I hesitate.

3.   You don't ever have to be a part of my job; our relationship is not a political move or talking point, and I will never publicly make reference to you without your prior knowledge and approval.

4.   I won't push you for last-minute plans, because I know you hate it; just because I live my life like this doesn't mean you need to as well. And I will give you plenty of time to make any decision. If you say no, I will stop trying to convince you.

You can suggest last-minute plans— your spontaneity is one of the reasons I fell in love with you, and I don't want to kill that part of you. Plus, sometimes they're excellent (e.g., Disneyland, Hawaii). I, in turn, will be more open, but I'll say no when I need to.

5.   I will stop and think whenever I'm either furious or very excited, and will try my best not to say the first thing that pops into my head.

6.   I will check in with my staff anytime we think their advice on dealing with the

media, etc., would be helpful so we'll know the smoothest path to take.

Or, so we can make an educated decision to take the harder path.

7. I will always order more than one dessert.

I will love you for the rest of my life.

I, Olivia Grace Monroe, agree to the following:

1. I will be open about my feelings to you when I'm anxious or scared or worried, even though that is hard for me. I understand that I don't have to fake it till I make it with you.

2. I will be open to talking to the press when you or your staff believes such a conversation will be helpful for your career, as long as I get significant assistance and prep in advance.

3. I will talk through my decisions with you, instead of just leaving you hanging for days or weeks or months—we are a team and I trust you to listen to me.

4. I will always support you in your pie-(or cake-?) making ventures.

5. I will attempt to learn how to relax and be more flexible—bear with me.

6. We will renegotiate this agreement

once a year every year in August, because I recognize that feelings and needs can change.

7.   I will love you for the rest of my life.

He fought back a grin at her edits and picked up a pen.

"I have just a few notes to make on your side of the contract," he said. He scribbled in the margins for a few moments, and then pushed the paper back over to her.

"Your thoughts?"

I, Olivia Grace Monroe, agree to the following:

1.   I will be open about my feelings to you when I'm anxious or scared or worried, even though that is hard for me. I understand that I don't have to fake it till I make it with you.

And I, Max, will always listen and pay attention.

2.   I will be open to talking to the press when you or your staff believes such a conversation will be helpful for your career, as long as I get significant assistance and prep in advance.

I will only take you up on this on very limited occasions, and will never push it.

3.   I will talk through my decisions with you, instead of just leaving you hanging for days or weeks or months—we are a team and I trust you to listen to me.

4.   I will always support you in your pie- (or cake-?) making ventures.

5.   I will attempt to learn how to relax and be more flexible—bear with me.

6.   We will renegotiate this agreement once a year every year in August, because I recognize that feelings and needs can change.

Some of my needs may change, but my feelings for you will not.

7.   I will love you for the rest of my life.

"I mean every single word. I swear," he said. "And if there's anything else you need, or want to add, please, please just tell me."

She looked down at the contract, then up at him. A smile spread across her face, and her eyes swam with tears.

"My feelings for you won't change, either, Max. I've missed you so much."

He practically jumped over his far-too-large desk and pulled her into his arms.

"I kept trying to think of living days and weeks and months without you, and it all seemed so empty and meaningless. I love you so much."

She looked up at him with so much joy and

laughter and love in her face that he almost couldn't believe it.

"I love you so much, too."

He kissed her like he'd never kissed her before, like he would be able to kiss her every day for the rest of his life.

Finally, he led her over to the couch, and they sat there, her head against his chest.

"I tried to get over you, but it was so hard." She let out a half sob, half laugh. "So much of this was my fault, too. I'm sorry I didn't tell you how hard all of that was for me so we could come up with a solution earlier."

He stroked her hair and kissed her again.

"I'm sorry it took me so long to figure out what to say. It took me two weeks and four conversations with Wes before I realized what I wanted to tell you, and then four days to write barely a hundred words that I hoped expressed some of what I thought and felt and wanted."

She lifted her head.

"I saw you on Maddow that night. When that guy tried to trap you into becoming vegan. I was sure you were going to do it, too."

He laughed. He couldn't believe she'd been watching that night.

"I was so mad, and I was so ready to take that asshole up on his dare, and then what you said about taking other people and their autonomy into account flashed into my mind, and I stopped myself." He grinned at her. "And the wild thing was, it made for a much better answer, and he had no idea how to respond to me. Thanks for that."

She gripped his fingers.

"I almost didn't even read what you wrote—I was so scared to hope that I wouldn't let myself read the attachment at first. When I finally did read it, I sat up all night thinking about it. I was going to email you back, but I wanted to see you, to really talk to you, first. I was going to wait until this weekend, but I texted Kara, to see what your schedule was like, and she said you were here all weekend. So I got on a red-eye last night and made it to DC first thing this morning."

Speaking of Kara . . .

Max jumped up off the couch and looked at his calendar. It was somehow, magically, empty.

"Kara cleared my schedule for the rest of the day." He pulled Olivia off the couch and handed her briefcase to her.

"Let's get out of here. We need to celebrate, and I know just the place."

Olivia held up her finger.

"Before we celebrate, I think we're forgetting something."

He laughed out loud and tossed her a pen.

"You're right, we are. Would you like to sign first?"

She grinned at him and bent over their agreement, and signed her name with a flourish at the bottom. He pulled out his favorite pen and signed right next to hers. They both looked at their names, side by side, and smiled at each other.

"There, signed and dated." He handed her their agreement, and she slid it into her briefcase. "Now, how would you feel about a slice of rich, decadent, luscious chocolate cake to celebrate?"

"How many layers?" she asked.

"Three," he said.

She grinned.

"Perfect."

Epilogue

They went back to Hawaii the next August during Max's recess. The year had been both hard as hell and better than Olivia could have ever imagined. They'd each had to push themselves—and sometimes each other—to follow their contract, but it got easier and easier each time. His job and hers had both had big ups and big downs, and then big ups again; they'd both traveled far too much; they'd seen each other not at all enough. But almost without fail, they saw each other at least once a week, unless there was some sort of emergency that got in their way—which had happened only three times, twice on Max's end and once on hers. One time she'd even surprised him and flown into DC for a night just to see him. She'd been to fundraisers and parties and town halls and concerts with him, and had actually found a number of them interesting, even fun—especially that time she'd managed to wangle an invitation for her sister and her husband, too. And she'd never, not for one second, doubted Max's love for her.

They went to the same hotel as the first time—

Olivia was less skittish about the press these days, but she drew the line at potential paparazzi shots on vacation—and ran down to the beach like fools again when they arrived. They spent the rest of the afternoon relaxing in a cabana, with pineapple drinks, and without their phones.

Midway through the afternoon, Max looked up from *The Economist*.

"What do you think about having dinner on the balcony of our room tonight, instead of down in the restaurant? I'm feeling lazy."

She looked up from her novel.

"That's an excellent idea. Plus, if we go down to dinner, someone might recognize you, and I want you all to myself."

Max picked up her hand and pressed a kiss on her palm.

"I want you all to myself, too."

Before dinner, Olivia showered and changed out of her swimsuit and cover-up, and into her favorite caftan. Aaah, this is why she loved Hawaii.

When she came out of the bathroom, the food was all set up on their oceanfront balcony.

"There you are," Max said as she walked out to join him. "Oh, by the way, since it's August, I thought we should take the opportunity to revisit this." He opened the folder sitting on the table, and there was their contract. They each had a copy, but this was the original.

"Oh." She supposed she couldn't argue with that; after all, the whole "we'll revisit every August" part had been on her list. "Yeah, that makes sense. I hadn't realized you brought this with you."

She was glad Max had thought about this. Though maybe it didn't have to be their first night in Hawaii?

"It felt wrong to do it with a copy," he said. "Let's get to it: is there anything you want to alter, or edit?"

She bit her lip and thought about it. She couldn't think of anything right now, but . . .

"Don't I get some time to consider that?"

Max laughed out loud.

"I should have expected that, shouldn't I?" He leaned over and kissed her. "Yes, of course you do. We'll be here all week, so you have plenty of time. It won't surprise you that I already know what my edits are."

She actually *was* kind of surprised by that. Did it mean something had been bothering Max for months and he hadn't wanted to bring it up until August? She hadn't intended to be quite so dogmatic about that. Maybe that's what her edit would be, that they'd discuss it every August, or at any other time if either party desired a reconsideration.

"Okay," she said. "What are your edits?"

Max took her hand.

"I want my last line to say, 'I will love you, and honor you, and cherish you, in sickness and in health, for as long as we both shall live.' Olivia. Will you marry me?"

So many tears streamed from her eyes she could barely see him.

He kissed her hand.

"And obviously, you get as much time as you need to give me an answer."

She swatted his hand away, and immediately grabbed it again.

"No!" She shook her head. "That's not—I mean, no, I don't need time, yes, yes, I'll marry you!"

He grabbed her and kissed her so hard she could barely breathe, but she didn't mind. They smiled at each other as they sat there together on a lounge chair. Olivia was so happy it hurt.

"I can't believe you and the fake-out with the contract! I thought you, I don't know, wanted flannel sheets in the winter or for me to stop waking you up late at night when I stay up too late or wanted me to move to DC or something."

Max laughed, and then reached into his pocket.

"None of those things, but speaking of sleep—thank goodness you're so hard to wake up in the morning; that way I got to measure your ring finger."

He snapped open the box and slid the ring on her finger.

"Oh thank God, it actually fits," he said.

He kissed her again, then disappeared back into their room.

"Hold on a second."

He came back out carrying a bottle of champagne in one hand and a cake box in the other.

"I was very nervous about getting the ring through security and to Hawaii without you seeing it, but I was almost as nervous about this."

Olivia saw the logo on the side of the cake box and smiled.

"You brought a cake all the way here?"

He carefully cut the tape on the box and nodded.

"Yes, which meant I had to pick it up yesterday, and keep it hidden from you the whole time I was packing, and remember to pack it, and . . . well, 'I'll bring a cake to Hawaii!' wasn't my best decision, I realize that now, but look!"

He flipped open the cake box to reveal . . . a chocolate cake, with blue smudges on top.

Max looked crestfallen.

"It was supposed to say 'Congratulations, Olivia and Max!' I guess it melted."

Olivia leaned over and kissed him.

"That's okay, it'll still be delicious. And even if it isn't, I love you even more than I love cake."

Max lifted the bottle of champagne in the air.

"I changed my mind: that whole ordeal with the cake was worth it, just to hear you say that."

They smiled at each other, and popped the champagne cork together.

Acknowledgments

✳

I somehow thought that writing and publishing would get easier after the first book. I was very wrong about that, but the incredible part is even though it gets harder and harder, it also becomes even more joyful and fulfilling. I'm so grateful for everyone who has helped me along this journey.

Holly Root, sometimes I imagine what it would be like to do this job without you as my agent, and shudder in horror. Thank you for everything you do, from the bottom of my heart. Cindy Hwang, I adore working with you; thank you for believing in me and guiding me. Team Berkley and Penguin Random House, I feel outrageously fortunate every day to have all of you in my corner. Thank you to Jessica Brock, Fareeda Bullert, Angela Kim, Craig Burke, Erin Galloway, Jin Yu, Megha Jain, Angelina Krahn, Vikki Chu, Jaci Updike, and Lauren Monaco for all of your hard work on behalf of me and my books.

I am full of gratitude toward other writers for their advice and counsel, and their friendship and companionship. Amy Spalding and Akilah Brown, thank you for your encouragement, edits, and enthusiasm. Ruby Lang, thank you for your constant wisdom. Kayla Cagan, thank you for coming up with this title. And eternal thanks to Jami Attenberg, Melissa Baumgart, Robin Benway, Heather Cocks, Alexis Coe, Nicole Chung, Roxane Gay, Tayari Jones, Lyz Lenz, Caille Millner, Jessica Morgan, Sarah Weinman, and Sara Zarr.

So many people took time out of their busy lives to talk to me as I researched this book; I appreciate that more than I can say. Thank you to Jane Friedman, Erin Clary Giglia, Betty Huang, Joyce Tong Oelrich, Jessica Palumbo, and Tere Ramos-Dunne for talking to me about starting your own businesses. Thanks to Julia Turshen, who told me so much about her experiences working with Angel Food East, which inspired the meal service work in this book. And many thanks to Sybil Grant for sharing so much of her research about criminal justice reform.

My friends have been there for me through everything, and I can't thank all of you enough. Jill Vizas, Janet Goode, Lisa McIntire, Joy Alferness and the whole Alferness family, Jessica Simmons, Julian Davis Mortenson, Nanita Cranford, Jina Kim, Melissa Sladden, Alicia Harris, Dana White, Samantha Powell, Nicole Cliffe, Kate Leos, Sarah Mackey, Maggie Levine,

Sara Kate Wilkinson, Margaret H. Willison, Rachel Fershleiser, Maret Orliss, Daniel Lavery, Toby Rugger, Kyle Wong, Lyette Mercier, Ryan Gallagher, Sarah Tiedeman, Sara Simon, Simi Patnaik, and Nicole Clouse. I'm so happy I have you all. Thank you especially to everyone who sent me cute pictures and videos of their children and dogs when I especially needed it.

Thank you so much to my big, sprawling, loud, joyful, argumentative family. I love you, Mom, Dad, and Sasha; all of my aunts and uncles, and all of my many wonderful cousins. I miss you, Granny and Papa, Grandma, Grandpa, and Stan. Thank you for everything.

Thank you, thank you, thank you to all of you who have read my books. Thank you for coming to my events and checking books out of the library and telling your friends and family about my books and sending me messages and telling me what my books have meant to you—I treasure all of this so much.

And finally, a special, heartfelt thank-you to all booksellers and librarians. Thank you for all of your hard work on behalf of books and literacy, and thank you for embracing me from the beginning. I've loved bookstores and libraries for my entire life, and didn't think there was any way I could love them more, but these past few years have accomplished that. You're all superstars—now more than ever.

Books are
produced in the
United States
using U.S.-based
materials

Books are printed
using a revolutionary
new process called
THINKtech™ that
lowers energy usage
by 70% and increases
overall quality

Books are
durable and
flexible
because of
Smyth-sewing

Paper is
sourced using
environmentally
responsible
foresting methods
and the
paper is acid-free

Center Point Large Print
600 Brooks Road / PO Box 1
Thorndike, ME 04986-0001 USA

(207) 568-3717

US & Canada:
1 800 929-9108
www.centerpointlargeprint.com